ACCOLADES AND PRAISE FOR

Little & Lion

"*Little & Lion* is beautifully insightful, honest, and compassionate. Brandy's ability to find larger meaning in small moments is **nothing short of dazzling**."
—National Book Award Finalist and #1 *New York Times* bestselling author Nicola Yoon

"*Little & Lion* is a **stunningly good** novel."
—Kiersten White, *New York Times* bestselling author of *And I Darken*

"This is a book and **a protagonist I will long remember**."
—Bill Konigsberg, award-winning author of *Openly Straight* and *Honestly Ben*

"A book full of **overwhelming love and courage**."
—Sara Farizan, author of *Tell Me Again How a Crush Should Feel*

★ "This **superbly written** novel teems with meaningful depth, which is perfectly balanced by romance and the languorous freedom of summer."
—*Booklist*, starred review

★ "**A moving, diverse exploration** of the challenges of growing up and the complicated nature of loyalty."
—*SLJ*, starred review

★ "Colbert sensitively confronts misconceptions about mental illness, bisexuality, and intersectional identity.... **A vibrantly depicted Los Angeles**."
—*Kirkus Reviews*, starred review

★ "From the threads of **love and romance**, to redefining family life, readers of all walks of life will find an entry point to this title."
—*The Bulletin*, starred review

"A **moving** and well-realized examination of secrecy, trust, and intimacy."
—*Publishers Weekly*

"Hand [*Little & Lion*] to readers who like **thoughtful, edgy stories** with no easy answers."
—*VOYA*

"With **compelling** honesty, Colbert portrays Suzette's evolving understanding of her sexuality, Lionel's longing for self-sufficiency alongside the challenges of his mental illness, and the difficulty of shifting familial relationships."
—*The Horn Book*

LITTLE & LION

Also by Brandy Colbert

Pointe

Finding Yvonne

LITTLE & LION

BRANDY COLBERT

LITTLE, BROWN AND COMPANY
New York Boston

Copyright © 2017 by Brandy Colbert
Excerpt from *Finding Yvonne* copyright © 2018 by Brandy Colbert

Cover art copyright © 2018 by Erin Robinson. Cover design by Marcie Lawrence.
Cover copyright © 2018 by Hachette Book Group, Inc.

Little, Brown and Company
Hachette Book Group
1290 Avenue of the Americas, New York, NY 10104
Visit us at LBYR.com

Originally published in hardcover and ebook by Little, Brown and Company in August 2017
First Trade Paperback Edition: July 2018

Little, Brown and Company is a division of Hachette Book Group, Inc. The Little, Brown name and logo are trademarks of Hachette Book Group, Inc.

The publisher is not responsible for websites (or their content) that are not owned by the publisher.

The Library of Congress has cataloged the hardcover edition as follows:
Names: Colbert, Brandy, author.
Title: Little & Lion / by Brandy Colbert.
Other titles: Little and Lion
Description: First edition. | New York ; Boston : Little, Brown and Company, 2017. | Summary: "Suzette returns home to Los Angeles from boarding school and grapples with her bisexual identity when she and her brother Lionel fall in love with the same girl, pushing Lionel's bipolar disorder to spin out of control and forcing Suzette to confront her own demons." —Provided by publisher.
Identifiers: LCCN 2016019838 | ISBN 9780316349000 (hardcover) | ISBN 9780316348980 (ebook) | ISBN 9780316318976 (library edition ebook)
Subjects: | CYAC: Brothers and sisters—Fiction. | Family life—California—Fiction. | Dating (Social customs)—Fiction. | Bisexuality—Fiction. | Manic-depressive illness— Fiction. | Mental illness—Fiction. | California—Fiction.
Classification: LCC PZ7.C66998 Lit 2017 | DDC [Fic]—dc23
LC record available at https://lccn.loc.gov/2016019838

ISBNs: 978-0-316-34901-7 (paperback), 978-0-316-34898-0 (ebook)

Printed in the United States of America

LSC-C

10 9 8 7 6 5 4

For Lena,
the best person and friend

one.

It's bizarre to be so nervous about seeing the person who knows me best, but the past year hasn't been so kind to Lionel and me.

I'm standing outside LAX on a sun-soaked afternoon in early June when my brother's navy-blue sedan screeches to a halt a few feet away. Part of me doesn't mind that he's thirty minutes late, because I needed time to get used to the idea of being back home. But now he's here and my heart is thumping like it's going to jump out of my mouth and there's nowhere to go.

Lionel bolts from the car and barely looks at me before he starts rummaging around in the trunk, shoving aside a plastic crate filled with used books to make room for my luggage. "I am so sorry," he mutters. "The freeway was a nightmare."

There really is no such thing as traffic back in Avalon, Massachusetts. People don't honk their horns. They put up with totally inconsiderate shit, like neighbors stopping their Volvos and Saabs in the middle of tree-lined streets to chat with friends, clogging up the road so no one else can pass. L.A. drivers would honk until their horns went dead while flipping them off and threatening murder—and I have missed that.

Lionel hoists my bags into the trunk, slams it closed, and turns to give me a quick hug. But it feels perfunctory and that makes me stiffen in his arms and I wonder why we're acting like strangers. I relax a bit when I notice he smells so much like he is supposed to smell, like the coziness of our house and the mustiness of his car, which is always filled with hiking shoes and old books. I'm almost overwhelmed with the reality of actually being home and standing next to Lionel. For a while now—not just a weekend or a few days clustered around a hectic holiday. I'm home for the summer.

"Good to see you, Little," he says, pulling away as he tugs one of the black dreadlocks that hang to the middle of my back.

That name never sounded so good. My brother calls me Suzette only when he's feeling anxious, and I'm relieved that he seems so calm right now.

I smile and pretend like I'm not examining every single inch of him for changes. "Yeah? I don't look too East Coast–y?" I glance down at his thumbs. Before, they were shredded, the sides of them forever bitten and spotted with red. Now they are smooth and the skin is clean, and I think that's a good thing, too.

He squints at me, blinks, shakes his head. "Nah. They haven't broken you yet. You—when the hell did you get *that*?"

My fingers automatically go up to the tiny gold hoop on my face. It's a septum piercing, "badass but still classy" according to the girl who put the needle through my nose at the only tattoo parlor in Avalon.

"Do you like it?"

He leans closer, his eyes glued to the jewelry. "Yeah. Never pictured it on you, but I dig it. Does Nadine know?"

Nadine doesn't know. She's my mother and she's been with Lionel's father, Saul, since I was six and Lion was seven; we merged households two years later. Lionel and I have called each other brother and sister since then, and that surprises some people at first, because he's white and I'm black. But we've been built-in best friends for practically our entire lives, until last fall—when boarding school separated the inseparable.

"Let's move it along, people!" a sturdy man wearing a fluorescent vest booms, gesturing toward the cars backed up in the lanes surrounding us.

We hustle to our respective sides of the car, and a few seconds later, Lionel successfully steers us out of the throng of airport traffic amid a cacophony of honking horns and hissing shuttle brakes.

"The parents are waiting for us," he says. "But I'm starving. Are you starving? Want to sneak off and grab a bite first?"

What I want is to go straight to my bed and collapse into a deep sleep for about twelve hours. But all I've had today is a pack of peanuts and two cans of cherry cola, and as soon as he mentions my favorite taco truck, I forget about my jet lag.

People back East would ask what I missed the most about California, and I never quite knew where to start. Of course I missed my family. It's never cool to say so, but even the little things I used to hate, like the way Saul hums Barry Manilow songs while he makes breakfast—I would've killed for that on the really bad days. I missed the towering palm trees that look a little ratty during the day and majestic against the inky skyline after the sun drops. I missed the blistering sunshine and the horrific traffic and the way nobody here gives a shit about what anyone else is up to because there are too many better things to be doing with your time.

"How are you?" I ask, looking over at Lion.

His dark red hair is in need of a cut, but he looks good. Healthy. His blue eyes are focused, and I feel like I am looking at the version of Lionel I truly know. The Lionel I've missed.

"Good," he says, shrugging as if the question isn't loaded. "Just finished this incredible article in the *New Yorker*. You read this week's issue?"

As if I am him, who has subscribed to the *New Yorker* since he was thirteen and saves the old issues in neat stacks at the back of his closet.

I shake my head. "It's no fun reading them if I'm not stealing yours."

He takes his hand off the steering wheel to flick my shoulder, and I grin. I needed that almost more than his hug.

"Besides, I don't really have time to read for fun anymore." A year ago I wouldn't have been able to fathom making such a statement.

Lionel turns left onto La Cienega and clutches at the front of his T-shirt. "Surely you jest."

Living in the same house, it was hard *not* to be a big reader, with Lionel's overflowing bookshelves and frequent trips to libraries and bookstores. But reading didn't relax me when I was at Dinsmore Hall. It mostly reminded me that my brother was no longer a few hundred feet away if I wanted to discuss the story I was into. I tried texting but it wasn't the same, with the three-hour time difference.

He sent me off with *One Flew Over the Cuckoo's Nest* last fall and...well, I put it on the top shelf of my closet after the first night, away from my other books. Lion meant it as a joke, as a way to let me know he still had a sense of humor about what was happening to him, but I didn't find it very funny or comforting.

"You really haven't been reading?"

"I know." I sigh. "I fully expect to be disowned."

He looks over and smirks. "Heavily judged but not disowned. Classes still tough?"

"Kind of. They were time-consuming, mostly."

And I did miss the unofficial book club I had with my brother, but I stopped having time for it less because of the studying and more because of a girl named Iris.

"Well, it's good you're here. Now things can go back to normal," he says.

Normal. But which is the *normal* Lionel, the old or the new? I wouldn't know anymore, considering how little I've been able to see him over the past year. It wasn't my choice to go away, and the guilt of not being here for him is almost debilitating. I want to remind him of that every second, even though I know he's aware I didn't want to leave him.

He pauses, not looking at me. "Are you glad to be back?"

"Yeah, I guess...." I stick my arm out the window to feel the California sun on my skin. "I mean, *yes*, but you know how you can get used to something, even if you don't like it all that much?"

"Yeah, Little," he says in a voice that holds too much weight. "I know."

The car is silent, save for the softest notes of indie rock

playing in the background. I turn to my window and zone out as we make our way from the west side of the city to the east, thinking about what I have to do now that I'm home. Hug DeeDee. Find out how Lionel has *really* been doing, because as much as I want to believe he's as well as he seems, deep down I don't think he is. Figure out if I want to go back to Massachusetts and face the mess I left or fight to stay here, where things are another kind of difficult.

My mouth starts watering the closer we get to the taco truck, and I'm prepared to ride around for a while, looking for parking, but then the most magical thing that can happen in L.A. occurs—we find an empty spot just two parking meters down. Lionel whips into the space and we bolt from the car to follow the intoxicating fragrance of marinated meat, fresh tortillas, and spices down the sidewalk. The ever-present line that curls around the front of the truck is discouraging but only reinforces how delicious the food is— definitely worth the wait.

Lionel orders our usual, and we barely make it back to his car before I'm digging into the bag, pulling out a foil-wrapped chorizo taco from the quartet squeezed inside. Lionel divvies up the wedges of limes and sliced radishes between us, and we lean against the back bumper to eat. Or, more accurately, I moan with appreciation as Lionel inhales carne asada and rolls his eyes.

"Don't look at me like that." I lick spicy-sweet salsa

from the corner of my mouth because wiping it with a napkin is a waste. "I've been deprived of good Mexican food for months."

"Yeah, but you get all that cool New England shit." Lion tips back his bottle of pineapple soda, identical to the one resting by my feet. He swallows. "Chowder and lobster rolls and—"

"And it's no comparison. Give me *this* over lobster any day."

My mother texts as we're finishing up our first tacos, asking if we're on our way back. Part of me wants to run right home and fold myself into her arms and never let go. But the part of me that remembers how helpless and angry and sad I felt when she told me last summer that I had to go away resurfaces in that moment.

Lionel watches as I balance the phone on my knees and clumsily text with my left hand, trying not to smear food on the screen. "This about her?" When I look up, he's pointing at my nose ring.

"Why does it have to *be* about anything? Why can't I just like jewelry?"

"I don't know... I never thought you were into piercings or whatever." Lionel starts in on his shrimp taco. "It's kind of front and center."

"People were getting things pierced." I shrug. "I guess I gave in to peer pressure. Do you hate it or something?"

By *people* I mean my roommate, Iris, and she didn't pressure me. We got tired of studying one day and took a walk in downtown Avalon and then we were upstairs in the piercing loft, watching the blue-haired girl snap on a pair of rubber gloves. Iris held my hand so I'd have something to grab on to when it hurt. It was the perfect distraction, because at first I couldn't stop thinking about how soft her palm felt against mine—until the needle pierced through the middle of my nose with a sharp prick and I felt like I was going to sneeze my face off.

"I don't hate it, Little. It's just different."

I don't like the way he doesn't look at me as he says the word *different*.

"Yeah, well. So am I."

My eyes sting as Lionel swings the car onto our street, and I tell myself I'm just tired, but *fuck*, I missed this place. I blink almost violently as our olive-green Victorian comes into view, with its fish-scale shingles and maroon trim and the turret at the top that houses my bedroom. We live in a historic district of L.A., the streets of our neighborhood lined with all types of gorgeous Victorian and Craftsman houses, but I swear, ours gets the most lingering looks when people drive or walk by. It's been six months since I was home, and now I'm the one who can't tear her eyes away.

Our parents are sitting close together on the wooden swing that hangs from the porch, but they pop right up when we pull into the drive. Saul comes bounding down first, his big arms engulfing me before I've even emerged from the car. "We missed you so much, kiddo."

"Missed you, too." I kind of can't wait to hear him humming "Copacabana" over fried eggs.

He gives me one last squeeze and pulls back, and I smile as I take in his strawberry-blond hair that's silvered at the temples, and the creases of laugh lines around his mouth. He has Lionel's same oceanic blue eyes, the ones that convey every ounce of emotion.

Father and son scoop up my bags and take them inside, leaving me alone with my mother. She looks pretty in wide-legged linen pants and a white top that contrasts perfectly with her warm brown skin and short Afro dyed the color of dark cherries. She notices my new piece of jewelry— her eyebrows rise slightly as her gaze sweeps over me—but she doesn't say anything about it.

Her eyes are wet as she blinks at me, as she smooths a palm softly over the side of my face. "Oh, sweet pea, I really missed you."

"I missed you, too," I say, folding myself into her hug.

I spent the first few weeks at school seething through the phone calls from her and Saul, but the longer I was there, the more my anger faded, until it mostly manifested on the days I particularly missed home and my brother.

I know she really thought she did what was best for all of us by sending me away.

I know how easy it is to believe you're doing the right thing if you say it to yourself often enough.

two.

I wake at six thirty the morning after I return. Every part of me is exhausted and I still can't escape the East Coast.

I blink at the rounded, soft gray wall of my bedroom, confused for a moment. I've always loved it up here, with the gauzy white curtains fluttering in front of big windows and the twinkle lights woven along the tops of them. And I missed the worn purple armchair, the one my mother has had since college and passed on to me years ago. My room is cozy, but today—well, I feel strange waking up in a turret. I used to think it was cool to sleep in a tower, but now it seems a little childish, like I never stopped playing princess.

Not to mention it felt even stranger falling asleep in a room by myself after so many months. It took me weeks to get used to sleeping across the room from Iris first semester . . . which is funny, considering everything that's happened.

I stretch from my toes to my fingertips, yawn until I see stars, then lie back and listen. The house is quiet. I curl my phone into my palm and walk down the short staircase that descends from my room, stopping at the middle-level bathroom. I peek into the shower to find my shampoo and conditioner sitting in the same spot where I left them at the end of winter break, back when Lionel seemed better—no frenzied footsteps heard through his door at two in the morning when I got up to use the bathroom, no trays of untouched food sitting outside his room at all hours of the day—but still not quite himself.

I pause on my way downstairs and press my ear to the door to see if I can hear him flipping the pages of the *New Yorker* or maybe an old novel by his new literary crush. All I hear is the soft whir of the fan he uses for white noise. He's asleep, like any other normal person on summer break.

In the kitchen I fill the robin's-egg-blue kettle with fresh water and turn on the flame under it. I keep waiting for light to peek over the mountaintops in the distance, but the sky remains hazy and gray and then I remember June Gloom. The sun won't be out until lunchtime, at least.

The whole world seems to be asleep. It's even too early for Mrs. Maldonado to be kneeling in her garden next door, obsessively checking her tomato plants for aphids. I should probably enjoy the silence, but it makes me uncomfortable in the same way I didn't feel right lying up in my room.

I bring my old yellow mug out to the front porch along with a spoon and a plastic bear filled with honey, then settle into the porch swing and rock back and forth, carefully, so I won't spill hot tea all over my legs. I started drinking tea in New England because that's what all the girls in my dorm drank, and it was always easier to do what they wanted than stick out even more than I already did.

I bring the yellow mug up to my lips to blow on my tea at the same time footsteps pound down our front walk, followed by a voice that's too loud for this morning.

"Suzette?"

"Shit!" The hot liquid scalds my upper lip, the tender, soft skin on the underside. The heat goes straight north to my nose, and I touch gingerly around my ring, still amazed that I haven't managed to accidentally rip it out in the few months I've had it.

"Hey, sorry. Didn't mean to scare you." Emil Choi is standing in front of our porch. "You okay?"

He's the son of my mother's best friend. His long brown legs stick out from a pair of gray running shorts, and the sneakers on his feet are scuffed and worn. He's already run at least a couple of miles if he's come from his house in Silver Lake, but he's barely broken a sweat.

"Hey, Emil. Yeah, I'll live." I go back to sucking on my lip.

"Heard you were coming back," he says, his nonchalance overpowering the air like a blast of cheap cologne. "When'd you get in?"

He knows exactly when I got in—our moms talk every day—but I decide to humor him. Because it's too early to be so bored and there's no one else to talk to and, well. Emil isn't so bad on the eyes. His mother is black and his father is Korean and he is the perfect combination of them, with his creamy brown skin and dark, serious eyes.

"Yesterday. Are you always up so early?"

He shrugs and plants his foot on the bottom step of the porch, leaning forward in a lunge. "It's better when not a lot of people are out. I have the sidewalks to myself."

"I can't believe you do this on purpose." I take a tiny sip of tea, keeping my eyes on him the whole time so there are no more surprises. But there is one more—the new shapes behind his ears. Hearing aids. Those are definitely new.

"I hated running at first." He scratches his head where thick black curls are beginning to crop up. "But then I kind of started to hate it less. Now I can't live without it."

I squeeze more honey into my mug. "That's fucked up."

"Never said it wasn't." Emil grins and I give him a small smile back. "What are *you* doing up so early?"

"Jet lag." I scoot back into the corner of the swing, suddenly self-conscious that I'm wearing my pajamas. They're just cotton shorts and one of Mom's old Wellesley T-shirts, but I feel exposed. I'm not even wearing a bra. And I want to ask about the hearing aids, but I don't know how.

Emil and I didn't exactly grow up as close as our mothers are. They've joked about us ending up together since we were babies, but I've always kept a safe distance. We were in the same crowd of bookish, artsy kids before I went away, but it would seem too easy to date Emil. I don't want my mother handpicking my boyfriend. And anyway, I'm not so sure Emil—or any other guy—is my type these days.

"So...DeeDee's tomorrow?" He's kind of hopping in place from foot to foot now, and when I give him a strange look, he says, "Gotta keep my heart rate up."

"Are you going?" DeeDee has been texting me about my welcome-back party for the past two weeks, and she was so excited I would've felt bad asking her to cancel it. I'd rather spend a night alone with her, rehashing all the stories that were too important not to text about immediately but that are better told in person, even if it's a retelling.

"Yeah, of course," Emil says. "I mean, I was planning on it. I could give you a ride if you want? We live so close and I'm already going that way, so—"

"Sure." He looks surprised at how quickly I agreed to it, and I guess I am, too.

I've always known my friendship with Emil could be more if I wanted it to be, and it's getting harder to ignore how much cuter I find him the older we get. I've never let myself give in to it because there would be no real surprises with Emil. I know everything there is to know about him.

But the summer already feels so uncertain, not knowing if I'll stay here or go back to Massachusetts at the end of August, so I figure it can't hurt to let my guard down for a few weeks. Besides, I haven't seen any of my old friends in months and I don't want to show up alone, even if they're all there to see me. I'm not much for entrances—grand, fashionably late, or otherwise.

"Okay, well...cool." Emil starts jogging backward, unable to hide the smile creeping up on his face. "Pick you up around seven tomorrow?"

I nod and, for a moment, let myself enjoy that I can make him smile like that. "Later, Emil."

He gives a wave and I watch his wiry frame jog away, and when he glances back over his shoulder, I am still looking in his direction.

then.

My stomach hurts when Mom tells me to wear my nice dress.

We're going to her boyfriend's house for dinner, and it's just him and Lionel. And Mom never tells me what to wear. She lets me pick out all my own clothes when we go school shopping.

"Why?"

She's laid out the dress on my bed with a pair of tights. I eye it like there might be a firecracker hiding underneath.

"Because Saul is cooking us dinner tonight and we should look nice for it." She kisses the top of my head before she leaves my room.

I sit on the end of my bed for a while, staring at the dress and feeling like something big is about to change.

Lionel opens the door to their house without looking up, his face covered by a thick book.

Mom smiles when he doesn't say anything and lightly clears her throat. "Hello, Lionel."

"Hi," he mumbles, and steps aside, his freckled hand wrapped around the book like a claw. I can't read the title.

I don't say hi to him as we pass. Our parents have been dating for almost two years now, and he's not always very nice to me. Mostly he doesn't say a whole lot. He's always reading, and he never wants to talk about the books, like he thinks I'm too dumb to understand them. He's only a year older than me.

Saul walks out from the kitchen. There's a dish towel hanging from his belt loop and flour on his nose. He kisses my mom on the lips and it still makes me feel funny, but not as much as the first time I saw it.

He gives me a big hug like every time I see him, but I think it lasts longer this time. Saul is always nice, and he doesn't talk to me like other grown-ups—when he asks me questions, I feel like he really wants to know the answer. And he always asks lots of questions. Not like Lionel.

"You have flour on your nose," I say when we pull away.

"You're a true friend, Suzette." He gives Mom a fake frown. "Your mother didn't even tell me."

"Maybe I thought it was cute," she says, and I giggle as he makes a big show of wiping at his nose.

From behind his book, Lionel's muffled voice says, "When's dinner? I'm starving."

Saul made lasagna and, like always, he serves Mom and me first before he moves over to Lionel.

"More, please," Lionel says, his head bowed. He's looking down at his lap, not even trying to hide the book sitting there.

Saul sighs. He scoops more lasagna onto Lionel's plate. "Son, put that away for now."

"Why? I can hear everything you're saying."

Saul gently puts a hand on his shoulder. "We're trying to have a nice dinner, and it's rude to read at the table when we have guests."

Lionel sighs now, and I know the look in his eyes. It's the same feeling I had when Mom told me to wear a nice dress. Why is everything so special all of a sudden? He slams the book closed, stabs his fork into his pasta, and starts eating without waiting for Saul to finish serving himself.

Mom and Saul keep giving each other looks. They mean something, but I don't know what. I try to catch Lionel's eye to see if he notices, but he's staring down at his plate and hasn't said a word since he put his book away.

Finally, after Saul has passed around the bread basket for the second time, he taps his water glass with his fork and says, "Kids, Nadine and I have an announcement."

My heart starts to beat fast. I want to know what he's going to say, but at the same time, I wish we could skip this part of the night.

Mom gives me a soft smile and looks back and forth between Lionel and me when she says, "We've decided to move in together. We're all going to live in the same house."

Lionel's fork falls to his plate with a clang. "So you're getting married?"

"No, we're not," says Saul. "We love each other very much, but we've both been married before and…we think it's best if we focus on one thing at a time."

"I don't want to move." Lionel's voice is flat. His blue eyes are darker than normal as he glares down at his plate like he wants to throw it against the wall.

"We're all going to move," Saul says. "Into a new place—new to all of us. Because we love both of you very much, too, and we want everyone to be happy."

Mom tilts her head as she looks at me. "What do you think, Suzette?"

I shrug, not quite looking at her or Saul but at a spot between them on the table. "I don't know. It's okay, I guess."

I don't think it's the answer she wants, but it's better than Lionel's. I'm not lying. It's not good or bad, just okay. I don't remember my dad. He died when I was three. And I like Saul, but I don't know what it's like to live with anyone besides Mom.

They bring out champagne for them and a bottle of sparkling apple juice for Lionel and me. We clink our glasses together, and I smile to match Mom's and Saul's faces. Lionel doesn't.

He disappears after dinner, and I walk all over the house trying to find him. Mom and Saul are in the kitchen, washing dishes and being lovey-dovey. I don't want to be in there, but I don't want to be alone, either.

I find him out in the garage, where Saul builds things from wood. A couple of scary-looking machines with big, sharp blades sit in the corner, which is why we aren't supposed to be out here alone. But Lionel isn't standing near them. He's in front of the table of projects that Saul hasn't finished. Smaller pieces, like shelves and bookends and some things I don't know the names of.

"Do you hate us?" I ask in a quiet voice.

Lionel's back is to me. It takes a long time, but he finally says, "No."

"Why are you so mad?"

He turns around. "Why aren't you more mad? Don't you like it with just you and your mom?"

"Yeah."

"Well, I like it being me and my dad. I don't like it when things change. The last time they changed, my parents got divorced."

I don't know what to say so I stay quiet.

Lionel picks up something from the table. His back is still facing me, so I can't see what it is. But he's pulling at it and smacking his hand against it, and then he smacks it against the table, too. Something chips off and falls to the ground.

I look at him with my mouth open, wondering if that was somehow a mistake. But he only hits it against the table harder and harder until large pieces start splintering off, flying into the air.

"What are you doing?" I walk closer to him. But not too close. He's scaring me now, more than the big machines in the room.

He doesn't say anything back, and he doesn't stop until the thing in his hand is in a half dozen pieces. He throws the chunk of wood to the ground with a clatter. I look down and see that it was a lamp. The lightbulb screws in on one side and the part he destroyed looks like a tree, except all the branches are gone now, scattered across the floor.

I put my hand over my mouth. "What did you do?"

He's breathing hard when he looks at me, his own mouth turned down so far it makes me sad.

The side door to the garage opens, and as soon as Lionel sees his father and my mother, his eyes go wide and wet with worry.

"You two know you're not supposed to be—" Saul stops as he sees the mess Lionel has made. "What happened?"

He moves across the room so quickly he's almost a blur. I watch him pick up what's left of the lamp and turn it over in his hands, inspecting every nook and cranny. He shakes his head as he looks at Lionel.

"Why would you do this?"

Lionel doesn't say anything, and the longer he stares at the floor, the madder Saul looks.

"Lionel, you knew this was for your grandmother's birthday. I can't believe you would ruin all my hard work like this." Saul's tone is steady, but that almost makes me feel guiltier than if he were raising his voice.

Lionel is almost always cranky, and he doesn't want Mom and me around. I don't think it would take all the fingers on one of my hands to count how many times I've seen him smile. But we have to live together, and I've never had anything like a brother. I think it will be easier if we're friends.

He still doesn't say anything, and then all of a sudden I start talking.

"He didn't. I dropped it, Saul. I'm sorry."

From across the garage, my mother says, "Suzette!"

Saul's face is confused. "You did this?"

"I wanted to hold it. It's really pretty." I swallow over and over. I don't lie and I'm not good at it. I've never had a reason to be. "Lionel told me not to...and it was too heavy and I dropped it. I'm really sorry, Saul."

He sighs. Runs his fingers over the broken edges and sighs again. "You're sure you did this, Suzette? Because if we're going to be a family, we need to be honest with each other about things. *All of us* need to be honest." His eyes drift over to Lionel, who won't look up at all.

"I didn't mean to." I feel sick inside. Because of the way Mom and Saul are looking at me, like I'm not the same girl I was a half hour ago. Because Saul's pretty lamp is ruined and it was a gift for his mother. Because I don't want him to become so angry with me that he breaks up with Mom and we never see him again.

Mom says my allowance will pay for the cost of the materials to remake it, and when we're in the car on our way home, she tells me I'll write and send another apology to Saul tomorrow.

But before we left, in between my mother saying good-bye to Saul and hustling me out the door, Lionel approached. He handed me a book, a collection of poems by someone named Shel Silverstein. A folded-up piece of paper was tucked into the first pages. Just one word written on notebook paper, in Lionel's big, blocky handwriting: *Thanks.*

three.

Lionel's bedroom door is cracked when I walk downstairs, so I stop and knock and he says to come in.

It looks the same: the forest-green comforter, rumpled and twisted up with his bedsheets; sneakers and sandals lying around the room where they were kicked off, none of them having landed anywhere near their match; the poster hanging above his bed, suggesting Hunter S. Thompson for sheriff. And books. Everywhere, there are books. Instead of shelving them alphabetically, he's sorted the spines by theme: Feminists reside next to the Dead White Guys (my brother has a sense of humor), and then there are the African novelists, who he has separated by country. Nonfiction takes up an entire three-shelf bookcase.

"What's up?" Lionel says from his spot near the foot of the bed. He's sprawled out on the floor with a book approximately the size of a telephone directory.

"What are you reading?" I ask, leaning against the doorframe.

"This is the year I'm finally doing it." He sticks his finger between the pages to hold his place. I give him a quizzical look until he turns the cover my way. *Infinite Jest.*

"Oh." I shake my head. "That looks like homework."

He shrugs. "I'm up to the challenge. What are you doing?"

"Going to see if they need any help with dinner," I say, pointing toward the stairs.

Lionel nods, then gives me a sly grin. "Heard you talking to Emil this morning."

My face instantly flushes. I forgot Lionel's bedroom is directly above the porch. "What were you doing up?" He didn't mention this at breakfast.

"I could ask you the same thing." He slides an envelope into the book for a more permanent marker and sits up. "Was that planned? For him to stop by?"

"Jesus. No, okay?" I touch my face to see if it's still warm, and I guess that answers any lingering questions of how I feel about Emil Choi. The last person I was with was a girl: Iris. But I know the feeling you get when you think about someone you want to kiss, and that feeling doesn't change when I replace Iris with Emil. "I haven't talked to Emil since

I was home last time. He saw me sitting out there and he stopped."

"*Okay*," Lionel says in the singsongy voice he uses specifically to irritate me, and I think how good this feels, my brother teasing me like he used to. For a while, everything with him was either urgent or miserable and there was no in-between. I saw hints of his old self coming back when I was home over winter break, but I felt like I'd let him down by leaving for Dinsmore, like he didn't trust me enough to completely be himself around me.

"What about you?" I ask. "Anyone special?"

"Nah."

I take a deep breath before I say what I say because I know he could be touchy about it. "Do you still talk to anyone?"

He blinks at me. "Like, a therapist? That's kind of part of the deal. Dr. Tarrasch and I are real tight."

"No, I mean...DeeDee says she doesn't really see you around anymore. You don't hang out with them?"

I know for a fact he's not hanging out with our friends. She told me last week that she hadn't seen my brother outside of school since I invited her over for dinner during winter break.

"People ask too many questions," Lionel says, looking down at the closed book in front of him.

"But they're your friends." I step into the room now. "They care. DeeDee asks about you all the time—"

"Well, Little, they stopped caring so much after you left."

He is not unkind, just matter-of-fact. "So maybe they're *your* friends now."

I open and close my mouth without speaking, but Lionel doesn't want a response. He's removing the envelope from the book, creasing down the page where he left off. "See you at dinner," he says without looking up, and before, I would have pushed him, urged him to talk about it.

But we're not back to where we were. Not yet.

And that was my cue to leave, so I step back into the hallway and shut the door.

Mom and Saul are down in the kitchen, tending to the food for Shabbat dinner. Saul always closed up his woodshop early on Fridays to come home and make the challah, and that hasn't changed. I find him pulling the ball of dough from a bowl that he set aside so it could rise.

"Hey, kiddo," he says, smiling as I walk over to the island.

Mom looks up from her post at the stove, protected by a black apron that sports bunches of dancing grapes. "Hi there, sweet pea."

"Can I help with the bread?"

"We've got everything under control," Mom says, bending down to peer into the oven window. "This is our first Shabbat dinner with you back, Suz. We want you to relax."

"I'm not a guest." I say it so fervently that they stop

looking my way to glance at each other. "I mean, I want to help, if I can. It's been a while . . . since I've been here for this."

"Of course," Saul says quickly, stepping aside to make room for me at the island. He will clean up before dinner, but right now he still smells like varnish and freshly cut wood from the shop, and that really does make this feel like old times. "Here, I'm just getting ready to separate this thing, and then we can start braiding."

I feel Mom watching me as I wash my hands and walk over to stand beside him. I see her looking at Saul as she talks about me with her eyes. Then she's by the island, looking at me and talking with her mouth.

"Suzette, I understand if you're still angry with me . . . with us," she says. "You know we never wanted to send you away, but—Lionel's illness took us all by surprise, and we could see how much it was eating at you, and I felt, at the time, that I needed to step in and do something about that. Ease your load."

"And ease your load, too?" I ask quietly, staring at the floor. I've never said as much to her, but I've always wondered.

We've talked about this before, but emotions were running so high last summer that I mostly pretended to listen when she talked about why I needed to go away. Now I can hear the sincerity and regret in her voice.

"Oh, Suzette. Oh, baby." She sounds so sad, and when I

look up, she's blinking like she might cry. "You've never been a burden, on me or Saul."

"Never," Saul adds, putting an arm around me.

"We never want you to think that. But we didn't know how to handle everything when this was all so new, when Lionel was still trying to figure out his routine. We didn't want you to start resenting your brother for something that isn't his fault, and we didn't handle that well, either."

They sent extravagant care packages and called all the time. I never once doubted that they loved me. But I didn't realize how much I needed to hear this—that I wasn't a burden—until I do. A lump rises in my throat. The sort that signals tears of relief, tears that release me from thinking there was ever a scenario in which my parents truly didn't want me around. I look down at the island to blink them away.

"We messed up," Mom says. "We thought not having to watch Lionel adjust to his treatment would be healthier for you. Allow you to concentrate more on your own life. But we should've talked to you more, kept you in the loop. And I'm sorry."

"We're both sorry," Saul says. "You're a good kid. You've always been honest, and you deserve the same from us."

"I don't know what to say." It's not every day your parents apologize to you for fucking up . . . even if that part about me always being honest isn't totally true.

"Just say you'll try to enjoy your summer as much as you can." Mom kisses my cheek.

"I think I can do that," I say with a smile.

Mom goes back to the stove. Saul pulls apart the dough in front of us and places a piece next to me on the butcher-block surface. I roll it into a long rope between my palms, set it aside, and wait for the next one. He looks over and grins at my quick work.

A few hours later we're all assembled around the table in nicer clothes, and Lionel and Saul are wearing their kippot. Mom and I light the candles and say the blessing together. My Hebrew is a little rusty, but the cadence of the words is so ingrained in me that it comes back after the first couple of lines.

We don't always do the blessing of the children, mostly because Lionel has complained that we're getting too old for it. But tonight, Mom and Saul ignore his grumblings and place their hands atop each of our heads as they recite the separate prayers for boys and girls. Saul whispers something to Lionel that I can't hear after his blessing, and when it's my turn, he says, "I love you and missed you very much."

After the kiddush, Mom turns and wraps her arms tightly around me. "Good Shabbos, baby."

I didn't tell many people in Avalon that I'm Jewish. I

wasn't the only Jewish person there, not by far, but people have too many questions when you're black and Jewish. My situation isn't really that hard to comprehend: Mom and Saul got together, we were slowly introduced to Saul's lifelong traditions, and Mom and I decided to convert when I was eleven. But it's too much for some people to handle, like you must offer up an extra-special reason for converting to Judaism if you have a certain type of brown skin. Not to mention the girls in my dorm weren't the most tolerant bunch, as I quickly learned. So I never joined the weekly van rides to the temple or the Shabbat dinners hosted by the Jewish student association, even though its presence was one of the reasons Mom and Saul chose Dinsmore in the first place.

Lionel has never been that into religion and does just enough to keep Saul happy. He thought it was funny how excited I was for my bat mitzvah, and rolled his eyes when I admitted I didn't mind the Hebrew lessons we took as kids. We're Reform Jews, and the Nussbaum-Mitchell household is more cultural than religious these days, but we still celebrate several of the holidays and eat Shabbat dinner each week, no exceptions, and I found myself missing every part of it while I was away.

"Good Shabbos," I say, and I hug Saul and Lion hugs Mom and Saul hugs my mother, and then it's Lion and me. His hug is tight but a little stiff, and I wonder if he's still annoyed from earlier. I called DeeDee to ask if there was something she wasn't telling me, but she didn't pick up; she texted later, reminding me that she was up in Los Olivos for the day with her dad.

"How does it feel being back, sweet pea?" Mom asks, passing the platter of roast chicken my way.

I slept through dinner last night, and now it's strange being with my family on a Friday evening instead of eating pizza in the dorm or bribing an upperclassman to drive us into town. I want to exaggerate, tell my mother this is the first time I've felt like myself since I was here for winter break, but that's not true. I felt like myself whenever I was with Iris.

"Good, except I can't shake the time change. It feels so late already."

Saul takes the challah that Lionel offers and breaks off a piece of the bread we made together. "Well, it seems like you managed to avoid picking up that hideous New England accent. My brother went away to Boston College when I was a kid and came back sounding like a Kennedy."

"Yeah, but they said I have a California accent. I didn't even think we had accents out here." I carefully scoop a hasselback potato onto my plate. The food was actually pretty good at Dinsmore, but we didn't have dinners like this. You can tell the difference when someone is cooking simply because it's a job and when the meal is lovingly prepared by people who missed having you around. "They think everything about L.A. is vapid."

"That's so lazy." Lionel finally speaks. "People who say that are the same ones who come out here and go to those shithead tourist spots and then complain that the city has no culture."

"Don't say *shithead*," Mom admonishes, but she smiles when she says it. "And I heard the same things from the girls at Wellesley, ages ago. They made L.A. sound soulless."

"Thank God you didn't listen to them," Saul says, winking when my mother looks over. She hides shyly behind her wineglass. They still have little moments like this, and it's embarrassing and kind of cute and gross all at once. Sometimes I wonder if I'll ever find anybody I like as much as my mother likes Saul. Not just love, but *like*. "And thank God *you're* back," he continues, looking at me. "I missed my museum buddy. Want to hit up LACMA next week?"

"Absolutely." I look over at Lionel, who's shoving roast chicken into his mouth. "Hey, what are you doing tomorrow night?"

"What I'm doing for the next three months of my life— hot date with David Foster Wallace," he says between mouthfuls. "Why?"

"DeeDee's having a party for me. A welcome-back thing. What do you think?"

He finishes chewing. Shrugs. "Maybe. Kind of feel like laying low this weekend."

"But I just got back," I say. Perhaps knowing I should

let it go but not wanting to. "It's going to be everyone you already know: Dee, Emil, Tommy, Catie—well, I guess Catie isn't exactly a selling point, but still. It won't be the same without you."

"I'll think about it, Little," he says, but his eyes tell me to drop it.

My mother starts talking then, and we spend the rest of dinner discussing what they've all been up to. She brings up the screenplay she's working on and, like she does every so often, says she still can't believe people pay her to make up stories, even though screenwriting has been her full-time job for a couple of years now. Saul tells us about the recent string of overbearing, eccentric clients at his woodshop. I glance at Lionel a couple of times, but he's zoned out. At the end of the meal, Saul says my return has granted Lionel and me a get-out-of-kitchen-duty pass for the evening.

"Hey," I say to my brother as we take our dishes to the sink. "I haven't been out to the tree house yet. Want to go up and hang for a while?"

It's our spot, a parent-free escape where we used to do homework and listen to music and talk about things we didn't want Mom and Saul to overhear. We're too old for it now, probably, but if Lionel doesn't want to hang out with our friends, the least I can do is get him to hang out with me.

Except I can't.

He scrapes and rinses his plate, shaking his head. "I'm

pretty tired, but I'll see you tomorrow, okay? Maybe we can bike over to the reservoir."

"Yeah, okay," I say, working hard to make sure he can't hear the hurt in my voice. Because before, it would've been *We'll bike over to the reservoir* without the preface of *maybe*. I start to ask him what's wrong, if he's feeling okay or if I've done something to piss him off. Our parents are still in the dining room, out of earshot and pouring the last of the sweet wine. But he brushes past me before I can get the words out and I wonder if anyone else has noticed.

That my brother looks like the old Lionel and sounds like him, too, but some part of him is missing.

four.

Emil is early the next evening and I'm late getting ready, so he's sitting with my parents when I get down to the living room.

"Sorry," I say, walking over quickly to rescue him.

But that's when I notice nobody looks at all put out that I'm running ten minutes behind. Of course Emil's been a friend of the family since forever, but the scene before me displays a level of comfort I wasn't expecting. He's sitting in the leather armchair across from Mom and Saul, chatting away like they're old friends. Emil is leaning forward, his hands animated as he tells them a story. Mom and Saul are totally engrossed, expectant smiles on their faces as they wait for him to get to the punch line.

He turns around, and I don't miss the way his eyes widen as they land on me. He stands. "Hey, no problem. I was just telling your parents about this guy down by the lake today."

"Yeah?" I say, waiting for him to go on because everyone in the room looks so amused and I want to be amused, too.

"So, he was—" He stops. "Honestly, it's kind of a long story if you don't already know about him."

"Oh." I look at Mom and Saul, who obviously know all about this random man who appeared at Echo Park Lake within the past nine months.

"But I can tell you on the way to DeeDee's," Emil says with an easy smile.

Mom and Saul walk us to the door, and I wonder if they think this is a date. It's more of a date than Iris and I ever had, but I don't know what Emil is thinking. Or what I want it to be.

"Curfew?" I say to Mom before I walk through the doorway.

She looks over at Saul and it's clear they haven't had to worry about this since I left. From what I can tell, Lionel doesn't seem to get out much anymore, if at all. I checked in with him tonight after dinner, just to make sure he hadn't changed his mind about DeeDee's. He hadn't.

"Well, you're almost seventeen," my mother says. "I think twelve thirty seems reasonable for the summer, doesn't it?"

"Totally reasonable." I begin inching out the door before

they can change their minds. My underclassman dorm curfew at Dinsmore was loads more conservative. "We'll just be at Dee's."

Out on the street, Emil unlocks the passenger door of his Jeep and holds it open for me. I hesitate, then look at him and say thank you. His attentiveness surprises me, but I like it. Lionel says holding the door open is more about not being an asshole than being chivalrous.

Emil gets in and starts the Jeep, and without looking at me, he says, "You look nice, Suzette."

I glance down at my outfit, a sapphire-blue romper with thin straps and tiny red roses dotting the fabric. I was wearing my pajamas the last time I saw him, so I guess I cleaned up well. "Thanks," I say again, feeling my face warm.

He looks nice, too, in a pair of army-green shorts, an oxford shirt with the sleeves rolled up, and navy boat shoes. I study his profile.

"So, when did you get your, um...?" I gesture to my ears even though he's not looking over, which seems really stupid when I think about it.

"These?" He lifts a hand from the steering wheel to lightly tap his right ear. "You can say *hearing aids*, Suzette. They're not bad words."

"Sorry." I clear my throat and try again. "When did you get your hearing aids?"

"A few months ago," he says, navigating toward Sunset Boulevard.

The top of the Jeep is off and the night breeze skims over my shoulders, rustling through the thick knot of dreadlocks gathered at the back of my neck.

"I started getting these dizzy spells, and then I would have to stay in bed for, like, days," Emil says. "My doctor thought it was just an extreme case of vertigo, but I have this thing called Ménière's disease."

"I guess I'm not familiar." Which makes me feel even dumber, that he's been dealing with this thing all year and I've never heard of it.

"Neither was I. It's an inner-ear disorder. There are different degrees of it, and not everyone loses some of their hearing, but..."

"I'm sorry, Emil." I've never thought about what it would be like to lose my hearing. Maybe he hadn't, either.

"Ménière's is...mostly manageable." He slows for a red light behind a beat-up old VW bus. "The aids aren't as bad as I thought they'd be. They're waterproof. And they help me hear better, which is the point, I guess."

He grins and I grin back and we ride quietly for a while, bumping along the asphalt in his graphite-colored Jeep. We take surface streets the whole way to Laurel Canyon, passing endless rows of strip malls and bars with flashing neon signs and fast-food places all crammed together at the busy inter-sections of Hollywood.

"What's going on with everyone now? Anything new?" I ask, realizing that I've been twisting my hands together so tightly the bones are starting to hurt.

I saw everyone over winter break, but that was back in January, and the only person I've talked to with any fre-quency is DeeDee. The party is for me, but like the last time I was home, I'm nervous that things will be too different. That I won't fit in, that everyone will have moved on and not made room for me. Especially since it seems like they already did that to my brother.

"Just the usual," Emil says, turning right on a red light. "The group hasn't really changed much since you left. Except there's more alcohol now."

I sit back as he navigates the twisty canyon roads with ease. Emil didn't even have his license when I left, and now he's basi-cally a pro driving through one of the trickier parts of L.A.

He maneuvers the Jeep up the hill at the top of DeeDee's street, parking in the dusty open space in front of the yellow DEAD END sign. He gets out of the driver's seat, and I should get out, too, because I know he's going to come around and open my door, which is so fucking nice it's unreal—but I can't move.

His face shows up on the other side of my door. He pulls it open, but I don't get out. "Ready?"

"Not really."

He raises an eyebrow. "What's wrong?"

"Emil." I finally turn to look at him. "Be honest: Did everyone stop talking to Lionel because of his...because of what happened?"

"What? Is that what he told you?"

I swallow. "He said you guys weren't there for him while I was gone. DeeDee says he stopped coming around, but— that doesn't sound like Lionel, to just stop talking to people...unless he has a reason."

"It's not as simple as that," Emil says. "DeeDee and I knew what happened with him, and everyone else knew something was up, but we didn't tell them exactly what it was...out of respect. So people may have come to their own conclusions."

I frown. "Their own conclusions? Like what? That he's dangerous or something?"

That's what a lot of people think about bipolar disorder. I found out when I was researching it online, when I wanted to find out more about what Lionel was going through than the information that filtered from his doctors and through my parents to me.

Emil shakes his head. "People aren't sitting around talking about your brother. I think...You weren't here, and no one knew the best way to handle it, and we just kind of drifted apart from him."

I gaze into the thicket of oak trees stationed behind the DEAD END sign: dark and leafy and quiet. "I never should have gone away."

"You can't blame yourself," he says firmly. "You don't know what would've happened if you'd stayed."

"I *do* know my brother would probably be in this car with us instead of staying home to read a thousand-page book."

"Maybe. Maybe not." Emil holds out his hand. "But you can't spend all night worrying about it. Come on."

He's right, even though I don't want to admit it. So I swallow down the contrary response on the tip of my tongue, and then I take Emil's hand and hop down from the Jeep.

DeeDee's mom is an architect, and the Sullivan house is designed to meet her every desire. She obviously has a deep, abiding love for glass, as the entire front wall of the house is made up of windows that stretch all the way to the second floor. A modern chandelier with vertical glass tubes housing skinny, soft blue lightbulbs hangs almost to the floor in the foyer, and every time I am here I think how DeeDee is tempting fate by letting us hang out. Someone would only have to step the wrong way for the whole thing to shatter, but DeeDee says she doesn't want to waste time worrying about bad things that *might* happen, and so far that's worked out for her.

The whole front of the house is empty, but I can hear a few people around back, voices floating through the open door off the kitchen that leads to the veranda. Still-sealed packages of hamburger and hot dog buns sit on the counter, nestled among bottles of liquor and cheap wine. DeeDee's parents are decidedly not here this evening.

I do a quick scan as we walk out to the patio, but I don't see her anywhere. The space is, however, dotted with my old group of friends: the creative types at school, ranging from modern dancers who are always moving, to brilliant, socially awkward musicians, to visual artists who create pieces that make adults complain at the school's gallery shows.

"Well, look who's back to grace us with her presence," Catie Ransom says in her trademark flat voice as she strolls over. She makes angry art, like the small-scale wire installation depicting abused laboratory animals that she presented at the end-of-year show last spring.

"Holy shit, it's Suzette." Tommy Ng walks up and strums a buoyant note on the guitar strapped over his shoulder as if he's ready to start busking for drinks. Tommy never goes anywhere without that thing.

"It's me," I say with a small smile, suddenly feeling alone even though I'm surrounded by the people I used to spend every weekend with.

Emil has drifted away a few feet, talking to his best friend, Justin, who's laying out rows of burgers and chicken breasts and soy dogs on the grill. All of us have known each other since middle school, but as soon as DeeDee transferred into our high school freshman year, I became closer to her than anyone. And I don't think it's my imagination that they've all seemed even more distant since I went away. We hung out during winter break, but they had private jokes that I wasn't a part of and new friends I didn't know, and I couldn't keep up with who was dating or fighting. It seemed like a totally different crowd.

Maybe I'm different to them, too. Not just because I went away, but because I've never talked openly with them about Lionel's illness. But really, was I supposed to tell them everything I shared with DeeDee, the person closest to me besides my brother? That I was scared and worried for him, and angry that I'd been forced to leave my life here?

"You seem upset." Catie is wearing a black cotton shirt-dress and floral combat boots, and when she raises her eyebrows at me, I notice the electric-blue color smeared across her eyelids. "Are you upset?"

"I'm not upset." I stifle a sigh because that would only prove her theory—which, by the way, is there a reason Catie Ransom of all people is analyzing my mood? "I can't get over this stupid jet lag."

"Cry me a fucking river, Suzette." Ah, there's the Catie I know, switching from concerned to vicious in mere seconds. "I'd give my left tit to go live across the country for most of the year. You do realize how disgustingly mundane it is being stuck here?"

"We don't live in some podunk town," I say, shaking my head. "L.A.'s worst day is still better than Avalon on its best."

Catie rolls her eyes and clomps away, muttering, "Whatever. You're still so ungrateful."

"Hey, Suzette, want to hear this new thing I'm working on?" Tommy asks, running his fingers gently over the guitar strings. "I started it a couple of months ago...."

"Um, I was just going to find DeeDee," I say, but the question was only a courtesy because Tommy is already strumming away, singing with the heart of someone performing in front of thousands. I slip away once someone else wanders over to listen.

The empty kitchen I passed through on the way in has been replaced with a roomful of people who've just arrived. Most of them I don't recognize—maybe soon-to-be sophomores or people who managed to fly under the radar my first year. One girl looks vaguely familiar; she has stringy, lime-colored hair and she's standing next to the fridge with two other girls I don't know. We see each other at the same time, and she narrows her eyes.

"I know you," she says, then snaps her fingers a few seconds later. "You were at my party with DeeDee."

I walk over to them slowly. "New Year's Eve?"

She nods and I remember.

"That was the best party," I say. And it was. We were on the beach and it was *freezing*, but we were all wrapped up in plaid woolen blankets and I shared a bottle of champagne with a group of people I didn't know as we raucously counted down to midnight. "Hey . . . are you here with Alicia?"

"Technically. She ditched us for DeeDee as soon as we got here," says a girl with big, curly black hair and the most badass tattoo I've ever seen in my life. Truly, it's fucking beautiful. A collage of various flowers is inked onto her pale skin, petals overlapping with stems on top of leaves, and all of it done in the most gorgeous, saturated hues of green and blue and pink and orange. I could stare at it for hours. She notices and smiles and that's what makes me look away.

"I, um, better go find DeeDee. Nice seeing you again," I say in the general direction of the green-haired girl as I make my way across the kitchen.

Climbing the stairs to DeeDee's room, I pass the same photos I've walked by probably hundreds of times—DeeDee and her parents, DeeDee standing solo on a hiking trail, fifth-grade DeeDee with her first French horn. I didn't know her back then, but she's looked the same since she was a kid: long, peachy-blond hair and sleepy brown eyes and skin that burns at the mention of sunlight. Seeing her smile makes me realize how much I've really missed her.

A soft light glows under her bedroom door at the end of the hallway. It's too quiet up here and I find myself tiptoeing down the hall even though her door is ajar. I lean forward to listen, to make sure she's not in the middle of something with Alicia. Voices carry across the room, but they don't sound intimate or angry. Just quiet and intense, and that's pretty much the nature of DeeDee and Alicia's relationship.

The door squeaks as I push it open and Alicia looks over, startled, alone on DeeDee's bed. The laptop in front of her is responsible for the voices, and she's watching whatever it is in the dark, the glow illuminating her round face. Her eyes go even larger when she sees that it's me.

"You're here!" She pauses the video and sits up straight.

"I'm here." I smile at her. I don't know Alicia well. She started dating my best friend while I was away, but she's always been nice to me, and she would have Dee tell me hi sometimes when we talked on the phone. "Is she up here?"

"Yeah, she's almost finished getting ready—"

The door to the attached bathroom opens at the far end of DeeDee's room and she steps out barefoot, a silky green skirt brushing the bottoms of her ankles. She gets halfway across the room before she sees me.

"Oh my *God*, how long have you been here? Why didn't you text me when you pulled up? I would've met you at the door. Oh my *God*, Suz." She rushes forward and pulls me into a warm, tight hug.

I look at Alicia. I like her, but I wish she weren't here, her angular bob falling across her face as she traces the music notes splashed over DeeDee's duvet. I was hoping to have a little alone time with my best friend, a few moments away from everyone else.

Dee understands what I'm thinking without me having to say a word. Just one of the many things I love about her.

"Babe, can you give us a minute? We'll be down in a bit," she says, her soft voice even sweeter than normal.

Alicia nods, closing the laptop before she stands. She smiles as she leaves the room, but there's a look she gives me. Not mean, but... curious. And a little skeptical.

"I'm so happy you're back." DeeDee reaches out to finger one of my dreadlocks. She's one of the few I'll allow to touch my hair without asking, a rule that sounds weird until you realize how many people are fascinated by black hair to the point of rudeness. "Your trip was good?"

"It was fine," I say, sinking down onto her bed, my back against the pillows. "I'm happy to be back, too."

"Everything okay yesterday?" She joins me on the bed, moving the laptop to the floor so she can stretch her long legs. "Sorry I couldn't talk. Dad had this meeting with a client and wanted me to go with him, and you know his rule about talking on the phone during a road trip."

"Everything's fine," I say. I don't want to get into the Lionel thing right now. I don't want her to think I'm accusing her of abandoning my brother. DeeDee is fiercely loyal; abandonment is not in her nature. But she's one of the few people who know Lionel's diagnosis, and a part of me can't help thinking maybe she didn't try hard enough with him.

She toys with the milkmaid braids wrapped around her head like a wreath. "So...anything new with Iris?"

I let out a breath. DeeDee knows about Iris—about *us*—but I didn't expect her to ask so directly. Or so soon. "She left the day before me and we said good-bye and...I don't know. She's back home in Michigan now."

DeeDee's mouth turns up at the corner. "Did you say good-bye or good-*bye*?"

"Dee..."

"*Suzette*," she mocks me. "Are you seriously trying to be shy with me?"

"I'm not trying to be anything, I just..." I pause, remembering the look on her girlfriend's face as she left the room. "Does Alicia know? About Iris?"

DeeDee looks at me with soft eyes. "I'm sorry. I was so excited for you and it slipped out and—well, I know she hasn't said anything to anyone. She doesn't even go to our school."

Even so, she's downstairs with all our friends right now; the news could slip out of her as easily as DeeDee revealed it, and then what? I have to explain myself for the rest of the summer to people I've barely seen for the past year?

But I say, "It's fine." Because Alicia doesn't seem like the gossipy type. And while I've always been able to trust

Dee with my secrets, a part of me assumed she would tell her girlfriend, if only to announce another initiate to the girls-liking-girls club. "But I feel like she thinks we're going to start hooking up now...."

DeeDee laughs loud and long, a laugh that comes from deep in her belly and makes me smile in spite of myself. "You and me? First of all, you're not my type; your boobs are way too big. But also, it's not like that, Suzette. Like, you start making out with girls and so we have to make out because I like girls, too."

"It was *one* girl," I say, sliding down the bed so I'm lying flat on my back, no longer supported by pillows. "And that's the thing: I haven't felt like that about any other girl. So maybe it was a one-time thing...an *Iris* thing."

If that's even possible, to like someone so wildly different from everyone else you've been attracted to. Were we just experimenting all those nights in our dorm room, under the covers, hands sliding over curves and lips exploring freely? Iris had been with other girls; she was *experienced*. But I'd only ever kissed boys, and only two at that, and always with our clothes on.

"That could be true," DeeDee says thoughtfully. She turns to face me. "Do you still like guys?"

"I don't know." I close my eyes and try to remember the last guy I thought about that way. Emil. My eyes fly open.

He doesn't count. He's cute and he looks really good tonight, but—he's *Emil*. "Maybe?"

"Well, you don't have to figure it out now." DeeDee touches my arm. "Or ever. Just like who you like."

"Says the girl who's known she was a lesbian since the day she was born," I say, rolling my eyes.

"I was eight, smartass," she replies. Then, with an exaggeratedly dreamy expression, she says, "I still think Ms. Bowling is one of the prettiest people I've ever seen. I looked her up a while ago. She was living up in Portland with some dude. Alas, we never could've been."

"Never mind that she was your third-grade teacher." I sit up. "Hey, Dee?"

"Yeah?"

"Can you not tell anyone else about Iris? I don't know if I can talk about it yet." There's still too much I don't understand, like why, even though everything I did with Iris felt good, I was still so shy about kissing or touching her first. Even after weeks of fooling around. Or why, after what happened a couple of weeks before we left Dinsmore, I'm scared of the same sort of judgment here, though I'm surrounded by queer friends and allies.

"Of course," DeeDee says. "And I know she hasn't told anyone, but I'm sorry I mentioned it to Alicia. That wasn't cool."

"It's okay." I squeeze her hand. "Really."

And it is.

Because the person I'm most worried about knowing the truth is myself.

More people have arrived and the scene downstairs is larger, louder. DeeDee gets pulled away almost as soon as we reach the first floor, and I stand still for a moment, holding on to the steel banister as I look around the room.

"So where's Lionel?" comes the voice I hoped I wouldn't have to hear again tonight.

Catie is standing in front of me with her arms crossed, and her red-ringed eyes tell me she's had a couple of drinks since I saw her out back.

"At home." I don't offer anything else, and most people would respect that, but not Catie.

"You know he never comes around anymore?" She eyes me as if I have something to do with this. "People are saying he's schizo."

My skin goes cold. "Who's saying that?"

She scratches at a spot on her shoulder. "Well, is he? If he's not schizo, what's wrong with him?"

"There's nothing *wrong* with him, first of all," I begin, stepping closer. Catie takes great joy in intimidating people, so it's best to remind her that I'm not scared. "And second, what makes you think it's any of your business?"

"It's creepy, how secretive you guys are about everything," she says, obviously not intimidated by me, either. She lifts her chin. "Like no one can break through your little duo."

I look her dead in the eye. "You're being an asshole, Catie."

Her lips twist together into a smile. "Well, at least I'm *honest*, Suzette."

She stomps off for the second time this evening, and I make a silent promise to stay as far away from her as possible this summer. But it's hard to get her snide tone out of my head, and I'm stuck on the last thing she said, about being honest. Does she know more about Lionel than she's letting on? Does she know something about me?

"Whoa, who pissed you off?"

I look up to see the tattooed girl leaning against the wall on the other side of the foyer, now in possession of a beer bottle. And realize I'm still glaring after Catie, fists clenched at my side.

"Nobody worth knowing, trust me." I feel my body relax and I try to smile at her, but it's easier to stare at the indelible ink on her arm rather than look at her face.

"Oh, I'm like a magnet for people not worth knowing," she says, and I don't normally think much about voices, but I like hers. Not quite deep, but throaty and sure, like she could be on the radio. "Attracting them is, like, my special skill."

She peels herself off the wall and steps closer, and I do look at her then. Her eyelids are rimmed with dark, heavy liner, but underneath, her eyes are a warm hazel. Friendly, which I didn't expect from someone who looks so tough. A *pretty* tough, but tough all the same, like people who don't know her probably wouldn't fuck with her, tiny as she is. And I'm almost paralyzed by how good she smells. Earthy and a little sweet.

"Why haven't I seen you around?" she asks before I can say anything back, and I'm glad, because I wasn't sure what to say to her. She seems so easygoing, so sure that she belongs here with these people I don't know at all or barely know anymore.

"I just got back from boarding school."

"Oh, shit, you're the best friend? This party is *for* you." She takes a swig of beer as she looks at me. "I've heard all about you."

"All good?" And I realize, with surprise, that I actually want it to be true, for her to think good things about me. I cared about what people in Avalon thought, but that was because everything was new—every place, person, experience. But here, I have almost too many people who actually care about me to worry about those who don't. So why is it so important for this girl I just met to like me?

"From what I hear, you're practically a saint."

"Really?"

"Not really," she says with a wry smile. Her lips are filled in with a dark purple color that hasn't smudged, even from the beer she's drinking. "But you are apparently the *best* friend ever, so . . . I'm Rafaela, by the way."

"I'm Suzette. How do you know DeeDee?" I ask, trying to remember if she's ever mentioned this girl.

"Through Alicia, actually. I went out with Grace for, like, five minutes," she says simply. "Thank Christ we realized we were better as friends, and I totally weaseled my way into her group." I must look confused because she grins and says, "The girl with the green hair?"

"Oh, right. Grace."

But I wasn't confused. I was processing the fact that she's dated a girl. I felt—well, relieved. To be back in a place where strangers openly discuss relationships that aren't just boy-girl, where a certain group of students don't whisper about the guys who were caught kissing in the woods behind Dinsmore Hall. And where two girls sleeping curled up in one bed wouldn't be gossip to make the rounds.

She drains her bottle and nods toward the kitchen. "Beer?"

I follow, palms sweating as we enter the kitchen, where her friends are still standing around. I glance at Grace, try-ing to picture the two of them together: going to see movies at the Vista and shows at the Echo and holding hands where anyone can see. It's not hard to imagine that for other girls— just for myself, since Iris and I were so private.

Rafaela hands me a beer and when she turns back to the fridge to get one for herself, I can't help staring. At the back of her head, where black curls bounce along the slope of her neck as she moves, at the flowers emblazoned across the back of her shoulder. I twist the cap off the bottle and take a big swallow, but I can't ignore the way my body thrums with nerves. My skin is warm and tingly and the feeling doesn't stop even when I look away from her.

Maybe it wasn't an Iris thing after all.

five.

The next morning I come downstairs to find Lionel making peanut butter toast.

Even though I can't let go of the words Catie used (*schizo, creepy, secretive*), I'm glad to see Lionel up and moving around. Last summer, when he was in the deepest trench of his depression, I would only see him at the table for dinner, if then. Mom and Saul didn't always make him eat with us, and I took it upon myself to bring meals to his room on those days, even if he wouldn't eat or acknowledge I was there when I opened the door to check on him.

"Hey, you want a piece?" he asks, hand poised over the bag of bread.

"Are we out of challah?" I look past him to the open

bread box. We usually have leftovers from Shabbat, and it makes the best French toast.

"Yeah, sorry. I used it to make a sandwich last night." He looks at me over his shoulder. "So...toast?"

"We should go up to the Brite Spot," I say, picturing the wood-paneled interior and shiny pleather booths of our favorite neighborhood diner. My stomach rumbles as I think about the vast menu, where I could choose from French toast or omelets or a breakfast burrito or—

"Or we could have peanut butter toast in the tree house?"

"Deal," I say, and a part of me lightens with relief. We didn't bike to the reservoir yesterday. In fact, I hardly saw him at all.

I prep a tray and pour two glasses of orange juice while he makes our breakfast. He's serious about it—the bread is toasted to a perfect golden brown, the thick globs of peanut butter applied with precision. We carry it all out to the tree house and I let Lionel go up first, then carefully pass the tray before I climb the wooden slats nailed against the tree to join him. It's a proper room, big enough to stand in. We've moved a few things up here: the old green rug that used to be in the living room, a small futon that lived in the garage. Lion and I used the tree house a lot the first few years after it was built, but now it looks like he hasn't been up here in months, maybe since I last left.

He kicks aside a few leaves and sneezes, then sits down cross-legged.

"When was the last time you were up here?" I take in the dust that's settled on every surface of the room before I brush at a spot on the rug and sit down with my back against the front of the futon.

"I don't know." He shrugs, pushing the tray between us. "It wasn't the same with you gone."

I know what he means. We didn't always come up here together; there were solo trips, and a few with people like DeeDee or Emil. But every time Lionel went to see his mom up in Northern California, I tried to sit in the tree house alone and didn't last more than a few minutes. The vibe was off. Empty. And it never occurred to me that Lionel would feel the same way with me gone.

I pick up my plate and pause before I take a bite of toast. "We missed you last night."

He looks up at the ceiling as he chews, then back at me. "You were probably the only one."

I consider mentioning that Catie asked about him, but he's no fool. He'll know that missing him wasn't the real focus of whatever she said. Instead, I ask, "Lion, what happened? Emil said you drifted apart from everyone and they haven't seen you in forever."

"*Drifted apart?* That's a nice way to put it." He washes down his toast with a swallow of orange juice. "I don't know. I missed a bunch of school and . . . People texted at first. A few emails. DeeDee was good about it, even after everyone else stopped. But then she wasn't, and school was weird as hell when I went back. Like, everyone was too scared to even ask what happened, so they wouldn't talk to me about anything real."

I frown as I set down my toast. "Why didn't you call them on it?"

"Because they already think I'm crazy! I shouldn't have to *make* people want to hang out with me. I'm still *me*." He shakes his head. "And you know, everybody drinks now and I can't do that. Doesn't really go with my meds."

"Oh." I hesitate before plowing ahead. "How is all that?"

We haven't talked much about the pills he takes, though I've seen the long plastic organizer he keeps on his dresser, separated into compartments with a different day of the week printed on each square. I can remember only one time he brought up the subject himself, a Sunday afternoon shortly after I'd arrived in Avalon my first semester.

His voice was thin and defeated over the phone as he told me they were changing his meds. That sometimes people have to try a few different combinations before they get it right. And that he wanted to believe them, but he felt like he was crawling out of his skin—that he would never feel better.

For a while, I regularly asked about his treatment each time we talked on the phone, wanting him to know I cared even if I couldn't be there. He'd answer, though it was always just enough information and nothing extra. But then one day, right around Halloween, he said he didn't want to talk about it—the bipolar, his meds, nothing. I said okay and bit my tongue so I wouldn't blurt out that I was worried about him, because if he wasn't talking to me, who else was left?

So I never brought up the topic again. Until now.

"They're working. Or at least that's what everyone tells me." Lion taps his fingers against the juice glass next to him as he talks. "But I hate feeling dependent on pills. This doesn't go away, you know.... Doctors say I have to take them for the rest of my life if I want to feel normal."

"They said that? *Normal?*" Of course I'm guilty of thinking that word myself, and I'm still not sure which one of the Lionels I've seen fits into that category. But I'm not a medical professional, and he's not my patient. I'm trying to learn how to be around the person I thought I'd figured out so many years ago.

"No, they said, 'You'll have to take some form of medication to live life to the best of your abilities,' or some shit like that," he says, slipping into a nasal tone.

"Well, you seem..." I look down at my feet. The soles are dirty, from walking barefoot outside and climbing the tree and scuffling around on the tree house floor, and that reminds me of long-ago summers, when Lionel and I could spend all day outside and hours up here, only needing each other's company. "You seem like you did before..."

"Before I went off the deep end?" he finishes, not giving

me time to find the right words. He smiles but his eyes are mirthless, his lips upturned in a plastic half-moon. "That's the thing. Everyone—Dad, Nadine, Dr. T—keeps saying this seems like the ideal combination, the right dosage, blah blah blah. But that only lasts until I have a bad day or week or month, or until the meds make me too sick to stay on them, or until Dr. T starts worrying about my blood levels. I'm tired of feeling like a fucking guinea pig."

"Maybe..." I pause, and it's hard to believe there was ever a time when I said whatever I wanted to Lion without thinking about it beforehand. "Maybe if you start hanging out with everyone again, that will get your mind off it."

"Right. So they can say stupid shit to my face instead of behind my back? No, thanks."

"The only ones saying stupid shit are stupid people, like Catie, and—" I clear my throat, try to rework my words, but Lionel latches on to them immediately.

"What is Catie Ransom saying?" He's trying to sound as if he doesn't care, as if we all know how offensive and clumsy-mouthed she can be and it doesn't really matter. But we both know how much more thoughtless words hurt when they come from someone who's supposed to be your friend.

"Nothing worth repeating." I touch the tip of my nose ring, where it peeks out between my nostrils. "She—"

"Little, come on."

I take a deep breath and tack my words onto the exhale.

"She said some people think you're schizophrenic and that's why you stopped coming around."

"They think I'm schizophrenic." He stares at me, shaking his head. "What if I were? Is there a hierarchy to mental illness? And how is what I have any of their business?"

"It's not. I never told anyone anything, I promise."

"Fucking typical," he says, standing up now, as if his agitation is too big to contain. "For someone who acts like they're so above it all, she sure seems to have something to say about everyone."

"Listen, fuck Catie. No one's really saying that. She's just trying to start shit. But really, there were so many new people there last night, and it wouldn't be as bad as you think, hanging out with everyone again. If I can come back and do it, you can, too."

I smile after I say this last part, but Lionel's eyebrows crease.

"The reasons we haven't been around them aren't exactly the same, Little."

"I know, I'm..." I'm trying to let him know I understand how difficult it can be to integrate back into a group that's moved on without us, but no matter what I say, it will sound patronizing. I was able to lie and tell people boarding school was my choice, but no one chooses a mental illness. No one will ever give our excuses the same weight.

Lionel starts walking toward the doorway and I want to

take everything back, to not ask him about the medicine or bring up our friends or anything else he doesn't want to discuss. All I've wanted since I got back was to sit up in the tree house with him like old times, and now that's ruined.

None of this would have been an issue, pre–boarding school. We talked about everything, but *especially* the things that made us hurt.

"Wait a minute." I stand, too. "I'm sorry. I just—"

He stops and turns, and his blue eyes are full of angry ocean waves as he looks at me. "Maybe Catie Ransom doesn't matter, but if she's saying shit like that out loud, other people are thinking it. And it really sucks to know people I haven't hung out with in a year are trying to guess how crazy I am."

He's down the tree before I can stop him and then stalking across the yard, and I wonder how I've managed to create a rift between us when I haven't been back even a week.

then.

I haven't thought of going shopping with anyone but my mom for my bat mitzvah dress, but when Catie Ransom offers to go with me, I know I have to say yes.

Catie is bold and unafraid, and everyone listens to her, even if they don't like what she has to say. Me included, I guess. Mom agrees to let us go alone but insists on dropping off Lionel, too, who is armed with a paperback copy of *Sula*. I don't protest because I always like having him around; he's sort of a lousy chaperone, though, being only a year older than Catie and me.

"Call me if you need anything," Mom says before we get out of the car, but she'd really rather we didn't. She works part-time as a copywriter, and this is one of her writing days, where she gets to stay home and work on her screenplay. I know it's a big deal for her to take time out of her schedule to drive me to the mall, but I still wish she could stay. I'm nervous about my bat mitzvah, worried I'm going to do everything wrong in front of everyone, including wearing the wrong dress.

"I've been to a million of these," Catie says in greeting. The worry must be plastered all over my face. "I could pick out a bat mitzvah dress in my sleep."

That only makes me sweat more—is there a specific type of dress I should wear, and would everyone notice if I didn't? I've been to my fair share of ceremonies, but it feels different now that it's my turn. And I know people will be watching me closer than the other girls in my Hebrew classes; I don't look like any of them.

For all her boasting, Catie is a reckless shopper. Not at all methodical and not at all interested in looking for my dress, at least not right away. My mother would have a set list of stores to go to and she'd look on the other side of the store from me to make sure we didn't miss anything and she'd stand outside the dressing room, available to give her honest opinion and grab different sizes. We'd find a dress by the time we got to the third store, and by the time we were sitting down to lunch, my anxiety would have faded.

Catie takes me into stores that don't sell anything in our size just to make fun of the clothing and rolls her eyes at me when I tell her she's being mean. We burn a quick path through a candy shop, Catie dipping her fingers into the bins when no one is looking so she can pop stolen candy into her mouth. I don't know why no one is looking. She wears all black and too much makeup and she's not a fan of inside voices.

"I really need to find a dress today," I say after an hour. We're in an electronics store now, where Catie is playing around with the display model of a computer, typing nonsensical emails to no one.

She sighs as if I've ruined her entire day but steps back from the computer and nods toward the door. "Come on. I know the perfect place."

And she does. It's a store I never would have thought about going into. From the outside, it looks like they only have two or three options, total, and everything is in muted colors—black and taupe and ivory, sometimes gray. But once I get inside, I see that all the clothes look better up close, with impeccable lace detailing and delicate beading and fabric so sumptuous I wish I could use it for my bedsheets. It's expensive, but when she handed over her credit card earlier today, Mom said, "I don't want you maxing out my account, but buy something nice, okay? It's a special day for you, sweet pea."

The sales associates know Catie, and they help us choose dresses for me to try on, fawning over us both like we're celebrities. It's kind of fun, after a while, emerging from the dressing room to all of their expectant eyes and having them fuss and fight over what looks best on me.

The dress we all agree on is the prettiest thing I've ever owned, by far. Fine gold thread is woven throughout the champagne-colored bodice, which has a sweetheart neckline and slender gold straps. The skirt is a soft, cream-colored tulle that stops above my knees and floats around me like air.

I'm smiling when I give them the credit card, pleasantly surprised that Catie came through for me. Maybe she isn't so bad.

"Mazel tov!" the blond girl calls out from behind the cash register as we leave. I wave at her in thanks, then duck my head when a woman appraising a pair of white pants gives me a strange look.

I'm suddenly ravenous and ask Catie if she wants to grab something to eat with Lionel and me before she leaves.

"Sure. But I have to give you something first." Before I can say anything, she pulls from her purse a long necklace with the most delicate gold chain and a violet-colored teardrop pendant hanging from the center. "Really pretty, right?"

It's beautiful. But why isn't it in a box? It takes me only a second to remember Catie looking at the jewelry while I paid for my dress. And that Catie never paid for anything in the store.

"For you," she says, holding it out between us. "It'll look amazing with your dress."

She pushes the necklace toward me, the pendant

swinging in the air, but I put my hands up and step back. My throat hurts as I say, "I don't want it."

"Oh, God. Are you really such a goody-goody? It's just a necklace." She shrugs, irritated. "It's not my fault those girls are so bad at their job. I practically took it from right under their noses."

"Catie, you can't . . ." I've never stolen anything in my life. "You have to take it back. They were so nice to us."

"They were nice to us because my mom spends a ton of money there. It's not like they own the place."

Nothing Catie can say will make me feel better about her having stolen that necklace, and nothing I say will make her return it. She's probably more pleased with herself the bigger a deal I make of it, so I stop talking about it. I refuse it one last time and say we should go meet Lionel, and I look away quickly from her downturned mouth.

Mom loves the dress, and when she's looking in the bag for the receipt, she says, "What's this?"

"What's what?" I turn around just in time to see her pulling out something small that sparkles when it hits the light.

The necklace.

"Oh, this is beautiful, sweet pea." She slowly untwists the chain and holds it up in front of her. "You bought it to go with the dress?"

My stomach jumps up and down. I don't know what to say. "I, um . . ."

"I know I told you to only get the dress, but—well, it's so pretty. And I want to see it on you." She walks behind me and drapes it over my neck. I wonder if she can feel my heart pulsing too fast in my chest, or the heat of anxiety clinging to my skin. The pendant is cool and smooth against my sternum, and Mom gasps when she sees it with the dress, says the two were meant to be. "You have to wear it to the bat mitzvah."

I'm glad when she heads back to her office. My throat is too dry to speak, and even after I've taken off the necklace, I can feel it burning a line across my skin.

Lionel is doing homework when I tell him we need a tree house meeting, but he puts down his pencil and follows me out to the backyard without another word.

I kick off my flip-flops and climb up ahead of him. The floor is scattered with the remnants of the Monopoly game we abandoned without crowning a winner the last time we were here.

I barely wait for him to get inside before I pull the necklace from my pocket and thrust it in his face. He frowns for a minute, looking back and forth from the jewelry to me, then shrugs. "It's nice?"

"Lion, it's stolen."

His mouth drops open. "You...?"

"Of course not. Catie."

"Damn." He touches the purple stone. "Looks expensive."

"It probably is. Catie won't take it back, and I guess she put it in my bag when we were eating, because I told her I didn't want it."

I place it on the futon, next to the Monopoly box. I don't want it in my hands anymore. The chain feels hot, like the dishonesty of its presence is searing my palm.

"You could tell her parents," Lionel muses. "Force her to take it back."

Sometimes I like it when he's so practical, but not now. He knows Catie just as well as I do, and he's not thinking about the consequences of getting her in trouble.

"She'd make my life miserable. Not worth it."

"So take it back to the store yourself. Explain that your friend took it."

"They won't believe me." I sink onto the futon, glaring at the necklace. "They love Catie's family. They'll think I took it."

I don't remember the first time Mom warned me about shopping while black, but I do remember the first time I noticed we were being followed around a store, even after we'd repeatedly told the sales associate we didn't need any help. I remember the look on Mom's face when we left the store. I'd never seen her so silently angry.

Lionel runs a hand over his hair. "You could blame it on

Nadine. Say she found it and threatened to ground you if you didn't tell her the truth. She could be the one to tell Catie's parents."

That's not a bad idea, but Catie would still be pissed and ready for revenge.

"I didn't say anything when Mom found it. She'll be mad if I tell her, and...what if she cancels my bat mitzvah? I know you think it's corny...that it doesn't really mean anything, but it's important to me."

What I don't say is that even though I've already converted, becoming a bat mitzvah feels, somehow, like it will bring me even closer to him and Saul. I know it doesn't matter that we don't look alike. I know that caring about each other is the most important part, but I like sharing something official with them.

I don't look up because I don't want to see him smirking or rolling his eyes, but Lion just nods. "I won't say anything, okay?"

I was hoping he'd come up with another solution. I can't think of a way to fix this that won't make someone mad. My only option is to shove the necklace into the bottom of my jewelry box and hope Mom forgets about it on the day of the party.

But I don't feel quite as yucky as I did before we came up to the tree house, knowing Lionel is aware of the secret now, too.

The morning of my bat mitzvah, I wake up to find a small black box on my nightstand. I'm still half asleep when I open it, but my eyes widen immediately once I see the silver Magen David lying on velvet.

I fumble with the clasp for a few minutes before I give up and run downstairs to Lionel's room for help. He's reading in bed like he does on the weekends; today, it's *The Shining*.

"Look at what Saul and Mom got me," I say, dangling the necklace in front of him. "I'll just wear this instead of the purple one. Problem solved, right?"

"Yeah, probably." He shrugs. "No one's going to ask why you're wearing a Star of David at your bat mitzvah."

"Will you help me put it on?"

He snaps the clasp together and I rush over to the mirror on his closet door to look. It's perfect.

I have my hand on the knob, ready to run downstairs and show Mom and Saul, when Lionel mumbles, "I got it for you."

I turn around to stare at him, fingering the edges of the star. "What?"

"I didn't want you to have to wear that stupid necklace or even think about it, and this one seemed like something you might be into or whatever, so . . ." He shrugs again and looks down at his book, but I know he's not reading. "I took care of that other necklace, so you don't have to worry about it."

"What'd you do with it?" I ask, nervous that he found some way to involve Catie.

"I put it in an envelope and took it to the store and dropped it on the counter when they weren't looking," he says, like returning stolen goods is the easiest thing in the world.

"They really didn't see you?"

"Nobody said anything if they did. I walked out and went to the bookstore."

"Lion..." I pause because I feel a little bit like I'm going to cry, and he'll tease me if I cry, especially over something he did for me. "This is really nice. The necklace and... everything. Thank you."

"It's no big deal." He looks at his feet, sticking up beneath the covers. "You're my sister."

I know that's what he's saying every time he calls me Little—acknowledging that we're siblings, even if we're not related by blood. But I like hearing him say it so plainly. It makes me think there'll never be a time when we question our bond.

six.

Saul makes good on that museum promise and we head out to LACMA after a late breakfast, determined to see as many exhibits as we can cram into our day.

"Your mom and I were talking about going on a family vacation this summer," he says as he backs the army-green station wagon out of the driveway. "Any suggestions?"

"Paris," I say immediately. It's my mother's favorite city in Europe. She's talked about it so often and with such love that I think I should see it, too.

"I like where your head's at, kiddo, but we were thinking about something closer to home. Yosemite, if we're all up to it. Or Joshua Tree."

"Maybe we should go to Nevada so you can relive your Burning Man days," I say with a straight face.

"It was *one* time." Saul shakes his head, laughing. "And you weren't even alive yet. My Burning Man days are long behind me."

"If we go to Yosemite, we might as well drive up and see Daphne." I grin.

"Your mother would love that."

He's not wrong. Daphne is Lionel's mother. She lives up in Humboldt County and knits these special wool blankets that sell for, like, a thousand dollars. She and my mom *do* get along, so well that anytime Daphne's in town, she makes a point to see my mother, too. They don't have a whole lot in common besides being overly proud of their Seven Sisters connection; Lionel's mom was majoring in gender studies at Mount Holyoke while mine was firmly entrenched in the English department at Wellesley. I think Saul is weirded out that they act like long-lost college friends, but Daphne scoffs when he gets awkward about it. "We were terrible together," she always says. "Honestly, we should've gotten a prize for signing divorce papers before we completely screwed up our kid."

"Well, at least Lionel will get to go to Europe next summer." I look at Saul out of the corner of my eye.

It's a promise they made to us when we started high school—as long as our college plans are set for the autumn after our graduation, they'll send us on a European trip for a month with one of our friends. I want it for Lionel. He needs that trip next year. Something to look forward to.

Saul is quiet. Too quiet, and I think he's doing that thing where he pretends to be preoccupied with traffic when he doesn't know what to say. But then he sighs. "That's on hold for now, Suzette."

"On hold? But it's a year from now. You don't think—"

Saul's cell phone rings then, sitting in the console, and his relief at not having to continue the conversation is palpable. Which I hate. He said he'd be honest with me about Lionel, but he still doesn't want to answer my questions.

He asks me to look at the screen for him.

"Ora?" I say, squinting at the last name.

"I'd better get that. The guys just delivered to her this morning." I pick up the call and put it on speaker while Saul gets his client voice ready. "Ora! How's that table working out? Beautiful, right? Looks perfect in the space?"

The woman who called sounds as if she's wringing her hands. Like so many people in L.A., she has a slight accent, a lyrical way of saying certain words that makes me think she grew up speaking Spanish, too. Saul pulls over to the side of the road, across from the lake, as he listens to her describe a strange patch on the table he made. We aren't anywhere close to LACMA and I don't think we will be anytime soon, which is confirmed when Saul offers to swing by and take a look.

"Sorry," he says once Ora has hung up the phone. "Slight detour. You into flower shops?"

"I'm not *not* into them." But people who are into flower shops seem like the people who would buy or receive flowers often, and I fall into neither category. Flowers seem inherently romantic, and I'm still a novice in that area. "Flowers are just so . . . temporary."

"Ah, you are your mother's daughter," he says as he does a clean U-turn to reroute us. "The first time I bought her roses she said she hoped they weren't a metaphor for our relationship because they'd be dead in a week."

"Ouch."

"She's a tough sell, kiddo," he says with a shrug.

The flower shop is a couple of miles away, in Silver Lake, near Emil's house. Like most of the shops in that area of Sunset Boulevard, it's part of a strip mall, linked to an upscale coffee shop on one side and a denim boutique on the other. The sign on the storefront is white with green script, advertising CASTILLO FLOWERS. A flash of orange in the front window catches my eye and I look over to see a fat ginger cat sunning himself, his stomach stretched out in all its fluffy glory.

A bell rings over the glass door as we walk in, and the first thing I notice is how cramped the shop is. Nearly every surface is bursting with rows of flowering bushes and potted plants and tropical flowers. The air is perfumed with a variety of scents that should conflict with each other but blend seamlessly into a fresh, clean fragrance.

What I notice next is the girl sitting behind the counter. I recognize the curves of ink that wind around her arm, and the black curls that fall just below her shoulders. And, of course, her purple lips. Rafaela. My stomach flips.

She hops off her stool when we walk in, but her expression is neutral, no recognition present. Her eyes only briefly sweep over my face before she looks at Saul and smiles. "You're here about the table, right?"

"Indeed."

He's barely gotten the word out of his mouth before a woman comes bounding through the swinging wooden door that separates the shop from the back room. She's wearing an apron over denim overalls, and her black hair is pulled into a messy, silver-streaked bun. She comes right over to Saul with arms outstretched and squeezes his forearms in a detached sort of hug.

"Thank you for coming. I realized I never said I love the table—I *do* love it, but it's just that patch…"

"Ora, I'm glad to take a look at it." Saul pats her shoulder when she lets go of him. "The shop was on our way, right, Suzette?"

Both Ora's and Rafaela's eyes shift toward me. I nod.

"This is your daughter?" I wait for Ora to ask all sorts of

personal questions or make an inappropriate comment about how our skin colors don't match, but she simply beams. Does that weird non-hug thing to me, too, and says, "Well, he never told me you were so beautiful."

I smile back at her and try not to glance over at Rafaela.

Ora looks at her. "Help Suzette pick out something— anything she wants."

"Oh, that's okay," I start to protest. "I mean, that's very nice, but I—"

"Beautiful girls should have beautiful flowers," she says as if that's the end.

And it is. She leads Saul to the back of the shop, babbling about the table as they disappear behind the swinging door.

"Beautiful girls should have beautiful flowers," Rafaela mutters from her post. I don't know if she's mocking Ora or the fact that she said it about me, but then Rafaela catches my eye and smiles.

I hope she can't see how embarrassed I am. "She's just being nice because of my... Saul."

"Your Saul?"

"He's with my mom but they're not married, so he's not really my stepdad," I say in one breath. It's easier to have some answers prepared.

"Oh. Well, my aunt Ora doesn't just tell people things they want to hear." She strides over to the cat lying in the window, and I remember how she said she dated Grace, and

I wonder, with an intensity that only makes my face hotter, if she endorses her aunt's statement. "So, you just disappeared at that party, huh?"

She does remember me. I move to the display of tropical flowers and examine their vibrant petals. "I...Sorry. It was my first night seeing everyone, and I got dragged away..."

The truth is that I practically ran into Tommy Ng's arms when he wandered by us. I couldn't tell if Rafaela was flirting with me or if it was going to go there eventually, and I'm not used to doing that—liking a girl in public. Everything with Iris was behind our dorm room door, or in town when we were sure none of the girls from our hall would see us. And even then, we weren't careful enough.

"Well, you heard about the drama?" Rafaela picks up the cat, who meows with his eyes closed and doesn't complain when she holds him like a baby, rubbing her cheek against his fur. "This dude I dated for, like, two seconds showed up wasted, acting like a complete asshole."

"That was about you?" We'd all had a few drinks by then and that part of the night was a little hazy, but I vaguely remember DeeDee proudly stating she'd kicked out some randoms. And I guess I'm surprised to know that Rafaela used to date guys, too.

"Yeah, some jerk from the Palisades. I thought we were just having fun, nothing serious...but he's taking this thing to stalker levels." Rafaela shakes her head.

I wander around the small shop, hesitant to open my mouth for fear of sounding stupid. Wishing I'd worn something a little nicer than my mustard-yellow shorts. Wondering if she can tell how nervous I am, and why.

She smooshes her lips into the cat's fur and sets him back on the window ledge, where he curls into a velvety orange ball in the corner, near a display of succulents. I look above him to where a sign is taped, and read, in letters that bleed through to the back of the sign, HELP WANTED.

I point to it. "You're looking for help?"

Her green-gold eyes follow my finger. "Oh, yeah. My aunt wants someone in here a couple of days a week so she can take some time to herself. Summers get kind of crazy with weddings and she always ends up working herself to exhaustion. She basically breathes this store—took it over from her mom, so she's super passionate about it." She looks at me. "Why? You interested?"

I shrug. "Maybe." This is the first summer I'm old enough to have a part-time job, but Mom and Saul aren't big on the idea. They're of the "kids should be kids" thinking and would rather we concentrate on school and enjoy our summers than spend our free time working for minimum wage. It's nice of them, but it would also be nice to earn my own money and have someplace to go a few times a week.

And to see Rafaela a few times a week, too, if I'm being honest.

"Well, it pays nothing," she says. "But I'd be your boss, so it'd be low-stress."

I look around at the green life surrounding us. "I don't know anything about flowers."

"They're not such a mystery." She beckons me over to a cooler full of pastel blooms, the petals bunched up to create a tight circle. Even among all the mingling scents of the flowers, up close I notice how good Rafaela smells. "These are peonies. We get a lot of orders for bridal bouquets made out of these. People freak out because they're not available year-round—but they're perennials, so if you plant them they'll come back every year."

She opens the cooler door and I lean my head in to smell them, close my eyes as I inhale their sweet fragrance. When I open them, Rafaela is watching me. I stand up straight. "So, you just know all that stuff off the top of your head?"

"Eh, you pick it up after a while." She closes the cooler door. "Ora doesn't make it easy to forget."

Her aunt comes out from the back a few seconds later, laughing with Saul. Rafaela reaches into the cooler again, extracts a handful of flowers, and takes them to the back room without another word. I stand off to the side while Saul and Ora wrap up, gazing around the room at the endless rows of petals and stems and leaves, wondering if I'd ever be able to keep track of anything more than roses.

"Ready to go, kiddo?" Saul says, and I don't mind that

nickname from him, but God am I glad Rafaela wasn't in the room to hear it.

"Um, yeah…" I look toward the back. I guess it isn't a big deal that she didn't stick around to say good-bye, but now I won't have a chance to ask her about the job, and I'm too shy to bring it up to her aunt myself. I turn to Ora. "Nice meeting you."

"Oh, nice meeting *you*, sweetheart," she says, this time kissing both my cheeks. "Stop by anytime you're in the neighborhood, okay?"

"Wait!" comes a muffled voice. Then the back door swings open and my heart jumps off beat. "You almost forgot these." Rafaela holds out a square glass vase full of pink and white peonies, water swirling around the thick stems in the bottom.

I wipe my palms on my shorts before I take them from her. "These are really gorgeous. Thank you." I don't quite make eye contact. I stop somewhere along the smooth line of her neck. Which doesn't do much to calm my nerves; it only makes me wonder what it would feel like to kiss her there.

"No problem," she says. "I'll get your number from Alicia and text you about the job."

I nod, and Saul waits until we're standing by the station wagon before he says, "Joining the workforce?"

"She said they need help part-time and I thought it might be a cool place to work. I could save for my Europe trip."

Which is impossibly far away, but maybe if I keep bringing it up, Saul and Mom will reconsider letting Lionel go next year.

He ignores that part, naturally. "Well, Ora is a good egg." He pauses, looking at me over the top of the wagon. "And that girl seems nice, too."

I can't read his tone. Does he know? He and Mom wouldn't care. I'm sure of it because for a while last year, they thought Lionel was acting so strange because he was hiding something; and they're sort of hippies, so they automatically assumed he was struggling over sexuality instead of, say, drugs or mental illness, and initiated a big, unsolicited talk.

But now isn't the time to tell Saul that I think I'm into girls. Not here on the side of Sunset Boulevard, with traffic whizzing past and people clasping iced coffees and an orange tabby sunbathing in the window of the shop behind us. Not when we're museum-bound. He can think what he wants, but I don't have to offer up anything he doesn't ask about.

Besides, I'm not sure what to think myself. Before Iris, I thought I liked guys exclusively, even though the little experience I had with them felt more like playing doctor. I haven't been attracted to any other girls...until now. Until Rafaela. And then there's Emil, who was so nice and good to me the other night. He's *always* been nice and good to me, but for some reason, this summer, I suddenly want to kiss him.

I'm jealous that DeeDee has known what she wants—*who* she wants—for most of her life. Even before I met Iris,

I was tired of all the jokes and assumptions I'd heard about bisexual people: that they're just being greedy or doing it for attention or trying it on for size "before they cross over to full-on gay." Even with the little experience I had, it wasn't so hard to imagine someone might be attracted to both—or more—options.

I don't think I'm selfish for liking both guys and girls. I just wish it didn't have to happen all at once.

seven.

I'm lying in bed, eyelids still heavy with sleep as I stare at the vase of peonies on my dresser, when there's a knock at my door.

"Come in," I say, grateful for the distraction. From thinking about the heady scent of the flowers and the position at the shop...and Rafaela.

Lionel pops his head in, hair still mussed from his pillow and sticking up in misshapen auburn spikes. "Hey, want to go for a hike over in Elysian?"

I rub at my eyes and sit up. I don't like hiking or mornings, but if it means everything will be okay between us again, I'll go. I look at him, try to gauge if he's still annoyed with me, but he doesn't seem upset. Lion and I never stay mad at each other for long, but after the way he left the tree house the other day, I wasn't sure if that was still true. I've been giving him space and he's been letting me.

I drop my feet to the floor. "Give me ten minutes?"

"Sure. And we can go to the diner after, if you want." He scratches at the back of his head, further messing up his hair. "My treat."

"Why are you trying to butter me up? Are we going on one of those hikes that makes me feel like I'm going to vomit the whole time?"

He grins. "No, it's a super-easy trail—you know, the one Dad used to take us on? I just...I need to tell you something."

I get a bad feeling in my chest, even though it's too early for that. But Lionel looks fine. Happy, even. "Everything okay?"

"Totally fine. Meet you downstairs."

He closes my door and I sit on the edge of my bed for a moment. I look at my flowers like they have the answers. They sit snug in their vase, pretty and useless. But I see why people like having them around. They will die, but for now their beauty is undeniable, and I take comfort in that.

Lionel is entirely too outdoorsy for such a bookish person. I blame Saul. My outdoor time increased exponentially once my mother began dating him. Sunday-morning hikes at

Runyon and walks at the lake and daylong trips to hang on the beach in Malibu—I think Saul would live in a tent if he could.

My brother's love of nature is one of the reasons I figured out he was sick. Before, he couldn't go more than a day without getting outside, taking long bike rides along the L.A. River or walking the path that borders the reservoir or, at the very least, taking a stroll around the tree-lined streets of our storybook neighborhood. It must have been gradual, but it seemed like one day he wasn't interested in anything he used to do, especially being outside. At first I thought he was mad at me. He never wanted to talk or hang out anymore. He'd sleep all day, and if he joined us for dinner, it was back to the sorts of meals we had in the first couple of years we knew him, when he barely said two words. But there were no books in his lap. That was another clue. Even if he was in a loner phase, Lionel always wanted to be with his books.

"Everyone kept telling me to get active...after the diagnosis," he says as we enter the park, squeezing through the narrow space next to an iron gate. "I used to think they were full of shit, but I don't know—it probably helps. The exercise. Fresh air."

I look at him with raised eyebrows. The last time we talked about this was a disaster. It was hard to give him the space he needed, but every time I went to knock on his door or text him, I remembered what Mom said last summer.

How she was afraid I was taking on too much emotionally for someone my age. How I couldn't worry so much about him that I missed out on my own life.

"You're feeling better?" I ask as we travel along the dirt trail spotted with black beetles, crunchy leaves, and the occasional cigarette butt. The path isn't crowded, but people are walking ahead of us, a couple of girls with bobbing ponytails and a guy running with an off-leash Labrador.

"I am," he says with a clarity that intrigues me. "I'm feeling a *lot* better."

I wait for him to explain, but he doesn't. He looks at peace as we walk along, and I run through the past few days in my head, wondering if I missed something that could have turned his mood around. He's not talking, not ready to tell me whatever it is, and the silence is making me uncomfortable. That anticipatory pause should remind me of how we used to be with each other—confidants, keepers of secrets with a bond that no one and nothing could sever. But our dynamic is different now. Our bond isn't broken, but it's been stretched too thin.

And I'm so unnerved by the quiet that I change the subject—to the only thing that seems to be on my mind lately, besides him. Maybe if I tell Lionel something secret of my own, he'll warm up.

"I like someone."

"No shit." He grins and I know he's thinking about Emil, which isn't wrong, but that's not who I'm talking about.

I open my mouth to continue but then bite my lip and pause. This is the first time I will say this to anyone besides DeeDee. And even if he is Lionel, that's still a big deal.

"That someone is . . . a girl."

"Wow. Really?" He glances at me before he pushes a piece of hair out of his eyes, the red strands blazing in the sun. "So I was way off base with Emil, huh? Sorry."

"No, that's the thing. . . . I think I'm into him, too."

"Huh." Lion doesn't say anything for a few seconds. Then: "What happened at boarding school?"

"What do you mean what *happened*?" I look down at the trail, not him, because I don't like the way he asked it. Accusatory, almost.

"Well, you liked guys before you went away."

"And?" I don't want to tell him about Iris. He doesn't sound like I want him to sound, and if he says something shitty about her, I might snap. I don't like hearing people talk badly about Iris.

He sighs. "It's, like, I thought everything would be the same when you got back, but you're different and . . . I don't know. It's weird."

My skin feels cold all of a sudden, unnaturally clammy under the heat. I never expected this from Lionel. My voice is somewhere between angry and humiliated as I ask, "Are you saying you don't think it's okay?"

He grabs my elbow and we pause on the trail. "Of course not. That was a dick thing to say. Sorry. I don't care if you like girls, it's just—so much has changed since you went away. None of it's good for me, not really, but it seems good for you. The time away. Like you really know who you are now."

"But I don't," I say, shaking my head. "I don't know anything except that I like Emil and I like a girl and I guess that means I'm bisexual, but...am I? Shouldn't I know for sure? You know you're straight. Dee knows she's gay. Other people know they don't fit into either of those categories...."

Lionel brings his shoulders up in a shrug. "I don't know. Maybe it's different for everyone. I know I'm straight, but I have a million people telling me my brain is dysfunctional."

"Have you ever liked more than one person at once?" I ask.

"Yeah, sure. Liking someone isn't the same as being in love."

"It just feels...People don't really care if you like more than one person if you're gay or straight, but if you say you're bi, it's different. Like the same rules don't apply."

He nods slowly. "I never thought about it like that, but yeah. You're right. It's pretty fucked up."

"Sometimes I wish I could go back to being ten years old. Even just for a day. Everything was easier then."

"I'd like to be six again. That was a great year," he says, looking wistfully at the brilliant blue sky.

"Hey!" I shove his shoulder. "We didn't know each other when you were six."

He smirks. "Sorry. Dad spoiled me a lot more before you two came around. Divorce guilt. So...who's the girl?"

"No one you know," I say quickly, though it's possible he'd have a vague idea if I mentioned the colorful tattoo that curves up and down and around her arm. He might have still been hanging out with our friends when Alicia and her girls started coming around, and Lionel is observant—he'd have noticed her.

I think of Iris again and consider telling him about her, now that I know he won't say something hurtful. I could go back to the beginning and tell him where and with whom these new feelings started, but thinking about Iris is painful. I haven't spoken to her since we left school, and there's still so much I don't know: if she's going back to Dinsmore next year, if I was as important to her as she was to me...if she ever wants to see me again.

Lionel kicks a small stick out of his path and looks at me. "You gonna tell the parents?"

"I don't know. Not yet. I mean, I don't even know if anything is going to happen. Seems like a bad idea to get them excited for no reason."

"Yeah," he says. "They'd probably throw a party."

Even if they hadn't stated it directly, it's always been obvious that Mom and Saul would be okay with whatever sexuality we claimed, but I never realized how much simpler that made my life until I met Iris. I imagine telling them, how thrilled they'd be that I felt comfortable enough to come out to them at sixteen, how Saul might say he knew from the moment we saw Rafaela in Castillo Flowers. But it's no small thing, and there will be several *talks*, and even if I know they'd be the supportive kind, I'm not up for that right now.

We move to the right to let a panting solo runner pass, and I look at Lionel as we position ourselves back on the trail. I don't know if it's because he needed to warm up or because of what I told him, but the silence between us seems more comfortable now. Enough for me to ask him directly: "What did you want to talk about?"

"Well, so." He breathes in deeply, slow and controlled like he's practicing yoga. "Remember how I said we can't find the right combination of meds?"

"Yeah," I reply, unable to ignore the sinking feeling in the pit of my stomach.

"I'm not taking them anymore," he says with a lightness I haven't heard from him in a year. Ironic, considering the weight of his words.

I stare at him, waiting for the punch line. And when it doesn't arrive, I play dumb.

"I'm sure Mom and Saul will understand if you need to

keep trying out new ones. Dr. Tarrasch will help you figure it out, right?"

But I knew exactly what he meant.

"No, I'm not taking any more pills at all." He removes his hand from his pocket, his freckled fingers wrapped around an orange pill bottle that glows in the light of the sun. Then he reaches down and produces another. "I'm done." He shakes the bottles for emphasis, one in each hand, like a thousand tiny maracas making music in his palms.

I stop walking, right in the middle of the trail. No one is behind us, at least not for now. "Are you sure that's a good idea?" I have to approach this with care rather than alarm, even if red strobe lights are dancing across my vision. "Didn't Dr. Tarrasch—"

"I don't care what she thinks," he says. "I don't. Maybe these work for some people, but I don't want to be on them. Not right now. I'm getting ready to start my senior year of high school. I'm tired of dealing with this shit. If it hasn't gotten better by now, I don't think it ever will."

"I think—"

But before I can finish, a woman with a sleek gray bob walks by, pumping hand weights by her sides. She gives us a smile and I do my best to return it, but it feels a bit like the sky is closing in around us, and I don't know why no one else sees it.

"I think maybe you should talk to the parents about this," I say once we're alone again.

His jaw clenches and he rolls the bottles around in his hands. "I'm not talking to them about anything. I'll be eighteen in a few months. They can't keep making decisions for me forever."

"Lion—"

"You think you know what's best for me. Everyone does. And I know that's supposed to feel good, like people care or whatever." He looks down at the ground while he speaks. "But nobody asks what I want. Sometimes it feels like I'm a science experiment, like my name is Bipolar Two instead of Lionel, and I fucking hate that."

I think back to when I started noticing the change in his behavior, how the thoughtful and always opinionated Lionel I'd known almost my whole life was hidden inside someone who didn't want to go anywhere or do anything, not even the things he loved. And how sometimes it seemed hard to believe that the same person could have days-long bursts of energy, or become irritated or angry at the smallest thing.

But the worst part was never knowing for sure how deep his sadness would go. Sometimes I felt it in my bones, and though I only found out he's at a higher risk of suicide after he was diagnosed, I think a part of me knew that I had to look out for him, even before it was confirmed. That feeling is what made me start sleeping in the guest room without telling our parents. It was across the hall instead of separated by a flight of stairs, and if anything had happened to him while

I was up in my tower, I never would have forgiven myself. Him being on his meds has felt like a type of insurance, like it's okay to have those extra few feet between us again.

"Don't look at me like that," he says, his voice softer. "I've thought about it a lot. The side effects suck, too. The first combination I was on made me gain weight, and these make me feel tired and sick to my stomach.... This is something I need to do, and I wanted to tell someone. You're the only one I trust, Little."

I don't mean to soften. I mean to stand strong, to become overly stern with him if I must, because what he's talking about is a bad fucking idea all around.

But he trusts me. Which is something I thought I'd lost forever when I went away.

"I brought them here to throw them out," he says when I still don't speak. He pops the childproof top on one of the bottles and shakes a mountain of pills into his hand. "Down in the ravine, so I'll know they're really gone."

I wonder why he didn't simply flush them, but this is likely more symbolic than anything else. Even with his moods regulated, Lioncl has never shied away from the most impactful approach. He starts to tread carefully down the slope along the side of the trail, trying to find the best angle to toss them for the farthest reach—

"Wait!" I call out before he can lift his hand, my objection weaving through the tangle of tree trunks and leaves and overgrown grass. "Give them to me."

I think of him sleeping all day and his chewed-up thumbs and the way he would look at me with blank eyes, the same way he looked at his books and out the window and at our parents.

His eyebrows knit together at the interruption. "Are you going to try to force them on me?"

I shake my head. "I won't. I promise. Just...don't throw them out yet, okay? I'll hold on to them in case you change your mind."

"I'm not changing my mind," he says with a conviction so strong I know it to be true.

"That's fine," I say. "But you shouldn't throw them out here, anyway. Bad for the wildlife."

"Wildlife? I don't think coyotes are interested in pills," he says with a smirk.

Normally I would shove him for making light of such a serious situation, but there's nothing normal about this. He's entrusting me with his biggest secret, and it all feels like a huge mistake.

Lionel dumps the pills back into one of the bottles and presses them both into my palm, staring at me hard before he lets go of my hand. "Promise you won't tell them."

I could lie. Say of course I won't tell Mom and Saul, with every intention of bringing the pill bottles to their bedroom this evening. I could flat-out refuse, even though I know he'd throw the pills straight down the ravine as soon as the words were out of my mouth.

But I promise him the secret is ours, knowing full well that I will keep it from our parents because that is the sort of thing we do for each other. I'll have the pills on hand if he needs them, and eventually, I'll be able to convince him to go back on them.

There are different levels of trust, and I need to get back to the point where he trusts me so much he no longer has to say it aloud.

eight.

The week is hot and long, and in the middle of it, DeeDee asks me over to swim.

"I don't have a good way to get there," I say from my position on the floor. It's the coolest spot up in my bedroom tower.

"Have Lionel come with you. It's been forever since we've seen him." Her voice seems sincere enough. She wants him around, and I'm glad. But I can't forget that she ultimately gave up on Lion, too. He's not DeeDee's responsibility, but she knows how important he is to me, and I'm uncomfortable thinking of her debating whether or not to invite Lionel to things and eventually deciding not to bother.

"He has therapy this afternoon." I move my legs out in

a sweeping arc and then inward, again and again, making angels without the snow on my lavender rug. "And he'd probably say no. He's not much into hanging out with anyone besides David Foster Wallace."

"Who's that?" DeeDee could talk for hours about the most famous and talented horn players in history, but she doesn't have the same love for literature.

"A genius who killed himself." That's how Lionel described him to me so long ago, when he first discovered Wallace's fiction in back issues of the *New Yorker*. And it didn't occur to me then to be worried that he was so captivated by someone who'd decided he'd had enough of this world.

"Sounds uplifting. Well, I invited Emil, so can you grab a ride with him?"

I hang up without asking what I really want to know: Will Alicia be there, and if so, is she bringing Rafaela? I haven't told DeeDee about her, and it's been only a few days, but I haven't heard from Rafaela about the job. It's hard to forget about her with the flower arrangement she made staring me down every time I'm in my room.

I text Emil, but it takes me entirely too long to write a simple message. I wouldn't have thought so much about it before, but now...things are different with him. And as I wait for him to respond, I wonder if it's obvious that I'm starting to look at him in a new way or if he thinks I'm just asking for a ride. I set down the phone and dig through my closet for my stack of swimsuits, hoping my favorite one from last summer, the white one with the yellow polka dots, still fits.

It does, and Emil texts back right when I'm adjusting the straps, and my cheeks fill with heat, as if he's standing here in the room with me. He'll be by to get me in twenty minutes. I pull my dreads back in a ponytail, throw on shorts and a cover-up, and toss sunscreen in my bag before I walk downstairs to wait for him.

I run into Lionel on the stairs. He's coming back from the kitchen with a cheese sandwich in one hand, his book in the other. I've been looking at him extra closely since he told me he went off his meds, but not enough time has passed to notice anything different—yet. He's not staying in bed and he's eating meals with us, and that is no small thing to be thankful for.

"Want to come swim at DeeDee's after therapy?" I'm hopeful for a few seconds that he will surprise me, say he'll meet me there, but he shakes his head.

"I don't think I'm ready to see people yet. Maybe next time, okay?" He smiles as he says it, and I think this time the *maybe* is good, that I have a reason to be hopeful things can go back to how they were.

I have to keep asking him to do things. Especially now, *especially* since he's gone off his meds. I know that's when he's most easily able to believe the lies in his head, the ones that tell him no one cares about him. Not asking seems like not caring, even if it's not true.

Emil and I go straight to the back of the Sullivans' house this time, passing DeeDee's father's old Land Rover parked in the driveway. We follow a stone path around the side of the house to an unlatched wooden gate. Emil holds it open for me and we round the corner to the backyard just as someone does a massive cannonball, sending water cascading onto the grass in front of the pool house.

I'm shocked when a green head pops up. Grace? She looks way too mellow for the display I just saw, but she takes high fives from the people in the pool around her, clearly proud. I look around for Rafaela, but she's nowhere to be found.

My disappointment must be audible; Emil turns to me. "What was that?"

I shake my head as I do another survey, making sure I haven't missed her in the pool or hanging off to the side. But I know I wouldn't have missed her the first time. "Nothing, it's just…hot."

"It is. I'm going in." He peels off his T-shirt, tosses it to the ground next to his towel, and jogs over to the deep end, slicing cleanly through the water. I'm alarmed to realize his hearing aids are still tucked behind his ears, then remember he said they were waterproof.

I try not to stare as he comes up shaking droplets from his shoulders, but my eyes don't get the message. Emil has the sort of body they put on the covers of men's magazines; I've always known he was in good shape, but watching him now makes my chest flush. His brown skin has taken on a golden hue in the sun, and I never noticed before, but there is something almost graceful about the way he moves. He knows how to use his long limbs and doesn't walk around gawkily like some of the other tall guys our age.

"I would totally try to get with him if I liked dudes." DeeDee comes up behind me so silently that I jump when she speaks.

"Hello to you, too," I say, turning to look at her.

She's wearing flowery board shorts over a red bikini and smells like coconut sunblock as she hugs me. "I'm just saying, I get why you're looking at him like he's your last chance on earth for sex."

"Would you stop that?" I whip my head around to see if anyone is standing within earshot, but we're safe.

"Relax, Suz. It's okay to think he's hot."

Maybe I should just let whatever happens happen—but I've never been very good at that.

"Yeah, but he's *Emil.*"

"And Emil just happens to be super kind and a total babe." She gives me a look. "You could do a lot worse."

She's right. When I take off my cover-up and lower

myself into the pool, I see Emil watching from the corner of my eye. I could face him, smile to let him know I don't mind him looking, but I'm too shy. Which is definitely new; I must have been around Emil in a bathing suit dozens of times and never thought twice about it.

I slip under the water until it covers my head.

A few minutes later, Grace and Tommy wade through the pool, trying to organize a tournament of chicken fighting. I can't think of anything that sounds worse right now, so I dip back under the surface when no one is looking and quietly travel to the shallow end. But as soon as I emerge for air, I hear my name.

"Come on, Emil needs a partner!" says Tommy, who is damn near unrecognizable without a guitar strapped across his body.

I shake my head and then, when he and Grace keep pestering me, I say no aloud. But they are relentless, starting up with a slow chant of "Su-zette, Su-zette" that only gets louder and grows in force until I say "Fine!" and meet them back in the deep end.

"I promise I had nothing to do with that," Emil says when I'm treading water next to him.

I don't know how much of that is true... or, for that matter, how much I want it to be.

"You'd better not drop me" is what I say in return, and he grins.

We're up against DeeDee and Alicia first, with Dee on top of her girlfriend's shoulders, facing me. I feel nervous about Emil supporting me—what if he slips and falls? Or gets tired of holding me up?—but his arms feel strong around my legs. He's not letting go.

Dee and I are useless competitors, giggling more than actually trying to defeat each other. She's taller than me, but after a few false starts, I grab hold of her long arms and, with Emil as my base, wrestle her off Alicia's shoulders with an unceremonious splash. They come up laughing and Emil says, "Nice work!" in a voice that's muffled below me. I ask if he needs a break between matches, but he says no, he's ready.

Grace and Tommy are up next, and as if the competitive gleam in her eye weren't enough, Grace says, "You guys are totally going down." I've never seen anyone take chicken fighting so seriously, and then I stop to wonder if this is about chicken fighting at all. Does she somehow know about Rafaela? Maybe she saw us talking at Dee's party. Or maybe Rafaela mentioned how she basically offered me the job at Castillo Flowers.

I'm still lost in my thoughts when the match officially starts. Grace swats hard at my shoulders, nearly knocking me off-balance in one try.

Or maybe this has nothing at all to do with Rafaela, and Grace just happens to be wildly overcompetitive.

We push and pull and twist at each other's arms while

Emil and Tommy faithfully keep us upright, and after a few minutes I wonder if either of us will ever give up or if this will go on all afternoon. If DeeDee's mom will come home from work to find us swatting at each other like wrinkly, exhausted prunes.

And then Grace gets distracted by a fat fly that buzzes near her ear. She stops fighting to smack it away, and it's only a brief respite, but I take the moment to push her hard and she goes tumbling off Tommy's shoulders backward, into the water with a resounding *thwack*.

"Still the champions!" Emil cheers as I raise my arms in victory.

"No fair," Grace says, splashing us as she finds her footing. "Black people aren't supposed to be able to swim."

A chill settles over me, starting at my shoulders and ending never. Emil's arms tighten around my calves instinctively. Sometimes it's easier to let things slide, to laugh along with them, to pretend like what they said to you wasn't really fucking offensive. But sometimes my mouth takes over first.

"What did you say?" My dreads are soaked, sending tubes of water cascading down my back every few seconds, and I'd like to get off Emil's shoulders, but this moment is frozen. Everyone heard her and no one is moving.

Grace laughs and wipes a few strands of green hair from her forehead. "I just mean... you know. Black people don't, like, swim."

"And yet here are two right in front of you," Emil says coolly.

"God, you guys, it's just a joke." She looks around for support, only to be met by downcast eyes and puzzled faces. Even Alicia is picking at her fingernails instead of looking at her friend.

"Did you know that black people weren't allowed to use public pools back in the day?" Emil says, his voice never wavering. "And that even if they weren't actually segregated, white people used to attack black people who tried to swim? But black people get made fun of for not swimming, like there's no fucking reason for that. Not all jokes are funny."

Grace's face is pure white and her bottom lip hangs down, but Emil doesn't wait for her response. I'm still balanced on his shoulders and he walks us over to the side of the pool, carefully depositing me on the edge. Then he jumps out, grabs his towel, and walks in the back door of DeeDee's house.

After a couple of seconds sitting in the collective silence of our friends, I do the same.

Inside, DeeDee's dad is sitting on a stool in the breakfast nook, sketching on a small pad. He designs bottle labels for wineries and breweries all over the state, but most of his clients are on the Central Coast.

"Hi, Mr. Sullivan." I flex my bare toes against the tile floor. I'm wrapped in my towel, but water still drips from my hair, pinging the floor next to my feet in fat drops.

He keeps sketching and doesn't look up, though I know he hears me. The slight quirk of his mouth gives him away.

I clear my throat and try again: "Hi, Rick."

"Suzette!" he booms loud enough to be heard outside as he jumps down from his seat to give me a hug. "Our DeeDee is real happy to have you back."

"I'm happy to be back."

Rick eases back onto the stool and slips on his glasses, peering at me over the top. "Massachusetts treat you okay?"

"Yeah, it was okay."

That's partially true. It was okay when no one had figured out what Iris and I were doing. Life has changed here in California, but I know I'm loved and safe and wanted. The only person who came close to providing that sort of comfort in Avalon was Iris, and all of that was ruined. What if we both go back but she wants nothing to do with me?

"The snow wasn't so bad," I say to DeeDee's father. "And I got to wear boots and sweaters for longer than two months."

"Well, sometimes you gotta leave a place to really appreciate it," he says, and I don't know if he's talking about the East or West Coast now. "You want a ginger ale? Iced tea?"

"I'm good." I twirl a loose string hanging from the

bottom of my towel. "I was actually... I just need to use the restroom."

"You know where to find it." He picks up his pencil again. "Good to see you, Suzette."

I don't need to use the bathroom, but I figure that's where Emil headed, so I walk down the hall and around the corner and—he's not there. I double back the way I came, branching off into the living room, but it's empty, and he's not in the family room, either. He wouldn't leave without telling me, but maybe he went to sit in his Jeep, even though it's baking under the afternoon sun. I cross the foyer, open the front door, and find him sitting on the curb, his towel draped over his shoulders. I close the door behind me and walk out to meet him.

"Hey." I use my towel to cover the curb and sit on top of it.

"I thought about leaving, like, a hundred times, but my keys are back there," he says, staring at the steep embankment that faces DeeDee's house. He pauses. "And so were you."

I try not to think about the way his voice changed when he said *you*. I try to ignore the shiver that runs up my legs, so close to his, because that's not why we're sitting here, at the opposite end of the house from our friends.

I glance at him. "Thanks... for saying what you did."

He bends his knees and rests his arms on them, elbows poking out from beneath the towel. "I didn't know I was going to. I mean, not until you said something. That helped."

"I didn't do anything." I focus on the cracked pavement.

"You did." He looks at me now, his eyebrows furrowed. "You called her out on it. It made something inside me snap and—I didn't know I was going to go off like that, but I'm not sorry I did."

"That's the part that sucks. When you feel bad for telling someone they were wrong."

Emil sighs. "Maybe it gets easier the more you do it."

The part of the curb where the Sullivans' house number is spray-painted sits squarely between us, but the digits are too faded to read. I trace the incomprehensible shapes. "Maybe it would be easier if people didn't say shitty things."

Emil smiles a familiar smile, one that I've seen too often on my mom and Saul and Emil's parents—black and Jewish and Korean, every one of us all too aware of the stupid things people say without thinking. A smile that says the only alternative is screaming with rage.

"I really don't want to go back there." He cocks his head toward the house. "But—"

"Your keys. And my clothes." I don't want to go back there, either. Dee must be mortified, and I don't hear anything from the backyard: no talking or splashing or shrieks of laughter. The whole vibe changed as soon as those words left Grace's mouth.

"Right. And maybe we shouldn't leave. This is our turf. She can't run us out of your best friend's house."

"True." I may have been gone for the past year, but I'll be damned if I'll let Grace start running things around here. "We have to go back there together."

"It's the only way," he says with a quick nod.

He reaches the door first and puts his hand on the knob but stops before he opens it. He looks at me. "Listen, I know we didn't hang out a lot before...I mean, not alone, but... would you want to, um, grab a bite sometime? Just you and me?"

The warmth I felt earlier returns, creeping from my chest all the way to my cheeks this time. Emil has never actually asked me out, but I have the feeling that he would have, if I'd paid him more attention. Has he realized that I'm noticing him in a different way now?

"Yeah," I say, hoping my voice doesn't give away my trepidation—not because I don't want to go out with him but because I very much do, and it's still a surprise, the way I see Emil now. Not only because I've always kept him at arm's length but because I like him more than I've liked any other guy, and it feels the way it did with Iris, like it could be something real. "Can we do sushi? That place over on Hyperion?"

He grins. "We can go wherever you want."

We won't leave Dee's for a while but we've still got a car ride ahead of us, and if the way I feel now is any indication, there's a possibility I might flush furiously the whole way home.

When we get back to the pool, Alicia and Grace are sitting off to the side, away from everyone. Alicia has her arms crossed while Grace silently picks at the grass. Part of me wants her to leave already, but another part is satisfied that she's forced to live with the uncomfortable aftermath.

The game of chicken fighting has stopped, but a few people are back in the pool again, throwing around an inflatable ball. DeeDee included. She sees us and sort of waves, but makes no attempt to get out and join us, which annoys me.

"Getting back in," Emil says. His tone is a little defiant, like he's still intent on proving Grace wrong, even though she saw us swimming long before she made her comment. "Coming?"

"I'm gonna talk to DeeDee for a minute. But promise you won't leave me here."

"Never that," he says, and he's smiling again.

I sit on the edge of the pool and dip only my feet in. DeeDee swims over a few seconds later, clearly aware that I'm here for her.

"Well, that was awkward," she says, wiping the water from her eyes.

"Yeah, I mean, who'd've thought someone could actually be worse than Catie?" I try to say it lightly, but there's an edge to my tone.

DeeDee swallows. "Are you mad? I don't think . . . I mean, Grace wasn't thinking. Clearly."

"What made it really awkward was that nobody said anything besides me and Emil." I keep my voice low, because this isn't a conversation we need to be having with anyone else. I wish *someone* had spoken up, but DeeDee is my best friend, not them. I don't expect as much from them as I do her.

She looks down at the pool and over at Alicia and Grace before she meets my eye. "I guess . . . I didn't know what to say. Nothing like that has really happened in front of me. Grace has never said anything like that when I was around."

"Well." I pause. Sigh. Maybe nothing she said could have made it better, but I want to know she cares enough to try. "I need you to have my back. I know Grace is your friend, but I'm your *best* friend."

She blinks at me a couple of times and I wonder if she's going to cry, but she doesn't. And I'm glad. That would make this more about her than me, and that wouldn't be fair. She lifts herself out of the pool and plops down next to me and wraps her dripping arms around me until my skin is almost as wet as hers.

"You *are* my best friend and I always have your back and I'm sorry." She pulls away to look at me, her hands still pressed against my spine. "Want me to kick her out? I'm getting pretty good at that, you know."

"Alicia would kill you. And no, I don't want to make things worse. She looks pretty miserable anyway." I swish my feet through the water. "Maybe one good thing came of it.... Emil asked me out."

DeeDee's grin is so big it makes me smile, like a reflex. "Finally, you guys are getting together!"

"Finally?"

"Don't play dumb. You know he's always had a thing for you."

"I guess. But...I still don't know how I feel about all of that. Guys. Girls."

"You'll figure it out," she says. "And would it be so bad if you had the best of both worlds?"

I know that's supposed to make me feel better, but right now I feel like I'm floating between both worlds with no idea of where I'm supposed to land.

nine.

Emil Choi and I have spent holidays together, taken joint family trips, and eaten more meals at the same table than either of us could count, but I'm still nervous Saturday afternoon, a few hours before we're supposed to go out.

"Ooh, a date," Mom said as soon as I told her, when I got home from the pool party. Because there was no way to *not* tell her. If she didn't find out from me that same night, Emil's mom surely would have said something, and I wanted my mom to hear it from my mouth—so I could stop her before she'd married us off and named our future children.

"We're just getting sushi," I said, leaning against the doorframe of her office. It's a little room off the kitchen, smaller than our bedrooms but bigger than a walk-in closet.

Large enough to hold a love seat and her small wooden desk. The mint-green walls are decorated with photographs from her childhood in Chicago and her years at Wellesley with Emil's mom.

"Okay, sweet pea," she said, and I knew she didn't believe I was as relaxed as I sounded. For good reason. "I hope you two will have fun 'just getting sushi.'"

"How's the writing going?" I nodded toward the laptop opened on the desk in front of her.

She pursed her lips. "Well, it's sort of like bleeding words from my fingers at this point. Thanks for asking." She followed that up with a smile. Then, "Everything okay since you've been back, Suz?"

"Everything's fine. It's great, being back here. I missed everything—every*one*—more than I'd realized."

"We missed you, too, baby." She brought her legs up so she was sitting cross-legged in her good-luck seat, which is really just a shabby chair from our old dining room set. She's written all of her screenplays in it. "I've been meaning to ask you...did it hurt?"

She was pointing to my nose ring.

"Not too bad." I paused. "Do you like it?"

"I think it suits you quite well." She smiled. "Let me know if you want to go shopping before your—sushi thing."

"Wouldn't that counteract the casual nature of a sushi thing?" I said before I left her alone with her latest project.

But now, staring into the closet of my bedroom tower, I wish I'd taken her up on that offer. Emil has seen me in most of these outfits; I haven't been shopping for new summer clothes since I've been back. I've narrowed down my choices to four pieces I don't completely hate when my phone buzzes.

I walk over to my bed and retrieve it, only to find a text from Emil saying he's sick: Ménière's kicking my ass today. So sorry but should stay home. Rain check?

I respond that of course we can postpone and I hope he feels better, but I realize then how much I was looking forward to seeing him, because my chest instantly feels weighed down with stones. And I'm glad Mom isn't around to see my face because she'd know for sure I was thinking of tonight as a date, that I wasn't feeling nearly as casual about it as I sounded.

I lie down, across the clothes stretched over the top of my bed. It's very warm up here and I suddenly feel sleepy, so I close my eyes. I think about Emil—all the times we've hung out together alone in the past, if I ever thought about him the way I do now, even for a second. If...

When I open my eyes an hour later, there's another text. This time from Rafaela: The job is yours if you want it

I sit up and look at the flowers across the room. They're dead now, the water thickened and murky, the petals dried out and drooping. But I couldn't bring myself to throw them away. I guess I sort of understand why people are so into flowers now that I have some of my own. Even if Rafaela didn't give them to me of her own accord, they're still the first flowers I've gotten from someone besides family. They're still just for me, and that feels special.

I try to think of something clever to write back, but I simply confirm that yes, I want it, and she tells me to show up at ten o'clock Monday morning. I think of her fingers typing out the text, long and pale with chipped black polish on the ends, and the rocks in my chest turn to backflips in my stomach.

A welcome distraction from the pill bottles hidden in my nightstand, inside a half-empty box of tissues. My eyes can't stop inspecting the box from up close and afar, checking to see if the pills are still there, though no one has been in my room to move them.

I decide to check on Lionel. I never said this to him, but ever since his decision, I feel like it's my responsibility to make sure he's okay. I'm the only one who knows he's stopped taking his meds.

He doesn't have therapy today, so I expect him to be stretched out on his floor or his bed with his increasingly worn copy of *Infinite Jest*, but the book is lying open, spine cracked, on top of his rumpled bedclothes. His car is parked out front, but he's not in the kitchen, living room, or dining room, either.

When I get up to the tree house, he's vigorously sweeping

at the dirty floor with a broom. I barely avoid catching a dust bunny in the eye as I pull myself up.

"This is exactly what it looks like," he starts before I can say anything. "I figure we might as well make this thing presentable this summer, while you're here."

Panic zaps through me, and it's only a moment, but I can't forget last year, when Lionel's hypomania kicked in. He had so much energy it was like he didn't know what to do with himself. A lot of times he just seemed irritable, like someone had interrupted him when he had a brilliant idea on the tip of his tongue. But often it was just a buzzing in the air, constantly surrounding him. The need to be up and about, always talking, always coming up with something new to achieve.

He never went full-on manic—that's not the form his bipolar takes. I know the real challenge is when he's feeling down and doesn't want to do anything at all—especially when that apathy turns inward. I know that without his meds that challenge could come sooner rather than later.

I look at his eyes to see if they tell me anything, but they're clear. Not brimming with too much energy, nor are they so dazed that I wonder if he's even aware I'm in front of him. So I send the panic back to its place and walk across the room to get out of his way.

"Looking good up here." I take a seat on the futon, curl my legs up beneath me. "Almost like the palace it once was."

"Aren't you supposed to be getting ready for your date?"

He didn't say anything about the girl I'd mentioned when I told him Emil asked me out, and I'm glad because I wouldn't know what to say to him. I thought I might never hear from Rafaela again, so I've tried to forget about her and concentrate on Emil. But now I'm going to be working side by side with her, and thinking about that makes me want to take deep breaths.

"He's sick, from his Ménière's," I say, trying not to sound as disappointed as I feel. Of course I want to see Emil, but I don't like that he's ill. He must be feeling really bad to have canceled.

"Ah, yeah." Lionel leans on his broom. "He missed a bunch of school when he was first diagnosed. Kind of made me feel like I wasn't such a freak for a while."

"But..." I pause. "Do you feel like that now, since you're not on your meds?"

"I felt like a freak after the diagnosis," he says, clasping and unclasping his hands around the broomstick. "When there was a name for it, and all these things to look out for.... Before that, I was just me."

I want to ask him how he's sure which him is the real him, but I shouldn't be asking questions I can't answer myself. I don't even know if I like girls or guys better or if it's really and truly both.

"Well, you're not a freak. Then or now," I say definitively. "How are you feeling... since you've been off your meds?"

He shrugs. "Do I seem any different?"

He doesn't, but he doesn't seem as lighthearted as the day he told me he was going to stop taking them, either. Maybe it's not working out like he wanted, and Lionel can be stubborn. What if he wants to take them but doesn't want to go back on his word?

"No, you don't." The reluctance swells through in my voice, but I can't help it. If he actually would have been fine without his meds this whole time, that means the last year was all for nothing. All the excessive worrying over his moods, and Mom worrying about my excessive worrying, and going away three thousand miles to Massachusetts.

But that's not true. His mood could swing so low so quickly, and I know how serious that is.

At least he's still seeing Dr. Tarrasch. He wouldn't be able to get away with missing their appointments—she'd call Saul right away if he didn't show. Lionel genuinely likes her, and if he doesn't dread going, maybe he'll want to take his meds again. They've gone hand in hand since the beginning, his pills and Dr. T.

"Good," he says, the word clipped and final, as if that wraps up this conversation, and maybe any future conversations, about his mental health.

The air feels awkward and so, like most times we talk about this, I know the way to clear it is to change the subject.

"I got a job," I say. "I'm going to hawk flowers."

"What?" He laughs, and then, as if someone snapped their fingers between us, the tension fades. "You hate flowers."

"I don't *hate* them," I say, and I'm surprised at how genuinely defensive I feel. "Peonies are nice."

"Peonies, huh? Is that what's dying on your dresser?"

"They were better when they were alive."

"Aren't most things?" And he sends the broom swishing across the floor once again.

ten.

My first day of work feels a bit like my first day of school.

Lionel offers to drop me off. The drive from our house to the flower shop is short, and my heart pounds faster the closer we get. I rest my palms on my jeans so the fabric will soak up some of the perspiration. I tell myself it's new-job anxiety, that I'm not actually so nervous about seeing Rafaela again.

But I am. I've only been around her twice, and each time was just a few minutes. Maybe I won't be attracted to her now that I've had some time away. It was the opposite with Emil; the months away from him made me realize how cute and sweet and strong he is, so maybe it could work the other way with Rafaela.

The sun is hitting the front window of the shop at the perfect angle for sunbathing, so I'm surprised to see the orange cat's spot empty as I walk up to the store. The coffee shop next door is bursting with customers, including two bearded guys at a wrought-iron table out front, holding a painfully intense conversation over a pair of iced lattes.

Rafaela is staring down at her phone when I walk in, absentmindedly stroking the cat. He sits complacently next to the cash register, his gravelly purrs traveling all the way to the door.

She looks up when the bell jingles. "You made it," she says, her mouth turning up in a small smile. Same plum lipstick.

I smile back and wonder if she can read my energy. Because her *lips*, they unnerve me. Being away from her a few days didn't make a difference. The way I like Emil is different from the way I like Rafaela. I can't explain it, but I know it's not the same. And yet I didn't expect that if I ever liked another girl it would feel so different from what I felt for Iris...and it does. Maybe it's because I don't know Rafaela well, but Iris reminds me more of Emil. Gentle and kind and a little bit serious.

Rafaela seems...very much her own person. Like she

doesn't care what people think of her. Maybe if I were more like her, I'd still be with Iris instead of wondering if returning to Dinsmore in the fall will ruin her entire year.

"Yeah, thanks." I stand by the door because I'm not sure where I should be standing. I'm awkward, like my first day at Dinsmore, when I constantly felt like I was in the wrong place and doing the wrong thing, no matter where I went. "It was cool of you to get me the job."

"Sorry it took me so long to get back to you." She scratches under the cat's collar and I look at her nails, at the polish still hanging on with jagged edges. "There was an incident."

I wait for her to go on, but instead, she reaches under the counter and pulls out a folded piece of navy-blue cloth and holds it out in front of her. I walk over to take it—it's my apron—and am reminded of how good she smells. Not any scent I'm used to. DeeDee is partial to floral fragrances, and Emil—well, he always smells like plain soap and I always notice that I like it. Iris wore nothing at all, but sometimes the scent of citrus would linger on her skin from the shower.

"You're not allergic to cats, are you?" Rafaela's eyes briefly flick to the ginger kitty still purring by her side. "Because Tucker kind of rules the roost around here."

"Not allergic." I set my leather messenger bag on the counter and carefully unfold the apron. "But my family isn't really into animals. I mean, we like them, but Saul is allergic to dander, so we've never had any."

"My aunt is a model cat lady. Tucker lives here at the shop, and she has two at home." Rafaela is wearing a white tank top, ribbed and fitted. She plays with the strap on her right shoulder, the part that covers the burst of daisies inked onto her skin.

"Do you live with Ora?"

"I do." Her voice changes, takes on a brusqueness I don't understand. "For now."

"Oh," I say, because there is nothing else to say. She has secrets of her own and clearly doesn't give them away so easily.

"I'm not a crazy cat lady like her, though." And just like that, her tone returns to normal. "I'm not a dog person, either. Don't you think it's weird, how there are so many beautiful, intelligent animals out there and we've confined ourselves to two species?"

"Well, domestication probably has something to do with it," I say with a grin.

Just then, as if Rafaela's comment registered with him, Tucker jerks away from her, stands tall on all fours, and struts to the other end of the counter, pointedly swishing his striped tail back and forth.

"All I'm saying is my mom should have been more open to the idea of getting that hedgehog."

I laugh. "Hedgehog? Do they even do anything?"

She purses her lips in mock agitation. "Suzette. You sound like my mother, and let me tell you, that's not a good thing. My friend growing up kept one as a pet and she was so affectionate and sweet. Better than a hamster but not as needy as a dog."

"My brother wanted a tarantula," I say, but Rafaela's not listening. She's leaning toward me, staring at my necklace.

"Is that a Star of David?" Her tone is unsure, like she's not certain she has the right name.

"Oh. Yeah." I hold it out so she can get a closer look. I call it a Magen David because that's what Saul has always called it. "My brother gave it to me."

"I didn't know you were Jewish." I can't read her voice this time, and I feel my chest tighten like it did every time I was sure the girls on my dorm floor were about to say something offensive.

"Since I was eleven. My mom and I converted." I don't mean the words to sound so short, but it's habit. I've had this conversation what seems like hundreds of times. It generally goes one of two ways, and I really don't want it to go the bad way with Rafaela.

She nods slowly, her eyes running over each point of the star. "That's cool. I grew up Catholic. My mom's a big believer. I'm...undecided."

"That's how my brother feels, too," I say, just as the shop phone rings.

I look at my messenger bag, wondering if I should be taking notes and if there's any paper left over in there from last semester. Next thing I know, she's picked up the phone and is shoving the receiver in my face. I shake my head. I haven't even been here five minutes and I've never answered a phone in any professional capacity.

But Rafaela won't take no for an answer, so a moment later I clear my throat and say in my best phone voice— one thus far reserved for elderly relatives and my parents' friends—"Good morning, Castillo Flowers."

She nods with smiling eyes and leans against the wall, watching me.

The customer on the other end wants to order two dozen roses: red. Simple enough. I repeat his order aloud and Rafaela slides a notepad in front of me, along with a pen. I jot down his information and then don't take my eyes off Rafaela, who guides me through the rest of the call: finding the next open delivery slot in the book by the register, taking down the message the customer wants written on the accompanying card.

"That was intense," I say after I've hung up the phone.

"No better way to learn than jump in, right? You were a total pro." She peers down at the pad of paper, inspecting the customer's note for the card. " 'For my sweet Darlene. My love for you is irreplaceable. My heart is for you, always.' Christ. That's pretty sappy, even for someone who'd order two dozen roses."

"They're not all like this?"

"You have no idea." She turns the book of scheduled deliveries back toward her. "*So* much of our business is apology bouquets. My favorite was the one that said, 'I didn't know she was your cousin. Sorry.'"

"Seriously?" My apron is hanging loose on the sides and the strings dangle by my legs, tickling the backs of my knees. I loop them around my waist, but my strings don't wrap around me twice, like Rafaela's do.

"It was my favorite, but not the worst I've seen, by far. It's amazing to me that people think flowers make up for acting like a fuckface."

"Well, what would you do?" I ask, genuinely curious. "You know, to apologize for acting like a fuckface."

She taps her pen against the delivery book. "All I'm saying is flowers are lazy. If I pissed off the person I was sleeping with, I'd *show* them I was sorry, not just say it. I'd cook their favorite meal and do something that they loved and I *hated*, like taking a long motorcycle ride, or going to the ballet. I would just—I don't know. Life's too short to be so predictable."

My arm tingles at her words.

Before I can think of a response, the front door opens: a woman wearing an armful of jangly bracelets who has wandered in to find a housewarming gift. Rafaela walks over to help her and I stand close by, observing the way she interacts with the customer. She sends her off with a wave and a potted plant I don't know the name of.

"What type of succulent was that?" I pick up an identical one sitting on the table. Its thick, waxy leaves are ringed with red, and the sturdy stems holding it up look like miniature tree trunks.

"You really don't know anything about flowers or plants, huh?" Rafaela says, coming to stand next to me. "That's a jade plant. *Crassula ovata*. They come from South Africa."

I gently finger the smooth, rounded leaves. "I knew it was a succulent!"

"You're cute," she says with a little smile.

And from the corner of my eye, I can see Rafaela watching me. I feel shy being watched by someone I have a crush on, and it reminds me of DeeDee's pool party when I wore my bikini in front of Emil. Did she mean I'm cute in the way people mean when you say something they think is funny? Or cute like she would be interested in kissing me, too?

I smile back, but I feel like I can barely breathe. My hands are starting to sweat again, and when I squeeze past her, pretending to need a drink from my water, our arms brush and mine tingles again from the contact. I don't know if I'll ever get used to how small it is in here, how Rafaela is close by almost anywhere she's standing in the room.

Ora walks in a couple of hours later, as I'm ringing up

what Rafaela informed me is a moth orchid. The cash register is old and I'm flustered trying to work it under the gaze of three sets of eyes, but I get through the transaction without needing help, if a bit slowly.

"First day and you've already sold an orchid?" Ora says after the customer has left. She smiles her warm smile at me. "Impressive."

I nod to my left. "Rafaela talked him into it."

"You're supposed to be lying on the beach," Rafaela says to her aunt.

"Oh, I never made it over there." Ora peers into a couple of the refrigerated cases, taking some sort of mental inventory. "Too much to do at home."

Rafaela rolls her eyes. "We hired someone so you wouldn't have to come in so much. What, you don't trust me to hold down the fort?"

"You know that's not true," Ora says in a voice that conveys it to be entirely true. "Where's Héctor?"

"Out on a delivery—imagine that!" Rafaela's mouth quirks up as Ora turns to her with a raised eyebrow.

"Okay, okay." Ora rearranges the glazed ceramic pots of African violets on a table near the front of the small room. "I know when I'm not wanted. Call me if you have any trouble locking up?"

"Will do. Want me to bring something home for dinner?"

Rafaela asks as her aunt leans over Tucker, planted in the window seat, and reaches down to give him a head rub.

"Well, with all this extra time I have now, I suppose I should cook something," Ora says thoughtfully. "I'll stop by the store."

We watch Ora cross the parking lot to her car. "You two seem to get along okay," I say.

"She's a little overbearing but not so bad most of the time." Rafaela shrugs but still offers up nothing else. She plants herself in front of the case of peony blooms, same as the first day I was here. "Want to learn how to do an arrangement? Ora's going to make you start doing them soon, probably. She makes me do two a week."

"Sure." I follow her to the back room, which is bigger than I thought it'd be. It has a long table with shelves above it, a refrigerated case full of blooms, boxes of unpacked vases and ribbon, and a small table with two chairs next to the same type of fridge Iris and I had in our dorm.

Rafaela clears the table of debris, sweeping cut stems and dead petals and loose leaves to the floor. Some of the potting soil sticks to her arms and I want to brush it away, find some excuse to touch her again. I don't think she'd mind, but I clasp my hands behind my back. I watch her place the burgundy-colored peonies on the table, along with a handful of broad, ribbed leaves that she tells me are called hosta.

"Are you right-handed?" she asks, and when I nod, she says, "Then you start making the arrangement in your left hand. Put the largest flower in the center...."

Rafaela may act like she doesn't care much about her job, but she's good at it. She treats the blooms and leaves with care and never takes her eyes off them, as if she's creating a work of art like the one inked on her arm. I guess she is, in a way.

I watch her instead of her hands forming the bouquet, taking in the small curves of her profile—the way her lips pout from the side and the smooth line of her tattooless shoulder. I'm not listening to what she's saying as she walks me through the composition and I'm certainly not retaining it for later. The bell from the shop floor snaps me out of my daze.

Rafaela wipes her hands on her apron. "Want to take care of this one?"

I walk out to the front and immediately stop when I see who's standing at the counter. "What are you doing here?"

Lionel's red hair and wrinkled gray pants and freckly arms look foreign in this room—too familiar in a place where I'm still getting my bearings. He usually avoids putting himself into new situations if he can help it, and him being inside the shop when he doesn't have to be makes me wonder if something is wrong.

He doesn't answer me, at least not right away. His eyes

are glued to a point behind me. And something in me drops when I realize he's looking at Rafaela.

"You told me to pick you up now," he finally says, his eyes moving to me. But only briefly, before they slide back to Rafaela, who's standing next to the bonsais, pretending not to notice the attention.

"Oh. It's already four?" I look at the clock above the counter. It's five past, and I can't believe how quickly the six hours have gone by, being in such a small space with just Rafaela, a snoozing cat, and countless containers of flowers and plants.

"I can come back if you're not ready . . . ?"

"No, it's okay." I begin untying my apron. "Rafaela, this is my brother, Lionel."

"Your brother——?" she begins, but then a flicker of understanding passes through her eyes as she remembers my explanation about Saul and my mother. "Oh, right. Cool." She walks toward Lionel and offers a hand. "I'm Rafaela."

The grin on his face is big enough to light up the sky, and I can't recall the last time I saw him this way: happy and hopeful and at a complete loss for words.

I didn't know you could identify such moments from the outside—that emotions that have nothing to do with you could be so evident, so tangible—but I am positive I just witnessed my brother falling in love at first sight.

eleven.

Before I left for work, Mom said Emil still isn't well, and I feel guilty about all the time I just spent with Rafaela, all the different points throughout the day when I thought about what it would be like if she and I were together. Would we sneak off to the back room to kiss, or would we flirt with each other all day, letting the tension build up until we could leave the shop for the evening?

"I want to bring Emil something," I say to Lionel as we pull away from Castillo Flowers. "Matzo ball soup, from Langer's."

It takes him a moment to respond, and I know it has everything to do with Rafaela. The dopey look on his face, the shine in his eyes, hasn't gone away, even after we walked out of the shop. He turns down the volume on the radio.

"Langer's, huh? You really like him."

"Lion." I flush because he's not making this easy for me. I can admit to myself that I like Emil, that things have changed between us this summer, but it's still not easy to talk about it. "He's sick, and I want to help. I'd do it for DeeDee."

"No, DeeDee's *girlfriend* would do it for DeeDee. And is he even the kind of sick that soup helps?" He takes a right onto a side street to turn us around. "But yeah, I'll drive you. Only because you look so desperate."

I shouldn't let him get away with that, but he's helping me, so I bite my tongue.

"Should I let Emil know we're coming?" I ask when we're headed toward the deli.

"I don't know, I'd probably like it if someone surprised me with food when I was sick," Lionel says contemplatively before a pause. "Especially if it was someone I liked back. Speaking of liking people..." He clears his throat and I know exactly what's coming next, but I feign ignorance. "What's up with that girl you work with...Rafaela?"

"What do you mean, what's up with her?"

He grins. "You know what I mean. What's she like?"

"I don't know her very well." I shrug and look out the window. I'm telling the truth, but I'm also trying to sound like I'm not interested in her. After the way Lion looked at her, I can't tell him about my crush. Although I wish I could admit I understand why he was so instantly smitten, I'm weirded out that we can like the same person. "She's friends with DeeDee's girlfriend."

"Oh." He pauses. "Is she into guys?"

I think of the guy from the Palisades, the one who showed up looking for her at Dee's party. "I think so. I know she's dated a guy and a girl... but just because she's friends with lesbians doesn't mean *she's* a lesbian."

"Thanks for stating the obvious, Little. It's a valid question." He looks at me. "What about you? You think she's cute?"

My face is so hot it's in danger of catching fire. He never would have asked me this before I came out as... whatever I am. I shift in my seat. "She's okay."

"Well, she seems cool, right?"

"If you want to ask her out, ask her out." I look straight ahead, at a faded pickup truck with ten thousand pieces of lawn equipment weighing down the bed.

"It wouldn't fuck things up at your new job?" He sounds genuinely concerned, and it seems unfair, withholding information from him, but telling him I have a crush on Rafaela seems pointless and a little cruel.

The last girl Lionel dated was shortly before he was diagnosed, and he hasn't expressed interest in anyone since then. Her name was Grayson and they had loud, passionate discussions about books and we all liked her a lot. He tried to hide it, but I know how upset he was after her family moved to New York the spring of his sophomore year.

So I can't say anything about Rafaela; I'd feel like I was crushing what little hope he has for normalcy these days. If he knew I was into her in even the smallest way, he'd step aside. He's good like that.

"You should do what you want. It's just a summer job." I shrug, and out of the corner of my eye, I see Lionel smile.

The deli isn't unreasonably far, but it's out of the way. Emil's house is in the same neighborhood as the flower shop; Lionel was nice to drive me. He complained during the trip to the deli and complains that the parking lot is a block away from the building, but he stops grumbling long enough to order a pastrami sandwich to go once we're inside. I get one, too, along with Emil's soup, which comes packaged in a tightly sealed mason jar.

Soon we're back on Sunset, heading up to Emil's house in the hills of Silver Lake. This stretch of the street isn't anything like the Sunset Strip, the flashy length of clubs and restaurants in West Hollywood, sunk down below the mansions on the hills. Over by us, on the eastern side of L.A., the street is a blend of bars with dark windows and brightly colored murals and strip malls that house everything from vegan restaurants to specialty sneaker shops.

The sandwiches sit next to me in their takeout containers,

snug inside a bag, but I'm balancing the soup on my lap. The warmth against my thighs contrasts with the air conditioner blasting in Lion's car. But as he makes a right turn and begins chugging up the hill, my legs start sweating, and I wonder if this is a mistake. Showing up at Emil's unannounced, bringing him food like we do this all the time. I don't even know what it means that he's sick from the Ménière's; he said he needed to stay home, but maybe he doesn't want to see anyone at all.

Too late now.

The car is crawling along the incline, the houses spreading out farther the higher we go. I pull down the sun visor so I can look in the mirror, realizing only now that I haven't seen my reflection since before I left work. Does it even matter, once someone has seen you in your pajamas after you just woke up, wrecked with jet lag? I guess it matters to me, because I run my fingers through my dreads and use the tube of peppermint lip balm sitting in Lionel's console as we near the steep driveway that leads to the Choi home.

"I'm gonna wait out here," my brother says once we've pulled up in front.

"You sure? Catherine will want to see you." I nod toward Emil's mom's car parked in the driveway ahead.

"Nah." He starts fiddling with his phone. "Catherine knows too much."

He doesn't have to say any more. There are no secrets

between our family and Emil's, and while we both like Catherine, it's easier to deal with that discomfiting fact the less we see her.

She greets me at the front door with a huge hug and a kiss. "Oh, honey, I have missed this *face*. Emil didn't tell me you were coming over—I thought he was sleeping."

"He doesn't know," I say, admiring the long, jet-black Senegalese twists that drape over her shoulders. "I'm here to bring by some soup. I probably should've called—"

"You should've done nothing of the sort, and your mother would be angry with me if she knew how long you've been standing on this porch. Come in, honey." She looks past me to the car. "Is that Lionel?"

I glance behind me, where my brother is now talking on his phone. I wonder if he's pretending to talk to someone, because he *hates* being on the phone. Even knowing how much he missed me, I think he barely tolerated our calls when I was at Dinsmore.

"He has to take care of something," I say, "and I just wanted to drop this off. I shouldn't bother Emil if he's sleeping."

Catherine holds the door wide open.

I step into the foyer and immediately take off my sandals, bending down to place them on the low shelf by the front door. Emil's dad—Appa, as he sometimes calls him—grew up with parents who emigrated from South Korea, and one of their traditions that's held strong in Emil's family is no shoes in the house. "It only makes sense—shoes are filthy," Mom said after the first time we visited them with Lionel and Saul. She tried to implement the rule in our home, but it wasn't a week before the Nussbaum men were once again stomping around on the hardwood floors in work boots and dirty sneakers.

Our house is big, but old and kind of rickety beneath all the historic charm. Emil's house is modern, with concrete floors and white shag rugs thrown around the Eames furniture in the main room. The front wall is enclosed by panels of steel and glass and has a gorgeous view of the houses that sit below the hill.

"Last night was pretty bad for Emil, but he's been better today. Sleeping, mostly." Catherine sighs. "He's been in remission for quite a while.... I hope this doesn't start happening more frequently."

"How long does it usually last?" I ask, wondering why, if there are no secrets between our families, nobody told me about Emil's condition while I was away.

"Oh, it depends," she says, leading me to the bottom of the stairs. "The episodes can last anywhere from a few hours to a few days. He might have another one next week or be fine for six months. It's hard to know."

"Maybe I should go. He can let me know when he's feeling better." I try to say it like it's no big deal, but Catherine sees right through me and my matzo ball soup.

"No, you should go up and see him. I think he's getting tired of me and his dad." She smiles. "He'll be happier to see you than either of us, trust me."

Emil's door is cracked, and through the sliver of space I can see he's lying on his side, facing away from the door and toward the big windows that overlook the backyard. His room is dark except for one panel of the wooden blind that's been pulled back. It sends a startling strip of sunlight across his desk, the bamboo floor, the corner of his bed.

I knock and watch him slowly turn over, draping an arm across his eyes as he says, "Come in."

"Hey." I push the door open after a slight pause, hoping he's not annoyed that I'm here. "It's Suzette."

The arm flies off his face and he sits up immediately, which was much too fast, judging by the pained expression that crosses his face. He grimaces for a moment, then turns it into a weak smile for me. "Hey."

"I brought you soup," I say, walking over to the bed as I thrust the mason jar forward. "Matzo ball. It always makes me feel better when I'm sick."

Emil blinks a couple of times and his smile deepens as he takes it from me. "No one's ever brought me soup before." He examines the jar's contents before setting it on his nightstand. "Thanks, Suzette."

"Are you feeling any better?" I ask, suddenly wishing I

had something to do with my hands. Like earlier, when I wanted to touch Rafaela's arm, I clasp them behind my back.

"Kind of." He reaches for his glass of water and nearly drains it before he sets it back on the nightstand, eyeing the pill bottle a few inches away. My heart jumps as I think about the pills I've hidden for Lion. "I really wanted to go out the other night, but I can't drive like this. I've been dizzy for the last couple of days. I lost my balance on the stairs after dinner Friday and almost fell."

"God, I'm sorry, Emil."

"The only thing that makes me feel better is the medicine, but then all I want to do is sleep." He taps the bottle in frustration before leaning back against the headboard. "Sorry. You don't want to hear all this."

I walk toward him then, because this is where I would pat his shoulder or touch his arm reassuringly—if he weren't sitting in bed. But he eases himself over and pats the space next to him on the mattress, and I hesitate only a moment before I sit down, my knees nearly touching the nightstand.

"Of course I want to hear this," I say. "What, you're supposed to pretend you're fine when you're not? You're my friend."

He looks at me for a long moment. "Just your friend?"

My heart is beating in my throat and my face is too hot and my God, if someone had told me a year ago that *Emil* could make me feel this way without even touching me, I would have laughed it off.

I'm still trying to think of how to respond when, again, he says, "Sorry. I'm just..." He covers my hand with his own. "I'm glad you're here."

"Me too," I say, my voice barely more than a whisper.

Emil slides his hand slowly up my arm, sending goose bumps tingling up and down my skin.

Catherine is downstairs and Lionel is waiting in the car, but I want to kiss Emil so badly that I don't care. And when he leans forward, I don't overthink it. My eyes close as his lips brush the slope of one cheekbone and then the other, followed by the spot below my right ear. He pauses and I wonder where he will go next, take in a breath as his mouth falls down to my neck and along the line of my chin before he kisses my lips. Slowly. Softly.

I kiss him back, resting one hand on his shoulder while I run a fingertip along the perimeter of his ear. I bump against a hearing aid and pull back, starting to apologize, but he shakes his head and kisses me again and then his arms wrap around my waist as he draws me closer. I like that I can feel his body heat through his T-shirt and how his skin smells like blankets and sleep, and I wonder if that's the scent I'd wake up to if we spent the night together. My skin burns even more at the thought.

Emil's hands move down my waist, sliding just under the thin fabric of my tank top to touch me on either side of my spine, and I realize he's searching for my dimples of Venus, the indentations in the small of my back. He must have seen them when I was in my bikini. "I like these," he murmurs.

I like you.

I kiss him harder so I won't be tempted to say it aloud.

then.

Iris and I are careful—until we aren't.

We've been locking our door at night because sometimes we fall asleep before one of us can move back to our own bed, and the girls on our floor don't always knock before they come in. We never touch outside our locked dorm room. Sometimes we have a slight reprieve, when we go into town, but it's hard to leave Dinsmore's grounds without the girls on our floor wanting to come along, too—and they're the very people we're trying to get away from.

But we slip up.

I don't know it at first. Neither of us understands that this morning is any different from the others. I wake up in her bed and yawn, my mouth cottony from too much vodka.

Iris got an A on her last chem test before the final in a couple of weeks, so we celebrated. And now she's spooning me, her cheek flat against my back, and I flush for a moment when I remember what I said last night. That I told her no one has ever made me feel the way she does.

My head is too foggy when I try to sit up, so I decide to skip breakfast in favor of lying here with Iris. I wait until the last possible moment to get up and take a shower in our private bathroom, and even then she tugs at my arm, silently begging me to stay. When that doesn't work she uses her lips, kissing along my naked skin, but I eventually, reluctantly pull away. I can't miss English lit.

When I walk out of our room, I don't think too hard about the girls hovering in the hallway outside my door. I smile, and I guess the hangover makes my brain slow, because I don't even think to follow their wide, disbelieving eyes, don't wonder too hard what they're doing here when none of them live on my floor. I don't think anything is out of the ordinary until one of them nods behind me to the door I've just pulled shut.

DYKES

My stomach goes sour. I realize that whoever wrote it took the time to go over the markered letters more than once. That whoever it was definitely wanted the word to be permanent.

Everyone in front of me, every door and corner of this

hallway that I've looked at nearly every day for the past nine months, goes blurry. And I think I'm going to be sick. The logical thing to do would be to go back into the room. Warn Iris. Stay in there until I know I'm not going to vomit.

But I take off. I push past the onlookers, because I'm sure everyone will know it's true once they see us together. And while I'd never think it was an insult to call someone a lesbian, this word isn't informing people of who we're attracted to—it's a hateful accusation.

I keep my head down while I walk to first period so I won't have to watch anyone react to seeing me. Hatred, confusion, sympathy—I don't want to see any of it. I don't want people to look at me any differently than they already do, though it's obviously too late for that.

I make it to the English hall bathroom before my stomach turns over. Afterward, I sit on the cold tile floor of the bathroom. There's no way I'm going to class today. Not one of them.

The first text from Iris comes in as I'm walking to the infirmary: What the fuck happened to our door???

I ignore it because I don't know what to say.

I lie down on a cot in the infirmary, but the nurse makes me leave my phone with her, so I can't check to see if Iris texts again. I try to sleep, but every time I close my eyes I think I hear my phone buzzing. And I can't stop seeing that word on our door.

I'm starving when the day is over, but by now surely everyone has seen or heard about what happened. The dining hall will be a shitshow, so I hurry to the library, keeping my earbuds shoved firmly into my ears, my eyes cast downward anytime I pass someone.

I wait until I've wedged myself into the stacks where anyone rarely goes, near the Latin texts, to check my phone again. I have thirty new messages. Most are from Iris, but some are from the few people I've grown to like while I'm here.

Iris's are the worst to read, though.

You've SEEN the door, right??
Suz where are you?
Well chem lab was hell
I really hate this and I can't believe you're ignoring me
I'm not pissed at you, ok? Just please come back to our room

When I get back, she's perched on the edge of her bed, facing the door. Her cheeks are flushed and I imagine they've been that way since this morning; her skin is pale and blushes easily and often. Her blond, curly hair is swept back into a French braid. Some pieces have started to work their way loose, and it makes me feel bad to think of her sitting here this morning, braiding her hair for the day and not knowing what was on the other side of the door.

"Someone scrubbed it off," I say, tossing my backpack onto my desk. My first instinct had been to lock the door, but we both know that's no longer necessary.

"Yeah, but you can still see it." Her voice is thin. "Not as well, but the letters are just faded, not gone. They'll have to paint over it."

I nod, staring down at the floor.

"Where have you been?" she asks, and the question isn't accusatory. It's more...sad than anything else. "I went to every single class and I didn't see you once."

"I got sick." I swallow, still not making eye contact. "Did people say anything to you?"

"Of course they did, Suzette. Everyone in our dorm has seen it. Every time I came back to the room to get something, someone was here staring. Some people I've never even talked to were asking me about us. About you."

She doesn't sound angry. Mostly frustrated.

"I'm sorry," I practically whisper. I should have been here with her. I know that.

"I can't believe I let them win," she mumbles. "I should have told everyone I was gay when I first got here." She pauses, then: "Did you know I was president of my middle school's gay-straight alliance? A couple of people told me they came out to their parents because I was so brave, so open. What would they think if they could see me now?"

"I'm sorry," I say again.

A couple of times Iris said we should walk out of our room holding hands, or kiss each other in the common room, and I'd agree in the moment. It was easier to think things would be all right when we were safely behind our locked door. When I was lying with my head against her shoulder and her arm was draped over my side, her fingertips tracing invisible patterns along the slope of my hip. I could pretend we were in California, in Los Angeles, where no one I knew cared who I was attracted to.

But as soon as we were out in the hall, under the watchful eyes of my classmates, my bravery vanished. All I wanted was to blend in as much as possible.

"Well, you don't have to worry," Iris says briskly as she stands up from her bed. "Nobody thinks you're a *real* dyke. I told them it was all me."

"You what?" I look straight at her for the first time since I've walked in, but now her back is to me. She's rearranging things on her already spotless desk, and I guess she doesn't want to look at me when she says this part.

"Lily and Bianca cornered me at lunch. Asked if it was true." She shakes her head and laughs a bit, but it's more like a bark—sharp and quick and unhappy. "They probably had something to do with it, or at least know for sure who did it. But I knew whatever I told them would get back to everyone else, so I said . . ."

The air is so quiet I can hear her breathing across the room. Like the many times I've listened to her when we were in our separate beds, counting her breaths and wanting to be near enough to feel them on my skin.

"I said I came on to you when we were drunk a couple of times and that it was all me. Everything." She clears her throat. "So it's all good, okay? Nobody thinks *that* about you."

That. As if girls liking girls is a disease. But it's how the girls on our floor think of it, and Iris is smart enough to know that nothing she says will change their minds.

"I don't care if they do," I say, but my voice is distant enough that we both know that statement is false.

The truth is that I already feel so on guard, I'm not sure I'm up for being put under a new lens to be examined. There's the fact that I'm one of less than a handful of black kids at the entire school, which is something I'm reminded of much more often than I think necessary. And while I don't feel great about the fact that I haven't so much as removed my Magen David from the bottom of my jewelry box since I've been here, the necklace that I've worn nearly every day since Lionel gave it to me, I know it's easier than explaining my background to the girls in our dorm. They're still trying to understand how my mother and Saul can make a family like ours without being married; they could never fathom my converting to the religion of a man who can't legally call himself my stepfather. They like clear-cut boxes, and I don't fit the one they know to be Jewish.

Iris turns and we look at each other, finally, her light brown eyes connecting with my own. "Do you…Did you ever feel like I was taking advantage of you?"

Her voice is so small that I want to go over and wrap my arms around her and kiss her until the pain goes away. But I know nothing will be the same between us now. I knew that the second I decided to walk away this morning.

"Never," I say firmly. "Not once."

"But we always drank. I know it made you more comfortable, and maybe that wasn't right…to be with you like that."

"I did everything I did because I wanted to, okay?" I say. "You didn't ever force me to do anything."

She nods, but I don't know if I've convinced her. She switches on her lamp and switches it off again. "You're off the hook." Her voice is the softest it's been since I came in. "We only have a couple more weeks here. Let them believe you were never into it…that you were never into me."

Maybe if I were a better person I would ignore her suggestion and tell everyone that she didn't take advantage of me, that I care about her, that being with Iris makes being cut off from the life I never wanted to leave enjoyable, not just bearable.

But I am the sort of person who, when I walk out of our

room the next day, finds it easier to let them believe what she said. I shut down Bianca immediately when, with the most concern I've ever seen her show toward another human being, she asks if I've been sexually assaulted and want to make a report. But I don't deny what Iris told them, and I don't correct them when they repeat it.

And the worst part is that I can't stop thinking how it's the nicest they've been to me all year.

twelve.

It's hard not to think of Iris whenever I drink.

We weren't even close to being the biggest drinkers in our dorm, but she kept a bottle of raspberry-flavored vodka under her bed that we sipped from during second semester. She'd procured it with the help of her older sister when she was home over winter break, smuggled back to school in a giant duffel bag with her lacrosse gear.

So when DeeDee says she'd like to get drunk because she's fighting with Alicia and I'm the only person she wants to see, I immediately think of Iris, the relationship between girls and liquor. Iris and I stopped drinking when everything fell apart between us, and it never occurred to me to use alcohol as a coping mechanism. We drank raspberry vodka on the nights I wanted to be closer to her.

DeeDee comes over armed with a fifth of spiced rum tucked in her overnight bag, and when she shows it to me up in my room, it reminds me so much of Iris that for a moment I can't breathe.

"What's wrong?" DeeDee asks.

"Nothing. I just..."

"You're not chickening out, are you?" She turns the bottle around so she can read the label. "It says it's premium. This is the good stuff."

I squint at the bottle. "Where'd you get that?"

"Someone left it at your welcome-back party. Totally unopened. Amazing, right?" She slips it back into her duffel, under her pajamas, and shoves the bag next to my bed. "Thanks for letting me come over. It feels good here. Cozy."

"Mom and Saul missed having you here," I say, linking my arm through hers as we head downstairs. Our bare feet press down on the squeaky hardwood floor as we walk in tandem.

"I missed *this*," DeeDee says as we step into the kitchen.

The room is heady with basil leaves and olive oil and fresh dough, which means only one thing: DeeDee's pilgrimage has warranted homemade pizza from Saul. He makes his own sauce, too, with tomatoes Mrs. Maldonado brings over by the bagful from her garden. The basil grows in a small plot of our own out back, across the yard from the tree house.

My whole family is hanging out in the kitchen: Mom carefully ladling sauce over a circle of rolled-out dough while Lionel and Saul line the top of the island with sausage and cheese and pepperoni and vegetables. We finish making the pizzas together, and DeeDee's right—there is something nice about being with my family and her like this. These were the sorts of moments that made me ache with loneliness at Dinsmore: tripping over each other in a too-crowded, flour-dusted kitchen that smells like the very essence of good food.

After dinner, DeeDee insists on helping clean up, even after my parents protest more than once. Maybe she's trying to solidify her spot on their good side, and I glance at her over the dual sinks as we rinse plates, wondering just how drunk she plans to get this evening.

Ten minutes later we're up in the tree with the bottle of rum, transported through the house wrapped in a blanket.

"God, it's weird being back up here." DeeDee walks around the small room to inspect what's changed and what's stayed the same since she was last here many months ago. She opens the cabinet that Saul built into the far wall and looks at the stack of dusty board games hanging out above Lionel's and my old sleeping bags. "Do you guys still come up all the time?"

"Not as much as we used to." I settle onto the futon and

place the blanket-wrapped bottle to the side. "It's all kind of different since—"

Just then, I hear Lionel's feet coming up the tree, and his flame-colored head pokes through the doorway a few seconds later. I asked DeeDee when we were washing dishes if she'd mind his company. I didn't think she would, but I wanted to check, and she said, "Why are you even asking?" like the best friend that she is. And he decided to come up, which isn't the choice I expected but the one I was hoping for. He's comfortable with DeeDee, and maybe starting small is the best way to reintegrate into our group of friends.

Lionel's eyes find the alcohol as soon as he's in the room. The blanket has slipped away, revealing part of the label. "Looks like I showed up at just the right time."

The first thing that comes to mind is his meds, but then I remember. And I know he's not taking them again, because I check my tissue box every day, and they were still lodged in the bottom before DeeDee came over.

"We're drinking because Alicia is being crazy," she says, joining me on the futon.

I stiffen, waiting to see if Lion will be offended. *Crazy* is the word he always uses when he talks about how other people view him, and I know how much he hates that label.

But he doesn't say anything or even flinch, and Dee tosses the blanket that we brought from inside over her legs. Los Angeles cools down after the sun has set, even in the summer. The two windows are sealed shut, but a chilly breeze winds through the cracks of the tree house. It's nothing compared to the bone-chilling winters of Massachusetts, but it is enough to make me ask Lion to pass over a sleeping bag.

He retrieves them both and shakes the dust out in the doorway before he slides mine over. I unzip the musty cotton roll; it's pink and purple and printed with sparkly-horned unicorns. Lion spreads his out, Transformers splashed against a navy-blue background, and sits on top of it, looking expectantly at the bottle.

DeeDee pops it open, taking a long swig before she passes it down to him. "Oh my God," she says, breathless after she swallows. "That's horrible. We need a chaser."

"Well, I've never had it, so I want the full experience." Lion sips, raises an eyebrow, and then takes a drink as long as DeeDee's. He gasps a bit and squeezes his eyes shut, but overall he takes it like a champ and I'm impressed, considering he doesn't have any practice. He moves his shoulders back and forth like he can shake the taste out of his mouth. "Fuck, that *is* horrible."

"The worst is over," I say, remembering what Iris told me when we drank together for the first time. I didn't think she could possibly be right, as medicinally awful as the vodka had tasted. But each drink went down smoother after that first one, every single time, even if I never did grow to like the taste.

I grab the bottle, tip it back, and send the honey-colored

fire tearing down my throat. This particular bottle of rum is *so* not fucking around. But I swallow it down; stick out my tongue and cough a bit as I hand it back to Dee.

"So, what's the deal with Alicia?" I ask as she rests the bottle in her lap. And I'm so glad I'm with my best friend and brother, because none of us are trying to impress each other. Lionel appears just as relieved that we're taking a break before round two. I'm already starting to feel fuzzy. "What did she do to earn your wrath?"

DeeDee traces her fingers around the edges of the label. "I want..." She pauses to glance at Lion but must quickly determine it's okay for him to hear this, because she blurts, "I want to date other people and Alicia isn't up for it."

"Why don't you just break up with her?" Lionel's voice is clear but looser than normal.

"That's the thing—I don't want to break up with her. I want her to see other people, too."

"Like an open relationship?" I say as the rum makes a slow, warm trip through my stomach and legs and arms, all the way to my fingertips and toes.

DeeDee's cheeks are flushed when I look over. "Yeah, I guess... if that's what you want to call it. I just don't want to be tied down to one person. I'm not even seventeen yet."

"What brought this on?" I raise my knees to my chest under the sleeping bag, pulling it tighter around me. "Do you like someone else?"

"I don't know." Dee shrugs. "I'm always looking at other girls, wondering what it would be like with them. And it doesn't feel right to hold her back, so I wanted to see if we could just keep things chill for a while. She completely freaked out."

"Doesn't that kind of freak *you* out, though? The thought of her being with other people when she's not with you?"

"Not really," Dee says, and I believe her. "God, sometimes I wish I were bi. Like, I definitely don't want to be with any dudes, no offense"—she looks at Lionel, who holds up his hands as if to say he gets it—"but it'd be so nice to just go back to a guy when you got tired of being with a girl. You'd never be bored."

I stare at her, waiting for the laugh, the one that makes it clear she was joking. It never comes. "Um, Dee, you know that's, like, one hundred percent not what being bi is."

"So, it's not about liking guys *and* girls?" She takes another drink of rum and Lion passes so now it's my turn, but I'm already feeling so hot inside that I don't know if another drink is a good idea.

She knows I've told Lionel, but I'm uncomfortable talking about this with him now. I still want to know if Rafaela would make me feel better than when I was with Iris, or if being with her wouldn't feel as exciting as when I'm with Emil, or if she'd make me feel something new altogether. But he likes her. He called her two days after they met, and they have a date this weekend. I haven't seen him so excited about anyone—anything, really—since he met Grayson, and I can't take that away from him.

"That's part of it, but…it's not about getting to switch between guys and girls when I'm *tired* of one of them. It's about being open to whatever happens with either one."

"I know a few girls who said they were bi and then, like, six months later they only wanted to date guys," she says. Her voice isn't mean, but she's challenging me, and I don't like it. "What if you're just experimenting?"

"What if I *am*, DeeDee?" I don't mean to sound defensive, but I don't appreciate the pressure, especially after she seemed so chill about it earlier. Maybe I'm bi, maybe I'm queer, maybe I'll never like another girl besides Iris and Rafaela. I'm not totally clear on my identity yet, and maybe DeeDee wouldn't be so skeptical if I told her about Rafaela. But I don't need her telling me what I am and what that means, best friend or not.

"Sorry." Her voice is unmistakably contrite, and I feel bad about snapping at her, especially in front of Lionel. "I'm just mad about Alicia. And this rum is really strong. And I thought—well, after you told me what happened with Emil…"

Lionel is holding back a smile, because when I returned to his car after delivering the soup to Emil, he took one look at me and said, "You were totally making out." I tried to protest, my hands fumbling with the takeout containers as I slipped into the passenger seat, but he knew he was right. Emil had walked me to the foot of the stairs and Catherine, grinning at us both, had said in a knowing voice that she was happy to see how much better he was feeling.

"I don't want to talk about Emil."

Not because I would take back what happened between us—I've thought about that afternoon so often since it happened, I'm embarrassed—but because I don't know what to do about my feelings. We hang out this summer, and then what? We have only a couple more months before school starts up again. I'm due back at Dinsmore in the fall, but of course I've thought about what will happen if I don't go back.

With my job and Lionel's therapy and the meds they think he's taking, Mom and Saul have no reason to think I'm missing out on my life or making his problems my own. They've already admitted they didn't handle things so well last year; I probably wouldn't have to fight so hard to stay. But then I might never see Iris again. And I don't want that, either. Because a voice I keep trying to squash deep down in me is wondering if I could ever be truly happy with Emil or Rafaela or anyone else if I never make things right with Iris.

"Little, seriously, what's your deal with him? You like him. Own it." Lionel's words slur just a little. He's had only a couple of swigs, but the alcohol is hitting him harder because he's new to it.

And he's chewing at the skin around his thumbs. I watch for a few moments before I swat his hand away from his face, and my stomach twitches as I wonder if this is the sign I've been waiting for. If that little tic, a common bad habit, was the switch that officially flipped him from Medicated to Nonmedicated Lionel. He frowns and swats back at my own wrist but he stops chewing his thumb.

"It's not *Emil*. I like him. It's…" I swallow hard. I'm with two of my favorite people in the world, but sometimes that makes saying uncomfortable things harder. I worry that they'll judge me, yell at me, tell me I'm a bad person. It's hard enough for me not to believe it myself sometimes. "I was a real shit to Iris before we left Massachusetts."

DeeDee looks at me. "What do you mean? Like, the breakup? Breakups are hard. Honestly, they should be outlawed. They're practically inhumane."

I forgot how much Dee talks when she's been drinking, how her soft voice gets raspy with overuse.

"We didn't break up," I say. "Technically."

Because technically, Iris and I were never a couple. Not in the traditional sense. We were locked doors and long, slow kisses that tasted of raspberry vodka and promises to keep whatever happened in our dorm between us.

Dee and Lion are staring at me and I feel sick to my stomach. I haven't had that much to drink. But it's not the rum. It's the fact that I've never mentioned this aloud to anyone since I left Dinsmore, and talking about it makes it real again. Harder to forget.

"I didn't stick up for her...for us," I say, not meeting their eyes.

"What do you mean?" DeeDee says again. From the corner of my eye, I see her head tilt.

"They wrote on our door. The word *dykes*," I say, grabbing the bottle from the center of our triangle. I take a long swig and it burns my tongue but it doesn't hurt so much going down this time. My body takes well to the liquor—to its warmth and the silent but steadfast promise that whatever I say out loud next won't hurt as much as it did at the time. "In black marker. They could've written it on our dry-erase board, but I guess they didn't want us to forget."

And then I tell them the whole story. DeeDee interrupts a few times to express disgust, saying she hoped we knocked those bitches out for what they did. But Lionel listens silently the whole time, until I'm finished.

"How'd you leave things with her?" he asks as he takes another turn with the bottle.

I am completely fuzzy now, and when I move my head to look at him, that part of the room takes a few extra seconds to align.

"She slept in the common room until we left," I say, remembering the first time it happened, when I woke in the middle of the night to find her gone and stumbled down the hall until I saw the faint glow of the television and Iris curled up under her yellow quilt on the couch. "And I let myself be off the hook."

"I can't believe you went to such a homophobic school," DeeDee says, shaking her head.

"It wasn't, though. Lots of people were out and there's a gay-straight alliance and... it wasn't even everyone on our floor. But the bigots made sure we all knew how they felt. Iris and I were new to Dinsmore and they'd been there a whole year before us and... it sounds stupid now, but it was easier not to stand up to them."

"Well, I still can't believe they treated you like that."

"I can't believe I treated *Iris* like that." I work my fingers around the edge of a faded unicorn hoof on the sleeping bag. "She was always nice to me. Always."

And patient and sweet. She was good to me, and a good person in general, and I didn't return the favor.

"She'll get over it. I feel like it sort of comes with the territory—dating a closeted person. You can't take it personally."

"But you've never dated anyone who was closeted."

"I might someday." She shrugs. "I mean, yeah, it wasn't ideal, or all that nice, but she gave you her blessing. Sometimes you can't think too hard about it when someone hands you a gift like that. Get out unscathed while you can, you know?"

It might be easier not to think about it, to just let it go because Iris did. She never mentioned it again, and when we parted ways, she was kind. She told me to have a good summer, that she hoped everything worked out okay with my brother.

But then I remember how much I hated not being open about my Judaism. We may be on the more liberal side of the religion, but it's a part of me and, especially, my connection to Saul, and I'm proud of that. Going back to Dinsmore and continuing to hide this other part of myself might actually kill my soul.

"It was a shitty thing to do," I say. "Iris shouldn't have to go through that. Not with me."

"Sometimes, when I'm getting all down on myself…" Lionel pauses to shove his hair out of his eyes, a task that suddenly requires absolute concentration. He begins again: "Sometimes Dr. Tarrasch makes me repeat this thing. She makes me say, *I'm doing the best I can*. I thought it was corny, but I don't know. It kind of works. Nobody's ever trying to do their worst, I guess."

But that doesn't mean it's any easier to do the right thing.

then.

Each year, our family goes to a Dodgers game to kick off the summer. None of us is a huge baseball fan, but it's fun to go as a family, and even I start to get into it once we're there, with the Dodger Dogs and the songs and all the fans dressed in bright blue and white.

Lionel seems particularly excited this year. He keeps talking about it to our friends, though none of them care because I'm pretty sure most people in that group have never attended a professional sporting event in their lives. He even bought us matching Dodgers shirts, the jersey kind that button up the front.

"Little. *Little!* Oh, good, you're wearing it," he said— or practically shouted—as he entered my room without knocking, something he's been doing more and more often. I'm trying not to let it bother me, because it means he's out of bed and talking to people and not looking at me with lifeless eyes. It means he's finally over Grayson, and we can get the old Lionel back.

The shirt is a nice gesture, but I can't see myself wearing it again after today. When I ask Lionel how much it cost, worried that he's spent too much on something I don't even want, he waves me off, insisting, "We can't just show up looking like casual fans!"

We always have before, and I don't know what's different this year, but before I can ask, he's running through the Dodgers' entire season of stats with fervor, occasionally interrupting himself with a non sequitur or to exclaim about a completely average fact that doesn't deserve the excitement. I try to stop him a couple of times, to ask if he's okay, but he's too far down the Dodgers rabbit hole. He's pacing my room as he talks, picking things up and walking around with them and putting them back in the wrong spot.

I'm relieved when Mom calls up to us from the middle floor. It feels claustrophobic in my room, like I'm being pushed out by Lion and his increasingly intense thoughts. He goes ahead of me down the stairs and I wonder, for a moment, if he's taken something—a pill, maybe, or even coke, though he once told me he has no intention of putting anything up his nose. But when I look at his hands, at the skin torn ragged around his thumbs—so badly in some places that I can tell they've been bleeding—I wonder if it means something.

"Guys, sorry to be the bearer of bad news, but Saul had a work emergency that's going to take up most of the afternoon," Mom says. Apparently Lionel has convinced her to dress for the occasion, too: A vibrant blue baseball cap with the Dodgers logo sits on top of her close-cropped hair.

"What?"

It's only then, when Lion is standing stock-still, staring at my mother, that I realize it's more than him bursting into my room and the rapid talking and the chewed skin around his thumbs. He's always up before me now, and he always has a million plans to execute before I've even finished my coffee. Yesterday, he was gone so long during the day that I started to worry, and he stayed up late once he was back home. The light was blazing in the space under his door when I got up to pee at four a.m.

Mom's eyes are apologetic as she looks at Lionel. "He's going to try to make it to the game if he can, sweetie. But we should probably head out now if we want to get there for the first pitch."

"Why didn't he call me?" Lionel sounds way too upset about this. He's not one to let a minor snag in a plan get under his skin, and up until this year—the past couple of weeks, even—I've never known him to be into baseball like this.

"He barely had time to talk," Mom says slowly. She can tell something is off, too. "We'll make it up to you, Lionel. We'll pick another day that we can all go, no excuses."

"This is bullshit," he mutters and then, without warning, he slams his open palm against the frame of the bathroom door. The smack is loud and angry and scary—something I never expected to see from Lion.

"Sweetie, I'm sorry." Mom's voice is measured but her eyes are wide with worry. "Why don't you take a minute and meet us downstairs when you're ready, okay?"

"*No!* This is fucking *bullshit*! We're all supposed to be together and this fucking ruins *everything*." His voice ricochets off the walls, at the loudest volume I think anyone has ever spoken in our house.

Mom looks at me then, and I realize by the unfamiliar expression on her face that she has no idea what to do. We are not a shouting family and we aren't a family that really loses control in any way. Problems are discussed rationally, and usually over food. Disagreements are settled by the end of the night. But we get along well, so those times are rare. And this, from Lionel, is unheard of.

He starts pacing then, back and forth from the door of the bathroom to the door of his room. His face is turning redder by the minute as he keeps pushing his hair back and muttering incomplete sentences. He's getting louder, too, and on the other side of him, standing at the top of the stairs to the first floor, Mom watches wordlessly.

"Lionel, I'm going to call your father, okay?" she says after it's clear he isn't going to stop anytime soon.

He doesn't hear her, or if he does, he doesn't acknowledge it. Two, three, four more paces and he stalks into his bedroom, slamming the door so hard I'm surprised it doesn't rock off the hinges.

Mom takes in a breath and doesn't look away from his door as she says, "Stay right here, baby. I'm going to get my phone."

I nod, my eyes glued to the door, too. He's still shouting, something about disrespect and honoring commitments, and I can hear other unidentifiable noises in the background as he moves around. I almost want it to be drugs, because my brother isn't just acting out of the norm for our family—he's acting like a completely different person.

My mother doesn't make it halfway down the stairs before the first crash comes. I shut my eyes, and my shoulders go up to my ears. It sounds like the roof has caved in on this part of the house.

"Lion!" I cry out, and Mom leaps back up the stairs in an instant. I hold my breath as she turns the knob, afraid he's locked us out, but the door opens at the exact moment an identical crash shakes the house.

She goes in first and I stand in the doorway, mouth open wide at the state of Lion's room. He hasn't been in here even thirty seconds, and the place is a complete wreck. He's swept everything off his desk and ripped his sheets from the mattress and torn posters from the wall. But the loud noises were his books. They're piled in massive heaps, crushed under the heavy bookcases, which he pushed away from the wall until they crashed to the floor.

"Everything is ruined," I can hear him saying.

Hear, because I can't look at him. Not now. I'm too afraid to look up and see that the person acting so erratically is actually my brother.

"*Ruined!*"

I don't see him make the fist but I catch him pulling it out of the wall. And then I see him do it again. And again. And I see his hand come back the last time with bloody knuckles.

He's breathing heavily, his chest heaving as if he's just run a marathon. He looks at my mother, who is frozen in shock, and my stomach sinks. I wonder if he'll turn his wrath on her next.

But he just whips his head back and forth as he says, "Why did he have to ruin everything? This is tradition and we're all supposed to be there and he ruined it. He fucking *ruined it*, Nadine."

"Oh, honey. He's so sorry, okay? So am I." She walks to him slowly and I stand on guard in case he lunges at the last minute and I have to step in. *Step in to defend my mother from my brother.* I keep thinking, hoping, that I'll wake up in my tower, drenched in sweat, but every time I blink, my eyes keep coming back to the incomprehensible scene in front of me.

Lionel doesn't do anything. He just stands still with his chest heaving and his injured hand curled at his side. When she reaches him she gathers him up quickly in her arms, perhaps too afraid of what will happen if she doesn't. She guides Lion over to the bare mattress and eases him down to a sitting position and holds him. She rocks him back and forth as he cries, his voice and tears muffled beneath her arms.

"It's okay, sweetheart," she murmurs to him, the same voice she used when I had bad dreams as a kid. "It's going to be okay." She looks over her shoulder then, not quite making eye contact as she says to me, her voice brisk and businesslike, "Suzette, go get your phone and call Saul. Keep calling back until he answers. Tell him we need him here. *Now.*"

Tears start streaming down my face as soon as Saul answers, and I'm crying so hard he can barely understand me. Even when I manage to hiccup out an explanation, it doesn't make sense. None of this makes sense. But Saul understands enough to know he is needed. He says he's leaving to come home right now.

Lionel's agitation has decreased by the time I get off the phone, but Mom never leaves his side, not even when Saul gets home. They talk to him, try to find out the root of the problem, but he keeps saying he doesn't know what happened, why he was so upset. He looks scared and sad, sitting between our parents in the middle of his debris-filled room, and I wish there was something I could do besides watch from the sidelines.

We don't talk that night, Lionel and me. He doesn't talk to anyone, really. We eat dinner, but no one is hungry. We all end up pushing food around our plates until Lionel says he'd like to be excused. Mom and Saul don't want to let him go; I can tell by the way they look at each other. But they can't keep him down here all night, either.

Later, after everyone is supposed to be in bed, I creep down the stairs to listen outside Lionel's room. When I slowly turn the knob, he's asleep. No late-night projects or lists to be made or whatever else he would do in here until the early hours of the morning. I'm not relieved, though. Something is wrong. Mom and Saul tried to disguise their worry, but they're clearly just as concerned as I am.

Saul and I picked up some of the mess in the room after dinner while Lionel took a shower, giving him enough space to get around without tripping over the books and their shelves. Still, Lion looks like he's sleeping in a cave made of books.

I close the door and tiptoe across the hall to Mom and Saul's room. Their light is off, but their voices murmur behind the door. I press my ear closer to hear what they're saying.

"...one of the scariest moments of my life," Mom is saying. "I didn't know what he was going to do. And he didn't, either. He looked so...outside of himself."

Saul sighs. "I'm so sorry I wasn't here, Nadine. You shouldn't have had to go through that by yourself."

"Don't apologize. He's my child, too. I just...I'm worried."

He sighs again and I hear rustling, like he's turning over. "We'll figure it out. Dr. Carver is going to get us in first thing tomorrow." He pauses, then says again, "We'll figure it out."

There's no space to sleep on the floor in Lionel's room, so I pad silently into the guest room and shut the door behind me. I don't sleep much, if at all, but that just makes it easier to get up and check on Lionel throughout the night.

I do so every hour until the sun rises. I have to leave before my parents get up, so I make the bed and close the door and slip back to my room without making a sound.

thirteen.

When I walk into Castillo Flowers two days later, I stop
as soon as I see Rafaela.

I dreamed about her, and I forgot until now. We were
at Dinsmore and we were rooming together and there was
no Iris. Rafaela and I held hands in public and kissed in
public and when we were alone, I wasn't shy about touching
her first. It was so real, not like a dream at all. I haven't ever
dreamed about Emil, not like that, and I wonder if that's my
subconscious trying to tell me something.

My neck and cheeks are hot, and I take a few seconds to
catch my breath. When I walk over to the counter, I'm sure
she'll ask me what's wrong. But she says nothing.

"Hi." I dump my bag on a shelf in the back room, squeeze

behind the register to grab my apron, and still, she doesn't respond.

She barely looks up. Her gaze never quite makes it to me; she's staring at the bonsais across the room and her expression is confused, as if she has no idea why she's not still looking down at the counter.

"Hello?" I try again, waving a hand in front of her face until her eyes snap into focus.

"Hey." She attempts a smile, but I'm not convinced.

I tie my apron around my waist and notice hers isn't even fastened. The strings dangle freely on either side of her. My eyes travel upward, to the black tank she's wearing with the oversized armholes that reveal the sides of a hot-pink bra underneath. I start talking so I'll look away.

"Everything okay? You seem a little out of it."

She leans against the wall behind the counter, her curls twining around a pushpin in the corkboard. The board is pinned with notes from satisfied customers, scrawled on everything from notebook paper to fancy monogrammed stationery. Most people send an email, but Ora is old-fashioned enough to attract customers with the same appreciation for handwritten praise.

"You know that guy...from the Palisades?" Rafaela sighs. "He's becoming a real problem. As in, he won't leave me the fuck alone. He—" She stops to look at me. "Are you okay with me telling you this?"

"Why wouldn't I be?"

"I'm going out with your brother tomorrow, and I know you guys are close, so . . . I just don't want it to be weird." She looks at me with raised eyebrows. "Is it weird?"

"God, no." And I probably sound a bit too chipper, considering she's talking about people she was or is interested in, and neither of them is me. But there's no point in her knowing how I feel, or that I've had dreams where she was with me instead of my brother. "Lion and I are cool about that stuff."

"*Lion?*" she repeats with a soft laugh. "That's damn cute. Anyway, this dude called me at Ora's—on her *landline*. And she answered the phone and I told her I didn't want to talk to him and now she's all upset because she's afraid—"

I think she's going to interrupt herself to ask if I'm still okay with her telling me this, but she doesn't finish. And when I prompt her, she shakes her head.

"It's nothing. She's just afraid I'm going to fuck up."

There's an *again* on the end of that, I know it. But the word never falls from Rafaela's lips, so I pretend it isn't dangling in the air between us.

"Let's just say that my date with *Lion* couldn't come at a better time." She flashes me an expression halfway between a smirk and a proper smile, and I decide to let her use my nickname for him just this once. A freebie. No one calls him that but me, not even DeeDee, and it would be just as strange if someone else started calling me Little.

The bell above the door comes to life and jars some-thing in Rafaela. She finishes tying her apron and steps from behind the counter just as a man wearing sunglasses enters and announces he's looking for something "exotic."

I came in later today, so for the first time since I started working here, I help her close up the shop. I even see the elu-sive Héctor, who rarely makes it farther than the back room when he's restocking for deliveries. He drops off the keys from the van and sticks his head in to say good night before he leaves.

Rafaela hums as we sweep the floors and wipe down the displays. Her humming grows louder as she looks at the delivery log, making sure everything is in the proper order for tomorrow. And then, by the time she removes her apron, she's singing under her breath. Even at such a low volume, it's clear she has a good voice.

"You sing?"

She looks up, startled, as if she'd forgotten I was in the room. "Oh. Sorry."

I finish scooping Tucker's litter box, which didn't turn out to be the horrific task I anticipated, though I found it somewhat insulting that he watched me the whole time from three feet away. "Sorry? You have an amazing voice."

She doesn't deny the compliment, but instead says thank you. I like that there's no false modesty. "I used to sing. I was in choir. At my old school...and my old church." She opens the register to begin removing the money, which she'll put in a locked box until first thing tomorrow morning when Ora drops it off at the bank. Then she looks at me and grins. "Just how amazing?"

"Really amazing." I'm tending to Tucker's overnight provisions now: fresh water and half a scoop of dry food in his stainless steel bowls. "But you know that."

"Yeah, maybe." I can tell she's still smiling without looking at her. "I like hearing it from you, though."

My skin burns like the moment I walked in, and I conjure my brother's face, force myself to think about how much he likes her. He sat in my room for thirty minutes last night, asking my opinion on everything from what he should wear on their date to whether he'll look cheap if he doesn't spring for valet.

There's a pause as Rafaela waits for me to respond. And I'm tempted to flirt back with her. Because it feels good to be open about it, and because I dreamed of her, and because of those gorgeous purple lips. But I don't. I scratch my fingers along Tucker's cheeks and ask her, "Are we just about done?"

"Yeah." She clears her throat as if she's realigning her train of thought. "Is Lionel picking you up tonight?"

"My mom," I say, relieved that I don't have to sit in a car with my brother and my guilt.

"Oh. Well...do you have to go home right away? Ora is going out tonight and...I'm probably being paranoid, but I can't stop thinking about how that guy called her house and he knows where I live and—I make really good pasta. I could cook dinner and drive you home later."

I'm surprised to see the anxiety is not just in her voice but reflected on her face, too. I know so little about Rafaela, but I never expected she'd be so vulnerable in front of me.

My family eats dinner together most nights, but I'm really thinking of Lionel. How he'd react if he knew I was feeling this way about Rafaela. How I'd worry that it would make him quieter and quieter until I never saw him anymore, until he lost interest in her and his books and the rest of his life, until he was so low that I wouldn't see even a couple of hours of sleep unless I was close to him, staying a few feet away in the guest room.

But just because I like her, that doesn't mean I have to act on it. I get the feeling she had to swallow a lot of pride to ask me to come over, and the guy from the Palisades clearly has no sense of boundaries. She shouldn't be alone when she's so scared.

I say yes and she smiles and I tell myself it's okay to stop thinking about Lionel's well-being for a few hours. I tell myself it's okay to take a break.

Ora's house is cute, a pale blue bungalow with comfortable furniture and art everywhere and just enough room for the two of them. It smells good, like someone dusted cinnamon around the rooms. Rafaela hangs her bag on a hook by the door and gestures for me to do the same. I instantly spy two cats, a small calico and one with lots of gray fur.

"That's Hall and Oates," Rafaela says as she heads toward the kitchen with them trotting along behind her. "It's their dinnertime now, too."

"Doesn't Tucker miss them?" I follow her to the kitchen, which is painted a warm yellow and has a checkerboard floor and a window box filled with potted succulents and cactuses, but no flowers.

Rafaela reaches into the pantry for a can of wet food and pops the top, splitting it evenly between two bowls with a fork. "Tucker lives at the shop because he's an asshole to other cats. Ora says he used to terrorize these two."

"Where is Ora?"

"At a movie. She's been out twice in the last week." Rafaela washes her hands as the cats devour their meal. "You could be single-handedly responsible for saving my aunt's social life."

She sets a big pot of water on the stove and assembles a cutting board full of vegetables. I offer to help, but she refuses to let me and instead pours us both a glass of white wine.

"Dump it if Ora comes in" is her only stipulation, so I try to relax and tell myself there's no reason at all to feel like I'm on a date with the girl my brother will be taking on a date tomorrow.

She chops and stirs and dices and sautés, and she does it all while talking, without missing a beat. She tells me about Castillo Flowers, how it was started by her grandmother, Ora's mom. How it's barely changed inside since it opened forty years ago, and how Ora threw herself so fully into her work after her mother died because the best way for her to grieve was to make sure she kept the family business alive.

Rafaela warms a loaf of bread in the oven while she takes down dishes and a pair of water glasses from cabinets with no doors on them. She's so confident in the kitchen, moving around as if she does this every day. She's good at a lot of things: singing, cooking, working with flowers. And there's still so much I don't know about her.

A couple of minutes later, she's placed a bowl of steaming pasta in front of me, bow ties surrounded by broccoli and bell peppers and zucchini and carrots and squash in a light sauce. It's delicious, as good as if it came from a restaurant.

When I tell her so, Rafaela doesn't look at me, but she smiles as she tears a piece of bread off the loaf. "Thanks, but if you think this is good, you should taste my mom's. Her pasta primavera is the best."

I sense an opening, and I don't know if I should go for it, but I do. "Did she teach you how to cook?"

"She taught me a lot of things. My dad took off when my sister was a baby, so she was obsessed with making sure we knew how to do everything for ourselves. I know how to cook, change a tire, drive a stick shift, and change a baby's diaper." She pauses. "I used to help out with my little sister."

She follows that up with a laugh, but it's strained and it makes me hold my forkful of pasta too long. I feel like she's talking in riddles. Part of me thinks she wouldn't have invited me over if she didn't trust me in some way, but the other part wonders if I'm going to have to dig for every piece of information about her life.

"How'd you end up here? At Ora's, I mean." I spread a generous amount of creamy butter onto my bread and take a bite.

Rafaela doesn't say anything, and I wonder if she was too lost in her own thoughts to hear the question, but no. She stares at the wood grain of the table for a few seconds, then sets down her fork and looks at me.

"I don't know why I'm telling you this, but you seem like one of the good ones, Suzette." She doesn't break my gaze. "You are, right?"

I nod right away, even though sometimes I wonder about that myself.

"The town I'm from, in Texas...it's really small. Like, one of those places you hear about or see on TV but you don't think actually exists. Barely any stoplights, everything shuts down by nine, and everyone knows everyone else. L.A. is like another world. I've been here for a year now and I still can't believe I can walk down the busiest street in the city and not run into someone I know."

She picks up her fork again, but only to push food around her bowl. I could eat the rest of my serving and another one right now, but it seems insensitive to be chewing when she's clearly about to tell me something important, so I abandon my fork and put my hands in my lap.

Rafaela looks at her pasta as she continues. "To be honest, the only things to do there were drink and get high and get in trouble, so that's what my friends and I did. There was this guy and he was a real piece of shit, but I only found that out after I slept with him. No . . . I found out he was an actual piece of shit after I got pregnant."

"Oh." I don't know anyone my age who's been pregnant . . . or at least no one who's told me.

"My mom refused to even discuss any option other than having it, and as far as I was concerned, that wasn't an option." She takes a long drink of wine and I follow suit, draining my glass. "My sister was my only other family there, and she's twelve. So I called Ora and she said she'd help me, and here I am."

I definitely don't know anyone who's had an abortion, but I don't tell her that. I don't want her to think I'm judging her, because I'm not. It's easy to think you know what you'd do if you were in a certain position until you find yourself there, feeling completely lost.

"Ora paid for it," she says slowly. "And we don't talk about it. And I was going to go home after that—just spend the summer here and go back to start the school year with my friends. But my mom told me I was a sinner, and that willful sinners aren't welcome under her roof."

"Your own mother?" When I was told I had to go away, to Dinsmore, I felt like I was being kicked out. But that's nothing compared with this, and I can't think of one reason my mother would kick me out of our house for good.

"Oh, it gets worse. She sent my Bible, with this passage in Hebrews highlighted: *For if we sin willfully after that we have received the knowledge of the truth, there remaineth no more sacrifice for sins.*" She looks at my surprised face and gives me a small smile. "I just kept looking at it, for hours, until Ora figured out what had happened and took it away from me. She dumped it in the trash bin outside."

"Ora kicks ass."

"Well, that part gets better," Rafaela says, and her smile widens. "She called my mom the next morning and told her she'd sic the devil himself on her if she sent any more of that religious propaganda to her house. Her own sister!"

I smile back at her, because Ora is one of the good ones, too.

"I don't regret it," Rafaela says, softly. "I still think about it a lot, and the only thing I wish is that I hadn't ever let that loser get anywhere near my naked body. I might want kids someday, but not now."

"I think you're brave." I don't mean it to sound trite or patronizing, and I hope she doesn't take it that way.

"Thanks," she says, and the openness of her face, of her voice, of those golden-green eyes, tells me that what I said was exactly right.

I hesitate before I ask my next question. "Do you think you'll ever go back?"

"I'll have to at some point, if only to see my sister. I miss the hell out of her." She picks up her fork and stabs another bite of pasta. "But I don't know if I'll ever talk to my mom again. Even if she got over the abortion, she wouldn't exactly agree with my *lifestyle*."

"But you're dating my brother."

"Okay, calm down—we haven't even been out yet. I think *dating* is a little too much right now. But even if I *do* date him, that doesn't mean I'll never kiss another girl."

My face flushes hot and I pick up my glass of water to distract myself from it, but I end up knocking over the glass. It sends a flood of liquid across the table, soaking our napkins and leaving wet rings under the bottoms of our dishes.

"Shit, sorry." I jump up to get a towel, but Rafaela waves me back into my chair.

"It's just water." She grabs two dish towels she was using

while she cooked and swiftly mops up the mess, then wrings them out in the sink and hangs them over the edge to dry. She gives me a funny look when she gets back to the table. "How do you ever talk to DeeDee about anything?"

"What?" My face still feels warm and now there's nothing to hide behind.

"I mentioned kissing a girl and you almost lost your shit....Are you weirded out by that?"

I see Iris's face as she hovers over me, her breasts bare and her blond curls messy and damp from our sweat. *If this weirds you out too much, we can stop. Anytime you want.*

"I've kissed a girl," I say. What I don't say is that if I had my way, I'd have kissed *her* by now, too. At least I know Dee was right: Alicia hasn't told anyone about me.

"You've kissed a girl? *Brava!*" Rafaela cheers, and it feels a bit like she's mocking me, but at least she doesn't think I'm a bigot. "Did you like it?"

I nod. "So...are you bi?"

"Pan," she says, and when I don't say anything right away, she clarifies, "Pansexual?"

"I know what it is." At least I think I do.

"I just don't really believe in restricting love to one or two genders." She shrugs and finally takes that bite of pasta, though now our food is cold and the table is still wet in some places. "What about you?"

"I don't know." I sit back in my chair. "There's only been

one girl, and she...she meant a lot to me. But now there's a guy I like..." I think of Emil, how he texted the day after I brought him the soup to say it was good, and that he was feeling better and wants to see me soon. I wonder, for a long moment, if he thinks of me as often as I've been thinking of him.

"Maybe you're bi," Rafaela says. "Maybe not. Maybe you're somewhere else on the spectrum."

"But I feel like I should know what to call myself."

"Why? Bi, queer...it doesn't really matter, as long as you're happy. Just make sure you don't let anyone tell you what you are. People can be real assholes about labels."

Later, when we've cleaned the kitchen and I'm grabbing my bag before she takes me home, I pull out my phone and see two new texts. Both from Lionel.

Feelin kinda off. Can you tell me where you put my meds?

Then, the next one, sent forty-five minutes later:

Never mind, false alarm.
I'm good

Fuck.

then.

Lionel has been quiet lately. Too quiet.

He hasn't talked much the past few weeks—to anyone, really. Not since his doctor appointments started. We used to hang out after dinner sometimes, even if we were just doing our homework in the tree house. But now he disappears immediately after we finish washing the dishes, straight up to his room with the door closed.

Tonight, I follow him. He doesn't invite me into his room but he doesn't close the door, either, so I step in, wordlessly. He sits on the edge of his bed, next to his newest issue of the *New Yorker*, but he doesn't look at it or me as he speaks.

"What's up?"

"I…I don't know. I wanted to make sure you're okay, I guess."

"That I'm okay?" He shrugs. "I'm fine."

I close his door and sit on the floor in front of him, leaning against his bookcase of nonfiction. "No, you're not. You can…You know you can still talk to me?"

He looks at me with blank eyes. Nods as he fingers the edge of the magazine cover. "I know. There's not much to talk about, I guess. I feel like shit all the time and everything sucks."

"Is it because of Grayson?" I've never dated anyone, so I don't know what it's like when that person moves all the way across the country. But I know how much he liked her. And I know how much he tried to hide the fact that he'd been crying about her after she left.

He shrugs. "Not really. I don't know. I wonder…Sometimes I think it might be the meds they have me on."

After the incident with the Dodgers game, Mom and Saul took him to our pediatrician, Dr. Carver, who referred him to another doctor. That doctor prescribed him meds for attention deficit hyperactivity disorder, and Lionel takes them every day but I know he hates them.

"Have you talked to Saul about it?" I ask, because I don't know any other solution. I've never been on meds. And I don't know how they're supposed to make you react, but I don't think his listlessness is one of the desired results.

He shrugs. "Kind of. He says I need time to adjust to them."

"I'm sorry." And when he doesn't say anything, I ask, "Do you want to take a walk?"

And for the first time ever, he says no. I think he'll give me an excuse, like there's a *New Yorker* story he's dying to start, but he just sits here. And the longer I sit here with him, the more I'm sure he's right. Whatever that doctor prescribed isn't working for him. This isn't Lionel. But neither was the one who trashed his room.

"Do you ever think..." He looks toward the door, as if double-checking to make sure I closed it. "Do you ever think about what will happen to your stuff when you're dead?"

I gasp. I don't mean to. It's not the strangest or even most morbid thing we've ever talked about. But the way he said it, as if he'd been considering this for a while now, is what scares me.

I stand and slide the magazine to the side so I can sit next to him. He doesn't move, doesn't look at me, just keeps staring at the floor.

"Are you trying to tell me something?" I ask in the calmest voice I can manage. Freaking out about this won't do either of us any good.

"I'm not going to kill myself or anything," he says, finally meeting my eyes. "I don't want to die. But...I hate that I feel like nothing good is ever going to happen to me again. And that sometimes I don't really feel anything at all. Like I'm just watching some dude who looks like me and it's really fucking boring to spy on him because all he wants to do is stay in bed."

I want to believe him when he says he doesn't want to kill himself, but I'm still scared.

"I think you need to talk to somebody—"

"I'm trying to talk to you." His eyes are pink and wet but no tears spill over. And they are . . . not clear, but I feel like he sees me. Like he needs me.

Lion isn't big on physical affection, so we're not the sort of siblings who greet each other every day with a hug and kiss on the cheek. Even during Shabbat dinner, when it's just the four of us, he always seems uncomfortable after the kiddush, when he knows we're all going to hug. But now, I take his hand and I wrap mine around it and he startles but doesn't move away.

"I don't know," I say. "I guess all the stuff goes to relatives or Goodwill or something."

"Would you take care of my books? If something happened to me?"

"Lionel—"

"You wouldn't have to keep them all. Just the ones you want, and then you can make sure the rest go to good homes or bookstores."

I've never really thought much about dying, outside the context of grandparents—and my father. He died when I was three, from sudden cardiac arrest. He had a heart condition. I don't like knowing that Lionel has thought about what my life would be like without him around, too.

I squeeze his hand and swallow hard. "I don't like this. I want you to talk to Mom and Saul. Or we can call one of those hotlines. But I can't sit here and—"

His hand pulses against mine. Not a squeeze, but a reminder that he's alive.

"I swear to you, I'm not going to do anything, okay? I'm going to sit here and read the *New Yorker* and go to bed. Sometimes I just need to say things to you that I can't say to anyone else."

I don't take my eyes off him. "I'm sleeping in here tonight."

If that was a serious cry for help, I think he'd appear more grateful, more relieved by my response. But all he does is shrug and say whatever.

I change into my pajamas and carry a book and a blanket down to his room. He's under the covers reading the magazine when I come back, and I lie on the other side, on top of the comforter, my head even with his feet, and pretend to read.

But I don't sleep once he turns off the light. And even after I hear him snoring lightly, I don't relax. Every time he rustles, I move. He coughs a couple of times and I sit up straight, staring at him until the snores resume.

And in the morning, I realize why I'm here, why I stayed in his room all night without sleeping. It wasn't the talk about dying. It was his apathy. Lionel not caring, not having an opinion about everything, isn't right. In a way, it's scarier to me than how he acted the day of the Dodgers game, because at least that Lionel cared about something.

The sun is still blurry, still making its way into the sky, but I hear Mom and Saul's door open across the hall.

I slip out of bed quietly, so Lionel won't wake, and tiptoe out into the hallway, where I see the back of my mother going down the stairs. I stumble down after her and she smiles when she sees me in the doorway to the kitchen.

"Well, you're up early," she says. "I have to finish my draft today. What's your excuse?"

"I..." This is one of the hardest things I've ever had to say. Lionel didn't tell me not to repeat our conversation, but it was implied. That's always implied with us when we talk about serious things. "I think you guys need to take Lionel back to the doctor."

"What? Why? Is he okay?" She looks at the ceiling and turns toward the stairs as if she's going up to his room.

"I think so. I mean, he's sleeping right now. I just wonder if maybe he should talk to someone or switch his meds or... I don't know."

"Suzette, if you know something, you need to tell me. Right now, baby."

"I don't know anything." I feel gross about lying to her like this, on such a large scale, but I'd feel grosser if I told her what he and I talked about. "But Lionel isn't himself. And I don't think he should be feeling the way he does, even if he's still getting used to the meds."

"If you don't know anything, then how do you know all this?" My mother doesn't usually sound so stern, but she obviously knows this is serious, even if I'm not telling her everything.

"Because he's my brother. I notice when something's off."

They take him to a different doctor—two different doctors, who both say they think his current depression, coupled with his episode earlier in the summer, is pointing to signs of bipolar disorder instead of ADHD.

He goes on different meds. He starts seeing a therapist, Dr. Tarrasch. He never says anything to me about why our parents hustled him to the doctor's office the day after our talk. He doesn't accuse me of betraying him.

But he doesn't talk to me about the bipolar, even though he knows I'm aware of the new diagnosis. And he doesn't seem that upset when I tell him Mom and Saul are sending me to boarding school in Massachusetts at the end of the summer.

I know what I did was right, that not saying anything would have been a mistake. But it isn't lost on me that Lionel doesn't share anything private with me for the rest of the summer—that in helping him, I've now caused him to alienate himself from the person he trusted most.

fourteen.

I cash in my rain check with Emil the night after I have dinner with Rafaela. It's the same night she goes out with my brother, and that's a coincidence, but once Emil and I are sitting across from each other at the sushi restaurant, I realize I couldn't have planned it better.

I was up this morning before the sun peeked over the mountains. I barely slept last night, even after I saw Lionel with my own eyes and knew he wasn't having an episode. He isn't humming with extra energy, but he hasn't slipped into the dark well of depression, either.

Yet.

He's irritable. I stared into his eyes for so long that he

turned away, told me I could get out of his room if I was going to keep treating him like he was sick.

I'm here with Emil, but I can't stop thinking about Lionel for more than a few moments at a time. Emil fills those moments with kindness. He told me I looked pretty when he picked me up, just before he kissed me right by my lips but not on them. He opens my car door every time we get in and out but he doesn't mind when I hold the door for him at the restaurant. His hand lightly touches the small of my back as we're led to our table and it's a small gesture, but I like that there's no mistaking we're together.

"I know you're going to offer to pay half," he says while we're looking at the menu. "But this is my treat, so get whatever you want."

"How are you so sure I'd offer to split it with you?" I ask, raising an eyebrow.

He laughs. "Because you're *you*, Suzette. You're one of the most stubborn people I've ever met."

"Me?"

He laughs again and takes a sip of water. "Come on."

I lift my chin. "Give me one example of when I was being stubborn, Emil Choi."

"Took you this long to go out with me, didn't it?" He's looking down at his menu, but there's no concealing that grin.

"What? You never asked me out until this summer!"

"Suzette, you knew I liked you. I did everything *but* ask you out."

"Well," I say, and then stop. Because he's right, and I don't want him to be right.

"We're here now," he says easily. "That's all that matters, yeah?"

"Yeah," I say, grateful that he's not pressing the matter.

We order an unreasonable amount of sushi with a large bowl of edamame. I don't realize how quiet I've been until Emil says, a piece of unagi roll balanced in his chopsticks, "Everything okay?"

His face comes into focus as if I've just noticed he's sitting here.

"Yeah, sorry." I swirl more wasabi through my bowl of soy sauce. "I..."

Lionel being off his meds is the biggest thing I've ever had to hide and it's heavy, a weight that's been stacked on my chest since the moment he confessed. I need to tell someone else. I need someone to talk to when I start to worry too much. And Emil seems safe. He already knows so much about my family, and me about his.

I take a quick breath. "Lion went off his meds a couple of weeks ago and I told him I'd hang on to them and he's seemed fine, but last night..." I swallow, nervous that Emil is going to lecture me on how stupid I've been. "Last night, I was out and he asked for them and I didn't see his text until it was too late."

Emil's eyes widen. "Too late? Is he okay?"

"Yeah, I mean, not like that. But now he says he doesn't want to take them, that it was a false alarm. What does that even mean?"

"I'm guessing your mom and Saul don't know about this," Emil says, but he nods before I can answer him because of course they don't know.

"I feel like I should tell them. Because of how Lionel was last year.... But then he'll be so mad at me, and I finally feel like we're back to where we were before I went away."

"How has he been? Have you noticed anything different?"

"Nothing that makes me too nervous," I say. "But it's not always easy to know how he's going to react or when his mood is going to change, and I'm scared. When things were really bad with him, when he was on the wrong meds and we didn't know he had bipolar... he was saying some really scary stuff."

"I didn't realize things got that bad with him." Emil sets down his chopsticks and looks at me, his face serious. "My parents didn't tell me. They said he was missing so much school because he was sick. And it wasn't hard to figure out that it was something with his mental health, but... I didn't know any of the details."

"I didn't know about your Ménière's," I say after a pause. "Not until you told me."

"Well…I asked your parents not to say anything." He meets my wide-eyed stare with a sheepish look. "You were so far away and couldn't see that I was mostly the same person and…I don't know, I guess I didn't want you to think I was weak, or whatever."

"Do you think that about Lionel?"

"God, no," Emil says so forcefully that a woman at the table next to us glances over. "I think he's strong as hell. The Ménière's is shitty and I hate it, but people see my hearing aids and they know something's wrong and they accept it. It's not the same for him."

Lionel said as much to me once, how so many of the same people who are quick to empathize with physical disabilities don't understand why someone with depression can't just get up and get on with their day like the rest of the world. *It's like they need a receipt that proves someone is actually going through some shit before they can care about them.*

I slide my hand across the table until our fingers are touching. "I don't think you're weak, either."

Emil takes my hand in his and squeezes. "Thanks."

I squeeze back.

"So, what are you going to do about your brother?"

"I'll tell Mom and Saul if things get bad." He doesn't say

anything, but I *feel* him wanting to say something, so I keep talking. "Lionel said I'm the only one he trusts."

"Yeah, but . . . some secrets aren't worth keeping, right?"

"Ours are."

"Why?" he presses me. "What's so special about your secrets? He could get really sick, Suzette."

My blood runs hot. Maybe irrationally so, but I don't like him talking as if he knows more about Lionel's illness than me. "Don't you think I know that?"

"Hey, hey," he says in a quiet voice. "I'm sorry. I just don't want you to regret this."

"I can't betray him, Emil. He feels . . . *defined* by his bipolar. Like he's lost himself somewhere in all the meds."

He nods but says nothing.

"Emil. You won't tell your parents?"

"I'm not a dick." He gives me a small smile. "Are we cool?"

I say yes and return his smile.

Later, when Emil brings me home, we tread the perimeter of the house, sidestepping Mom and Saul in the living room, and go up to the tree house.

I climb up first and feel around in the darkness for the lantern we usually keep by the doorway. Lionel must have moved it. Emil is right behind me, and before I can tell him to wait for me to find the light, his hands are on my hips. Turning me around to face him. I can't see him, but I can tell he is smiling, just from his energy. I like the moment before we kiss; his warmth becomes my warmth, and its combined force envelops me before I even touch him, like we're in a cocoon built for two.

Emil gathers my dreads in one hand and pushes them away from my shoulders. His lips start at my neck and graze across my earlobe, and my skin ripples with goose bumps as his mouth meets my own. We stand in place for a while. A breeze skips across the night, lighting on our skin and fluttering the chimes above the back porch as we kiss.

We feel our way across the room and onto the futon, and then we're lying down. I silently marvel at how Emil's lips can touch mine in the softest, sweetest way, and then in the next instant leave me breathless. We pull apart after a while and we are still. The room is softly lit by the dim moonlight filtering in through the windows, and I look at the outline of Emil beside me, run my fingertip along his temple and over the hearing aid behind his left ear.

I trail my finger down his neck and shoulder and along the soft part of his arm until he shivers. He lightly catches my arm by the wrist and pulls it toward him, and I rest my palm flat on his chest, against his heart.

"Suzette," he says with an ache in his voice.

It's cool up here, almost cold, but I want to be as close to him as possible, so I begin to unbutton his shirt. Once the buttons are undone, he shrugs it off and peels off his undershirt, too. I sit up and turn my back to him, holding my dreads up with one hand while I gesture with the other to the zipper that falls down the back of my dress. Emil has it undone in seconds and, when I point to the clasp, my bra, too.

I slowly push down the top of my dress and toss my bra to the floor, and I almost wish the moon were hidden behind clouds tonight because when I turn back around he's looking at me so intently that it makes me self-conscious. I want to cross my arms over my chest; no one has seen me without clothes on since Iris, and she was the first. But I sit here, completely still, and I let him look at me.

I breathe out as he touches my breasts, first with his hands and then with his mouth. It feels so good that I moan softly, and I'm embarrassed at being so audible, but he kisses just above my navel and says my name again. I lie back and his hands move to my thighs, to the hem of my dress and then under it. He bends his head to kiss between my legs and I jerk away.

"Sorry," he says, sitting up and moving his hands away from me.

I sit up, too. "No, it's okay. I'm..."

"It's cool if you're not ready. Sorry if that was too fast."

He keeps his hands clasped together in his lap. "I didn't mean to push you into anything."

"You didn't. I'm just..."

Do I explain how it wasn't too fast but how that reminded me too much of Iris, and how jarring it was to see her face when I liked, so much, what I was doing with Emil?

I don't have to tell him about her. It wouldn't change anything between us, either way. But I trust Emil. So much that it freaks me out, thinking about how open I want to be with him. Maybe I won't overthink the physical if I tell him.

"The last person I was with was a girl." I pause in case he wants to say something, but he just waits for me to continue. And in that pause I wonder if I would have stopped him if he were Rafaela; I wonder if I would have been uncomfortable, if I would have felt the need to explain why. "She was my roommate at school and we're not together anymore and...we had sex. I liked her. And I think I like girls."

"Okay." Emil nods. "Okay," he says again. "But it feels like what's been going on with us...you seem into it. Is this...?"

"I'm into it." I place my hand on top of his, still firmly glued to his lap. "I just wanted you to know because...I'm still figuring things out. And if I'm weird about some things, I don't want you to think it's because of anything you've done." I swallow. "I like you, Emil."

He looks down at my hand before threading his fingers

through my own. "Good. Because I like you, too. A lot, Suzette."

He leans over to kiss the apples of my cheeks. Then he presses his mouth to mine, just as the wind chimes dance their way through a new song.

fifteen.

The next morning, my mother offers to drive me to work and I'm probably happier about that than I should be. I don't want to talk to Lionel about his date because I'm feeling strange about what happened with Emil. We didn't have sex, but we would have, if I hadn't stopped it.

The drive to the shop isn't long, but I'm actually glad for the time alone with Mom. We haven't seen much of each other since I've been back. She keeps saying she'll knock out a draft of her script in a few days, by the Fourth of July, and then I'm hers for the rest of the month, but part of me doesn't mind that she's been so busy. It's easier to hide what's going on with Lionel, and also what happened with Iris.

Riding along in the passenger seat next to Mom reminds me

of when I was little and it was just the two of us. I don't remember much about those years between my father and Saul, and even less about my father. But Mom talks about those years sometimes; she'll look at me with tear-filled eyes and say how happy she is that we're part of a unit, but that we used to make a good team. I always like when she reminisces; there's a fondness in her voice that I never hear when she talks about anything else. Only us.

"Did you and Lionel compare dates before you went to bed?" she asks as we pull out of the driveway. We pass his car parked on the street in front of the house as we drive away.

"No," I say, but I don't tell her that when I heard him come home, about an hour after Emil left, I quickly turned off my bedside lamp and pretended to be asleep, even when he tapped lightly on my door and said, "Little, you awake?"

"Well, I think it's great that he's getting out and meeting new people." She pauses, then: "I think you being home this summer is good for him, Suz. He seems more like his old self than he has in a long time."

I want to feel better about hearing that from the person who sent me away *because* of my brother, but I don't know which Lionel she means. The one who was supposedly on the right combination of pills for his disorder or the one who went off them cold turkey?

"I like being home," I say. *I like being here for him.* But I keep that to myself because if we continue talking about

Lionel and his health, I'm going to slip. I know Mom and Saul monitor his moods, but if they don't think he's off his meds, they have less of a reason to worry.

"The school called yesterday." Mom stops at a red light and turns to look at me. "They haven't gotten your dorm request. Are you not rooming with Iris next semester?"

Shit.

"Um, we haven't really talked about it." I look down at my nails instead of at her. "We're both so busy, being back at home."

"Well." She clears her throat and when I look over, she's smiling. "You do seem to have a lot going on here, with your new job... your new friends... your new *Emil*."

"Mom."

"Sorry." The light turns green and we're moving again. "What I'm trying to say is that things are different now. This summer isn't the same as last year, and Lionel is doing so well.... What would you think about staying home for your junior year? Going back to your old school with all your old friends?"

"What?" My voice is too loud for the car, but I don't actually believe I just heard what I did. I didn't know they'd make it so easy on me.

"Only if you want to. We're done making decisions for you."

"So that means I can start setting my own curfew?" I grin over at her.

"You wish." She glances at me with a smile of her own. "You don't have to figure out school right now, but...soon, so we can make some arrangements. The choice is totally yours, Suz."

When I arrive at the shop, Ora is bending over the display of tropical plants with Tucker sitting tall at her feet, his orange striped tail curled regally around his legs.

"Do I have the wrong day?" I ask, looking behind me to see my mother's car already pulling out onto the street.

"No, just a change in plans." Ora moves a potted plant on the table and points to it. "What is this?"

I step closer and squint at it, taking in the wide leaves and pom-poms of flowers made up of tiny blue petals. Then I try to remember everything Rafaela has ever told me about the flowers in this room. "Hydrangea?"

"Good girl. Now, how do you care for it?"

"I, um..."

Ora pats my shoulder and smiles. "You're still learning. When you drop your things, go out back and start helping Rafaela load up the van, please. Héctor's sick today, so you two are taking over the deliveries."

I blink at her. "Really?"

Her attention is already back on the table of flowering plants, so she doesn't look up as she says, "I can't believe I'm trusting her with it, either, but we don't have much of a choice. You'll keep an eye on her?" She looks over then and winks.

"I'll do my best."

In the back room, the door that leads to the parking lot is propped open with a brick. I poke my head out to see the delivery van backed up as close as Rafaela could get it, with the two doors in the rear wide open. Rafaela is perched on the back ledge, looking at her phone.

"We're really doing this?" I nod toward the tops of flowers peeking out of the crates stacked behind her.

She looks up and grins as she sets her phone next to her. Some people, once you've known them for a while, start to look different from when you first met them. Like their face has blurred, become a thing you simply recognize instead of a landscape of the features that once made them stand out. But with Rafaela, it's like I'm seeing her for the first time every time. I notice each part of her like it's the first night we met—the vibrancy of her eyes, the bounce of her curls, the soft curves of her figure and the elegant lines of ink on her arm. I was hoping that sensation would go away when she started seeing Lionel or after I realized how I felt about Emil, and yet.

"We are *so* doing this," she says. "Help me get the last few packed in here?"

I take the rest of the morning deliveries from the refrigerated case in the back room and carefully hand them to her as she secures them in the van. After we leave, Ora will restock the case with any deliveries scheduled for the afternoon.

"Why are both of us going out on deliveries when Héctor does this by himself every day?" I ask once we're sitting in the front of the van, Rafaela behind the wheel.

"Because I told Ora I didn't want to go out by myself." She turns the key so the engine starts up with a rumble. "And Ora would rather hold down the shop than have anything to do with this."

We have deliveries in two different directions and head west first, toward the office suite in Los Feliz, near the library. Rafaela says they have a business account, so we deliver to them pretty regularly. "Boring, but reliable business," she muses, turning right from Sunset onto Hillhurst. "Weddings are the best because everyone wants something different, and you never know who you're going to get."

I'm prepared to wait in the van, but she shakes her head and motions for me to get out with her. "I'm not driving *and* doing the dirty work of talking to people by myself."

We walk into the building, each holding a bouquet, and are greeted at the front desk by a girl with big green eyes and long, glossy dark hair. A man stands to the side of her chair; he's tall and good-looking, which always feels weird to admit when someone appears to be Saul's age.

"Hi, we're delivering from Castillo Flowers." Rafaela sets her vase down on the desk. I place mine next to hers. "We just need a signature."

"The flowers look amazing," says the man. He walks out from behind the counter, looking from Rafaela to me. "And no offense to the usual guy, but rarely do we get them carried in by pretty girls."

Rafaela stiffens next to me, her back straightening even more than it already was. She looks him square in the eye as she says, "Héctor is sick today. I'll pass along your well wishes."

That just makes him grin. "Stephanie, why don't you sign for these while I talk to the girls for a minute?" He turns to Rafaela. "You do have a minute? I wanted to discuss our account...."

He's practically touching Rafaela, he's standing so close. Her body is visibly tense, but it doesn't deter him. The girl behind the desk is pretending to look at something on her computer but the tight pull of her mouth tells me she's been on the receiving end of his unwanted attention more than once.

"You'll need to discuss anything business-related with my aunt." Rafaela steps back from him.

"But your aunt isn't here." He tries to cover up his gross persistence with a playful tone. "Couldn't you pass along the message?"

"I'm sorry, but we have to go," she says firmly. "We're on a tight schedule, but I'll have my aunt call you right away to discuss the account."

She's practically through the door before I can blink. I follow her, looking over my shoulder at the girl behind the desk.

"*Fuck* that dude." Rafaela slams her hand on the steering wheel as soon as I'm back in the van.

"Have you met him before?"

"No, but anytime I go on deliveries, it's the same shit. Doesn't matter who it is. Like we've showed up solely to be ogled by them." She lets out a breath. "I swear, if it weren't for guys like your brother, I'd be one hundred percent into girls forever because sometimes it is so not worth the bullshit of dealing with men."

"That guy was, like, fifty," I say, especially embarrassed that I'd thought he was attractive for even a moment. "It's not like you'd go out with him."

"That shit doesn't start with fifty-year-old guys, Suzette. It starts when they're, like, four years old and everyone laughs when they're pulling girls' hair on the playground because, you know, there's no better compliment than a boy's attention, unwanted or not, right?" She smiles when I look over.

218

"Well, I suppose you can check *feminist rant* off your list today."

I smile back to mask whatever I'm feeling—is it jealousy that she was out with Lionel and not me, or something more? "So, I'm guessing the date went well?"

"I figured he'd already told you everything... *Little*."

I feel my face turning hot but ignore that last part. "I was asleep when he got home."

Rafaela buckles her seat belt, then programs her GPS to the next destination and starts out on our route. "I'll spare you the details, but your brother is... a nice guy. Not the kind of guy who can't stop telling everyone how nice he is to cover up his raging misogyny, but a bona fide nice guy."

"He is," I affirm. I chew on my lip so I won't be tempted to ask her if he acted weird in any way. I can't do that to him, no matter how badly I want someone else to be looking out for him. Or how much I wish Rafaela had a reason to like me better than him.

"And he barely stopped talking about you all night."

I look at her with raised eyebrows. "Really?"

"He just about thinks you're the best person he knows. So I guess you *are* one of the good ones." She pauses. "He told me about his condition."

"It's an illness," I say automatically.

"I know. I think it's... My aunt always uses the word *admirable* for anyone she thinks is cool." Rafaela sighs. "So,

219

I know it makes me sound old as fuck, but it's pretty damn admirable of him to be so open about it. And I can't imagine being on meds like that."

"He told you he's on meds?" My voice is too sharp, but I can't believe Lionel would lie, especially when he didn't have to bring it up in the first place.

"I'm not some delicate flower. Even in my hometown, where people pretend like ignoring things or only God himself will cure you, some kids our age were on medication."

I look out the windshield at the long line of cars blanketing Los Feliz Boulevard. "I guess I'm just surprised he told you all that on your first date."

She slows down behind a Mercedes convertible with a bald head shining out from the driver's seat. "He said… Wait, you're *sure* you're okay with hearing this stuff? I don't want to make things weird."

"You're the one making things weird," I say, and I sound too irritable, because she turns to look at me. "I mean, just talk about whatever. I'll tell you if it's weird."

But I'm irritable because I don't know what she means. Is the hesitation because I'm Lion's sister and she still doesn't understand that we share everything, or is it because of us? I know I haven't simply imagined her flirting with me. And I don't know for sure, but I think something could have happened between us by now, if I'd been brave enough to let her know I was interested.

"Fair enough," she continues. "Well, he said it feels like he's known me his whole life, and I *know* how cheesy that sounds. Guys have said it before and it felt like they were just trying to get into my pants. But...I believe him. And I feel the same way." When I glance to my left, her hazel eyes are huge and a little scared. "Is that stupid?"

"Not stupid," I say quietly. "Honest."

then.

I ris finds me in the dark.

We've just finished taking turns sipping from the vodka bottle and she's turned off the light. On the floor I sit completely still, my back straight and flat against the edge of my bed.

She kneels next to me. My skin is warm and the coolness of her fingertips makes me shiver. Her lips find me, too, and it's the second night we've done this, but this time I'm not so tense. I let myself lean into her and my mouth opens with hers and I kiss her like I wanted to the first time.

Her palms slip behind my neck and she pulls me closer, kissing me so deeply I feel as if I might burst into flames. I push my fingers through her curls, thinking how strange and good this is, how unexpected even though it's the second time. I pull away, slowly.

"What are we doing?" It's the same question I asked last night, except I remember the mild panic in my voice, shocked that one minute we'd been drinking and complaining about the girls on our floor and the next I was pressed against the wall, her lips moving in a swift line from my chin to my collarbone. Tonight there is no panic, just lazy wonder; more of an excuse to prolong what's happening rather than stop it.

"What do you want to do?" Her voice is serious as she sits back on her knees and looks at me.

"I don't know, I... This is new for me."

We're whispering even though it's late, even though everyone is in their dorm rooms like they're supposed to be.

"New bad or new good?"

"New good," I say without hesitation.

"I didn't know you were into girls," she says as we remove our shirts, as my hands slide hesitantly over the side of her body.

"I didn't, either," I say, and when I look at her, she smiles.

When we're both in just our underwear, we sit on the edge of her bed for a while. Just looking at each other.

"You can touch me," she says.

And I do, because it's odd that I've been around other girls my whole life and never felt like this. So many gym periods and sleepovers spent changing in front of one another and I never felt this urge. The citrus shower gel I've smelled on her since our first morning at Dinsmore is different now. It is so distinctly her and it is the best thing I've ever smelled and I keep dipping my head toward the space between her collarbone and her neck to fill my nose with the scent.

My hand shakes as my fingers skate across Iris's skin— her incredibly soft skin. I slide my fingers across the smoothness of her stomach and linger around her breasts until she exhales and kisses me again. After a few moments, she takes my hand in her own and holds them both over her heart.

"I've been with other girls," she says. "I've *only* been with girls."

"I know."

"But—do you feel that?" Her heart. It's beating as fast as my own. "None of them have done this to me."

I move her hand to my chest. "*No one* has ever done this to me."

She gently pushes me back on the bed and we start kissing again and when her hand moves between my legs I don't stop her. When my breathing changes, when she asks if I want her to stop, but it is so clear she doesn't want to stop, I say no. And when we're lying there, after the space around us has transformed from a small, dark dorm room into an explosion of fireworks only I can see and then back again, she asks if it was okay.

"That was amazing," I say, breathless and wondering if I

should feel more embarrassed about what just happened. One of the boys I kissed back in L.A. had tried to put his hand down my jeans and I got too nervous, so I pushed him away. He seemed to know what he was doing up to that point, but I can't imagine anyone ever making me feel as good as Iris did.

"Lily and Bianca would be losing their shit right now," she says, kissing my shoulder.

Should I be losing my shit? Maybe, but the only thing I feel nervous about is how inexperienced I am, how I don't know if Iris expects me to return the favor tonight.

"Lily and Bianca need to get laid," I say, and Iris laughs with me.

"Really, though...how much do you think they'd freak out if they knew about this? About us?" she says in a serious tone.

"I don't know, but...I'm not sure I want them to find out. I mean, not yet."

She's quiet. I wonder if I've said something wrong.

"I like you," I say, turning on my side to face her. "But—"

"But new good is still new. I get it." Iris pauses. "Are *you* okay with what happened?"

"I am. I just..." I put my hand over my heart to see if it's still beating so rapidly. It's slowed, but not much. "I need some time to figure out what this is...what I am, before we tell anyone, okay?"

"Sure," she says. And she doesn't sound any different than

she normally does, but I wonder if she was hoping I'd say we should ignore the girls on our floor and figure out whatever this is without hiding.

Or maybe that's what I was thinking. Because I'm tired of not being my true self around here. I'm tired of hiding things—secrets about me and secrets for other people. And I know better than anyone how dangerous it is to start any kind of relationship based on secrets.

sixteen.

Echo Park Lake isn't a proper lake, but it's the first lake I ever saw and one of my favorite places in the city.

It's just around the corner from home, so I find myself there whenever I need a hit of nature. The day before July Fourth, I'm there with Lionel. This is not the sort of lake people swim in, but you can rent pedal boats and admire the lotus flowers that are so beloved they get their own festival each year. The water is surrounded by golden medallion trees, little bursts of sun sitting among the bushy groups of green fronds. There's a boathouse that serves coffee and snacks, and an enormous fountain that looks like magic from afar as it shoots up higher than the spindly palm trees and the buildings of the downtown skyline in the distance.

Lionel and I edge down the small embankment that leads to the paved pathway. We just finished breakfast, lox and cream cheese on bagels from the place Saul says is the only bakery in Los Angeles with any integrity. Lionel complained that the meal felt heavy this morning, that he wanted to walk it off, so I invited myself to come with him, even though his reason makes no sense. We have that exact meal once a week, a tradition from Saul's childhood, and Lionel has never complained before.

I breathe in the smell of the water. "You look happy."

He shrugs, as if the bounce in his step isn't new and noticeable. "I guess I am happy. See? Told you I'd be fine. Better than fine."

My heart speeds at the tone of his voice. It's overconfident, more assured than the Lionel I've heard in a while. I start to say something but there's a lecture on the tip of my tongue and we've only just started our walk.

"Do you think..." He pauses and glances at me, then looks straight ahead before I can make eye contact. "Do you think people can be like medicine?"

"People?"

"Like, being around someone."

I smile, thinking of what my mother said, that me being home is good for him. I wonder if she said something to him, too.

But before I can ask, he says, "I've never felt better than when I'm with Rafaela."

Different parts of my heart crumble for different reasons.

"I just feel like...not like she's the *one*. We're not old enough for that. But she gets me. She likes me for me."

"Lots of people like you for you."

"Not like Rafaela. She says I have a gorgeous mind." His voice is inflated with pride.

"Does she know you're off your meds?"

"No." I look at him just in time to see his face closing off—his eyes turning a stony blue, his freckles somehow disappearing more into his skin. "I want her to like me for me, not some doped-up version."

"Lion..." But I don't finish and he doesn't prompt me to continue.

We walk without talking for a while and stop when we're halfway around the lake. I sit down on the grass. I can see his knee jerking, like he's itching to keep moving, but he plops down next to me after a few seconds.

"You want me to go back on them," he says, so matter-of-fact that it disturbs me.

"I'm worried about you."

"Why? I'm not doing anything wrong." He picks at a blade of grass. Across the lake from us, a group of people with yoga mats under their arms starts to assemble.

"No, but...your energy has been up lately. You've been staying up late the last couple of nights." I swallow hard, aware that I sound more like his babysitter than his sister. "And this morning..."

He was sitting at the table, making a list of tasks to complete and books to buy and potential places to take Rafaela on future dates. He tried to hide it—the pad of paper was covered in more doodles than writing. But I looked at the page when he was rinsing his plate and I saw all the lists, separated into three boxes that blended into the rest of the scribbles.

"Little, I don't need anyone keeping tabs on me and I don't need a lecture, not even from you."

"I wouldn't say anything if I didn't think..." I take a breath and start over. "You know what could happen after this."

"How do you know this is hypomania? How do you know I'm not different because I met the best girl ever? You're not a doctor. And you know, nobody ever asked if maybe I *like* this part of being off the meds. It's not all bad, you know—I'm more productive and I get shit done and don't you think that's better than staying in bed all day?"

"I think that...maybe it's good now, but what if you don't know how bad it can get? You've been on meds since the first episode and—"

He lightly drums his fingers against his thighs. "Sometimes...sometimes I think you're jealous of me."

My lips part while I pause, try to think of how I can possibly respond to that without sounding as rude as he did. "I don't know why you'd say that to me."

"Because I'm happy!" he says, throwing his arms wide. "Because I'm with Rafaela and she's amazing."

"Well, I'm with Emil and he's amazing," I say, wishing I didn't sound like I'm trying to one-up him.

"But you think she's amazing, too. Rafaela. *Right?*" He's staring at me now and I'm afraid to meet his eyes, afraid to confirm that he's saying what I think he's saying. That somehow, he knows. Sometimes I forget that being so close with him means we can read each other in the same ways.

"I think she's cool," I say. "I like working with her."

"So you should be happy. That we're together."

The force behind his voice makes me look at him and I wish I hadn't.

He knows.

"I am happy for you." I sound like I'm choking on the words, but there is no other acceptable response. Even if he doesn't believe me, I have to say it.

"Good." He stands and brushes off his pants and now he's the one not looking at me. "I didn't come to sit. Let's walk."

So we do. In silence.

And with each step I take, I am pounding out a regret: that I ever met Rafaela, that I ever started working at the flower shop, that I ever trusted that the abandoned meds are a secret of Lionel's that I can handle.

I've never questioned my loyalty to my brother, not since that day so long ago, in Saul's garage. The flip side of loyalty is betrayal and Lionel deserves better than that. Even when I told our parents they needed to take him to the doctor, I didn't repeat my conversation with him. I never told.

But even I know I can't stay in the middle forever, that when it comes to him and his health, there is no in-between. I have to make a choice.

seventeen.

DeeDee and her girlfriend are back on again, just in time for Alicia's big Fourth of July party. We missed it last summer because they hadn't yet met, but DeeDee says the party has been going on for years, started by Alicia's older sister when she was in high school and still thriving since Alicia took the reins.

"Her parents go up to Big Bear every year," Dee says when we're up in her bedroom, getting ready before the party. We're sitting together in front of her vanity, our butts perched on the small, velvet-covered seat. "So I guess it can get kinda wild sometimes."

"Lion is meeting us there. With Rafaela." I brush a curved mascara wand across the length of my eyelashes. Emil will be there, too.

It's the first time I'll be in the same place as both Rafaela and Emil and I'm trying not to think too hard about it, but I can't help feeling anxious. If Lionel has noticed how I feel about her, Emil can't be far behind. DeeDee, too. It's probably best to stay away from her tonight—as much as I can without being obvious.

"Showing up at parties together, huh? *And* this is the first party he's been to in God knows how long." Dee runs a brush through her thick, reddish-blond hair. "Did he do a total one-eighty or what?"

I shake my head, though it's hard to watch his behavior as closely when we're not really talking. He's upset with me, with the fact that I brought up his meds again. He's not spinning out and I don't sense he's depressed, either, but I know it could go either way in an instant. I watch Mom and Saul when the four of us are together, but they haven't noticed anything. So maybe Lionel is right. Maybe it's not hypomania. Maybe he is managing his illness alone. But the rational part of me knows that would be too lucky, that more often than not, it doesn't work that way.

"Lionel's in love."

"Wow." Dee turns to look at me, her eyes wide. "Do you approve?"

"Rafaela is cool."

Dee toys with the hairbrush in her hand. "Grace says she has shit taste in guys, so maybe she's turning over a new leaf with your brother."

"Maybe Grace is just jealous that Rafaela is with someone besides her." I'm sure DeeDee isn't aware of Rafaela's whole story, but I feel the need to defend her.

"They're not like that. Clean breakup." She hesitates. "Are you still mad at Grace?"

I hold the mascara wand in midair. "Not mad. I'm not thinking about her or what happened all the time, but it's not like she ever apologized."

"Well, she's embarrassed," DeeDee says slowly. "Alicia told me she feels terrible."

"How does she think Emil and I felt? She never said anything to us."

DeeDee looks down at the cluttered top of the vanity. "Everyone fucks up, though, right?"

"Yeah, everyone fucks up." I sigh. "But when you fuck up, you say you're sorry."

"You're right. Do you want me to ask Alicia if she'll apologize?"

"No." I shake my head. "A forced apology is worse than nothing at all. Just…listening is good. Thanks for doing that."

Alicia lives in the Valley, the utter bane of DeeDee's existence.

"It's just Studio City," I say as we pass the little market off Laurel Canyon Boulevard. "That's basically your neighborhood."

"Oh, my dear, sweet Suzette," she says with a sigh. "You act as if I'd date anyone who lived any deeper into the Valley. Alicia barely passed my test."

"So things are good with you two now?"

"Eh, good enough." She grits her teeth and taps her fingers against the steering wheel as we crawl up the winding road behind a small white car that brakes at nearly every turn, the driver clearly uncomfortable with the sharply curved roads of the canyon. "She convinced me that we don't need to date other people, at least not for the rest of the summer."

"How'd she do that?"

DeeDee looks over with a sly smile.

We aren't the first to arrive, but the house is still in pristine condition and everyone is still sober. A giant American flag is planted on the front of the house, waving in the slight breeze. Inside, Alicia has decorated with red, white, and blue streamers, patriotic paper fans, and ceramic bowls with stars and stripes painted along the outside that hold pretzels and chips. American flag–themed pinwheels are piled in the corner of the coffee table.

Alicia herself is decked out in a pair of white shorts flecked with blue stars, a red tank top, and a metallic Uncle Sam hat. She pulls DeeDee in for a kiss as soon as we walk inside. I do a quick scan of the room to see if anyone I know is here, and notice Grace watching me from across the living room, next to the stone fireplace. We nod at each other, but no attempt to talk is made from either end. I'm grateful when Emil and Justin show up a couple of minutes later, though I can't stop wondering when Lion and Rafaela will be here, too.

Justin immediately walks out back to check on the keg and, with DeeDee distracted by Alicia, Emil and I have this corner of the room to ourselves. He kisses me, directly on the lips, and I think how good it feels, to be so open about what we're becoming…whatever that is. And then how guilty I feel, too, because I was never brave enough to have this with Iris.

A few more of Alicia's friends show up, all strangers to me; people who go to school with her and Rafaela and Grace. It's a different crowd than the one we hang with from my old school. There's lots of hair dyed bright colors and black clothes and plenty of piercings and tattoos, but there's a different vibe than our crowd. Maybe that they're not so much artsy as they are badass. I'm slightly intimidated by them.

Catie Ransom slips through the door not long after we've arrived and surveys the scene with a look on her face like she's tasted something bad. I try to discreetly move from her line of vision, but she sees us right away and walks over in her boots and black shorts and crocheted black crop top.

"What is this?" She points her finger back and forth between Emil and me.

I frown, even less in the mood for her than I normally am. "What is what?"

"Are you guys, like, together?"

"What if we are?" Emil says, parroting the derision of her tone.

Catie steps back for a moment, looks at him with surprise and a tiny bit of respect. Emil usually doesn't let Catie bother him and he doesn't talk to people the way she does, and I think she likes this side of him, no matter how brief.

"Hey, whatever makes you happy." She shrugs before walking past us to the kitchen.

I don't like how this night is starting out.

Rafaela and Lionel are among the last of the "first-tier crowd" (Alicia's words) to show up, and I breathe a sigh of relief when I see his red head ducking through the doorway. Rafaela's arm is looped through his and despite the fact that I'm holding Emil's hand, it makes my heart jump with envy. But I feel a sting when I look at Lionel, too, and I realize it's bugging me that his first official outing this summer is with her and not us, the people he's known forever.

They walk over to us, both beaming, and I try to hide all the feelings I shouldn't be feeling. I wonder if Lionel will act like the other day didn't happen, like everything is good between us.

But then Catie is back from the kitchen in what seems like record time, a can of beer in hand and eyes wide as she stares at my brother. "Holy shit. You *are* alive."

Lionel blinks at her. "Nobody said I wasn't."

"Well, I haven't seen you out in forever." She takes a long drink. "And it's not like your sister over here ever tells us anything."

I stand tall and glare at her but, true to Catie's statement, keep my mouth shut.

"If you have something to say to me, just say it." There's not a hint of playfulness in Lionel's tone.

She swigs from her beer again as she appraises him, but she doesn't respond.

"Right." He stares hard at her. "You'd rather say it when I'm not around."

"Fine." She holds his gaze, a battle of steely blue eyes. "What's wrong with you?"

Everyone in our group is silent. No, speechless.

"What's wrong with me? Right now it's that I'm standing here talking to a waste of time like you," Lionel says coolly.

Catie's mouth drops open. "How dare you, Li—"

"Fuck off, Catie. I know what you've been saying. Stop talking shit behind my back."

She doesn't recover. Catie always recovers. And if she was impressed by Emil standing up to her earlier, she seems almost scared of Lionel. I've never seen her so caught off guard, her mouth still hanging open as she waits for a response that doesn't come.

Lionel turns his back, edging her out of the circle, and

behind him I see her retreating to the front of the room, still looking stunned.

"Uh, so you're kind of super sexy when you're mad," Rafaela says, grinning up at my brother like he's Prince Charming.

He blushes, returning her smile.

"What's in there?" I gesture to the brown paper bag in his left hand to change the subject. I don't know how much everyone understood from that conversation, and I don't want to linger on it.

"Liquor, fireworks, cake," he ticks off, holding open the bag so I can see.

Rafaela smiles at me, squeezing my brother's arm. "All the essentials."

"Cake?" Emil peers down. I look, too. The cake is from a grocery store, round and covered in a plastic dome. The icing is thick and white, decorated with holiday-themed sprinkles.

"Wait." I look at my brother. "Where'd you get fireworks?"

He waves his hand back and forth a few times. "I don't know, some stand I passed on the way home from Boyle Heights."

"What were you doing in Boyle Heights?"

They ignore my question as Rafaela tugs on his arm. "It's dark out," she says, and when I look over her eyes are shining.

But not like she's been drinking—more like she's fueled by the mere presence of my brother. "We should start setting it up."

"Setting what up?" I ask, looking back and forth between the two of them.

Rafaela grins at me. "Don't look so worried, Little."

"Don't call me that," I snap. And I look to Lionel to see if he will back me up, but he doesn't seem to notice. He's preoccupied, digging in the bottom of the paper bag.

Rafaela just keeps grinning and starts to drag him away, toward the back of the house. But not before she says to me, "You don't have to be so serious. It's the Fourth of July!"

I watch them until they disappear completely, and I can feel Emil watching me, but I don't look over. He leans in close and asks if I'm okay. I say yes, but both of us know I'm lying.

A tray of Jell-O shots starts a path around the room and Emil intercepts it before they can cruise by us. He looks at me questioningly and takes two red ones when I nod. "Cheers," he says, tapping the rim of his against mine.

The pat of cherry Jell-O slides easily down my throat with a tang from the alcohol that makes my lips smack. Emil crushes my cup with the one in his hand and takes them to a nearby trash can. DeeDee swoops in as soon as he's gone, eyes wide and smile huge. "Holding *hands*. You guys are the real deal, huh?"

"We haven't talked about it, really." My face is hot like

I'm talking to an audience instead of my best friend. "I don't know what we are."

"Whatever, I'm just glad you finally realized what a goddamn catch he is," she whispers, bouncing away as Emil returns.

The sound system in Alicia's house plays through every room, the recessed speakers emitting a mix of patriotic music that's almost never played outside of this holiday and sporting events. Emil and I wander through the house, examining the intimate belongings of a person we only know peripherally. Family pictures cover the walls of the living room and front hallway, framed photos of Alicia, her mother, and her older sister. The dining room and kitchen are practically bursting with alcohol, more than I've ever seen in one place and certainly more than we usually have at our parties.

Justin finds us in the dining room next to a half dozen types of tequila. He's carefully holding three plastic cups of beer, the foam almost brimming over the top.

"Have you seen Lionel?" I try to sound casual as I ask, but I see Emil's head turn slightly toward me and he must sense my worry.

"He's outside with his girl. They're hanging all over each other."

"Oh," I say flatly.

Emil looks at me again. "You don't like her?" he asks,

and I realize I never introduced them, that the only thing he knows about her is she's my coworker and Lionel's girlfriend.

But before I can answer, a loud pop interrupts my train of thought—not as loud as I'd imagine a shotgun sounds, but definitely not a car backfiring, either.

"What the fuck is that?" Alicia says, pressing down on her hat. She's standing a few feet away with DeeDee, but when the popping noise doesn't stop she cuts her way through the people in the room, heading out to the backyard.

We all follow and as soon as I see Lionel and Rafaela standing with a lighter and the paper bag between them, I stop by the door. Alicia keeps walking out to them, and I think maybe she'll be angry, but instead she laughs and says, "Oh my God, you got fireworks? Yes!"

"Your neighbors are going to be so pissed," DeeDee calls out, standing next to me.

"So what?" Rafaela calls back, doing a little shimmy. A fireworks dance. "It's not even midnight. We'll set them all off at once. Come on!"

And DeeDee does. So does Justin, and then it's just Emil and me, watching silently as the five of them light up the contents of the bag in a steady stream of hissing, whistling sparks and pops that make my heart beat too fast. I want to walk away but I'm afraid of what will happen if I do, so I plug my ears and stand next to Emil.

"Happy fucking Fourth of July!" Lionel yells at the top of his lungs, and everyone laughs and joins in his cheers, and I wonder if one of the neighbors *will* call the cops if this keeps up.

"Is your brother..." Emil pauses, careful with his words. "Is he doing all right?"

I don't say anything, which is an answer in itself.

They save the sparklers for last, Rafaela lighting them up and handing them out as if she's a mom distributing Halloween candy. She dances over to us with a sparkler in each hand, twirling the fiery sticks like pyrotechnic batons. I shake my head when she holds one out to me and Emil does the same, and she shrugs and smirks as if to say it's our loss.

Soon the ground is littered with debris and the air smells like rotten eggs and Rafaela is pirouetting across the yard with the last sparkler in one hand and my brother's hand in the other as he twirls her around and around.

Justin wanders back over to us, swirling a finger through the head on his topped-off beer. "Some people are getting a game of flip cup going in the garage. You guys game?"

"I'll watch," I say, but I'm not looking at him. I'm still watching Rafaela and Lion, hoping their excessive energy will die out with the sparkler.

"Dude, you drove us here." Emil raises an eyebrow at Justin. They exchange a couple of looks until Emil sighs. "And I guess I'm driving us home."

We follow Justin to the garage, where a long card table

has been set up in the middle, away from the dusty boxes and bicycles and crates filled to bursting stacked alongside the walls. Two pitchers of beer are set up on either end of the table and teams are assembling, a tangle of arms and plastic cups attempting to find their way to the appropriate side. I try not to look for Lionel, and Emil tries to pretend like he doesn't notice me looking, but it's obvious every time I whip my head around when someone new comes into view.

And then Lionel is standing on the end farthest from us and I tense up instantly. I remember what he said at the lake: *I'm not doing anything wrong.* And right now, he's not. He's laughing and holding a beer like everyone else, taking sips as he talks to Rafaela. The shouting, firework-shooting guy from just a few minutes ago seems to have calmed down, which calms me down, at least for a moment. I remind myself that this is what I wanted—for him to be back out again, hanging with our friends, acting like he belongs with everyone else.

But now that he is, I'm worried. He was supposed to be around us as his new self—pills, regulated moods, and all. Not off his meds and glued to Rafaela and already way too comfortable with partying. I was nervous in the tree house when we drank the rum with DeeDee, but that was controlled. Close to home, with people he knows. Now I think he might be trying to keep up with everyone else, pretending he's had more experience with alcohol than he really has.

The hand not holding a beer involuntarily tightens at my side, perhaps because I'm so tempted to walk across the room and pull him away—from Rafaela and the game and all the buzzing in this room that he doesn't need to soak up.

I can't stop squeezing my hand into a fist because I can't stop looking at and thinking of Lionel, so as the game officially starts, I reach for Emil's hand. He startles for a moment and it sends relief flooding through me. This is all still new to him, too. We're both figuring out what we are. He looks over and smiles.

Even as the crisp, cold beer starts to soften the edges of the room, it's impossible to relax. I'm keeping an eye on Lionel, but I'm also watching Rafaela. I haven't seen them together since he first met her at the shop, and everything she told me the other day rings true in their actions. They're always attached to each other in some way: Lionel grabbing her hand or Rafaela standing behind him with her arms around his waist, her cheek flat against his back; after he takes his turn at flip cup he swivels around and they kiss for a few beats longer than necessary. They're so comfortable with each other, but it doesn't seem honest, their relationship. She doesn't even know about his meds.

The first round goes to Justin's team, which also happens to be Lion's team. Rafaela steps back to let someone else take her place and then she's standing next to me, saying she needs an escort to the bathroom. Emil doesn't let go of my hand, though, and that sick feeling comes back when I realize I have to introduce them.

"Emil, this is Rafaela. Lion's...and we work together." I couldn't say it. *Girlfriend.* I don't know if they've said it yet. But even if they haven't, anyone who sees them together would know the word applies. "Rafaela, this is Emil."

"Nice to meet you," he says, politely holding out his hand.

She smiles at him, her mouth twisted to the side. "Oh, I think I've heard about you."

He glances at me before shooting a nervous grin her way. "You have?"

But Rafaela doesn't respond. She takes my arm and whisks me away, and I barely have time to look over my shoulder, to mouth *Sorry* to Emil before we're heading inside and up the stairs. We stop at the doorway to the master bedroom and I fumble my way after her in the dark until she mercifully flips the switch in the bathroom, flooding my path with light.

I step through the doorway to find a marble bathroom with a gleaming shower stall big enough for five people, and double sinks under the mirror. The towels hanging from the rack are impossibly fluffy and monogrammed.

"So that's the guy?" Rafaela asks, lifting her maxiskirt before she plops down on the toilet. Her underwear slides down to her ankles, pooling under the hem of the skirt. "Emil?"

I lean against the sinks and face the shower, talking over the sound of her peeing. "Yeah, Emil. He's..."

"Cute?" I can hear the smile in her voice.

"Yeah." My mouth turns up, too. "I don't know what we are. I've known him my whole life, practically, but something changed when I came back. And I told him I'm not totally straight."

"He's chill about it?"

"Completely."

"Well, lucky for you." She flushes and walks to the sink to wash her hands. "One of the scariest things about that Palisades dude was that he flipped after I told him *I'm* not totally straight. He started getting super possessive and would watch me when we were around other girls to see if I was checking them out."

"Wow. Have you seen him lately?"

"He's been scarce, thank God. Although he did send a text today."

She dries her hands on one of the fancy towels hanging by the sink and fluffs her curls with her fingers. Then she reaches into the pocket of her skirt and pulls out a tube of lipstick. When she clicks it open, I see the purple shade that I so love on her.

I don't realize I'm staring until she stops, midapplication, and looks at me in the mirror. "What?"

"Nothing." I don't really have to pee but I walk over to the toilet to escape her gaze.

Rafaela is quiet as I flush and wash my hands. She carefully scrapes the excess color from the edge of her lips with the side of her fingernail before blotting with a tissue. Then she says, "Come here." She's brandishing the lipstick in one hand while studying my face.

I stand in front of her, almost disturbed by the vibrancy of her gold-flecked eyes when we're this close. She touches the center of my top lip, briefly rests her finger in the little groove right under my nose ring, and I close my eyes out of instinct, like the moment I know I'm about to be kissed. I hold my breath while she glides the tip of her finger around the edge of my mouth.

"You have great lips," she says, and I finally open my eyes, finally exhale.

"I do?" My voice is shaky, and I know she notices, by the way she smiles.

"They're full, perfectly shaped. Makeup artist's dream." She touches my face then, but only so she can angle my chin where she needs it to be. "Don't move." She holds up the lipstick and slowly paints the color along my bottom lip. I close my eyes again. Partly because it seems like the thing to do when someone is putting makeup on your face, but mostly because I want to savor the soft but assured touch of her hands on my skin.

She does the top lip and then goes over my whole mouth again with the lipstick. When I open my eyes, she's holding out a fresh tissue. "Blot."

We look in the mirror together with our matching lips, and I think how easy it would be to kiss her now. How my brother or Emil wouldn't have to know. How easily I could hide the evidence on our equally stained lips.

"That color looks amazing on you," she says.

"Yeah?" I silently agree, though I think it looks better on her.

"Emil will love it." She steps away then, breaking the temporary spell that made me think I'd actually be brave enough to kiss her, to trace the elegant lines of her flowered tattoo. She pockets the lipstick. "Ready?"

I nod, but she stops before she opens the door. Turns to face me.

"I've never cheated on anyone I've been with," she says carefully.

I frown. "Neither have I."

"And I'm not in the habit of coming between family members."

I almost drop my beer. She stares and stares like she wants me to say something, but the only thing I can come up with is "I never said you were."

"Sometimes I say things out loud when I need a reminder. So...I don't cheat. Okay?"

But I think it's a lie. I think that if I'd made a move, she would have kissed me back. That we might be pressed against the cool marble sinks, touching and still kissing and not just wanting. But she's with Lionel and I am sort of with Emil. So I nod again and follow her, clutching so tightly to my beer I'm surprised the cup doesn't splinter in my hands.

I meet up with Emil again downstairs, and we walk out to the keg to refill our cups. We get in line behind two girls with tattoos that cover more skin than Rafaela's, and I'm trying to discern what they are when Emil nudges my shoulder and says, "Hey."

I look up at him. "Hey."

"New lip stuff?"

I nod. I don't normally wear anything so dark and I wondered if he'd notice—especially that it's the same shade as Rafaela's. "Do you like it?"

He kisses me in response. Soft and sweet and unexpected, square on the lips. I kiss him back, and when we pull away, I smile.

"What was that for?"

He shrugs. "Do I need a reason?"

He doesn't, but I have to wonder if he could tell there was something different when Rafaela was around. If he felt the need to remind me that I'm with him tonight.

Just then a guy lopes over from the porch and announces

to the entire line of people waiting for the keg: "Fight! In the garage!"

Lionel's face flashes in front of me. I send it away. He was angry with Catie earlier, but they only ever fight with words. And he wouldn't hit a girl. And maybe there's a point when you have to stop worrying, when you have to believe everything will turn out okay in the end.

Half of the line disperses and follows him back to the house. Mostly guys, but a few girls scurry off, too. The ones in front of us stand strong for only a few more seconds before one of them looks at the other, shrugs, and they walk away, too. Emil and I have just reached the front of the line, him instructing me to hold my cup while he pumps the keg, when Justin comes tearing toward us.

"You guys should get to the garage." He's jogging in place like Emil did the first day I saw him this summer. Like he wants to be here but has somewhere more urgent to go.

"We heard about the fight," Emil says. "I'll pass."

"Yeah." I hold my cup steady as the tap slowly fills it at an angle. "What's the point of watching people we don't know get into it?"

But I know. It's too early to stop worrying. I know there's a good chance it's—

"Guys, it's *Lionel*."

My cup crashes to the ground, soaking my feet in fresh beer.

We race inside. Emil pulls me along after him so fast that I feel like I'm floating. But we're nearly the last to arrive. The garage is full, the center of the room obscured by a thick wall of backs nearly pressing up to all four corners.

"Let us through!" I shout, loud as I can. "We need to get through! That's my *brother*!"

But they can't hear me over the cheering and yelling. Even if they can, no one parts the crowd for us. Everyone is too invested in what's going on up front or trying to *see* what's going on up front or just getting swept up in the commotion of it all. My heart is thumping so loudly that the voices coming at me from all sides fade into the distance.

We push our way up a millimeter a minute. I feel like I'm going to be sick. Maybe Justin was wrong. Maybe it isn't Lionel. Maybe there was some other guy with red hair hanging out in the garage. But I can't ask him; he's ahead of Emil, who's ahead of me, still tightly gripping my hand so we don't get separated.

Lionel isn't a fighter. And so my stomach turns even more when I think about him getting bruised up by some guy who's actually had practice. The closer I get, the more I can hear the sounds from the actual fight: grunts, breathless curses, the ripping of clothes.

But by the time we finally make our way to the head of the crowd, it's over. And it's not the scene I thought I'd find. A guy with long, dark hair is lying on the floor of the garage, holding his arms around his head like a helmet. He raises his elbows just high enough for me to see that his nose is gushing blood: a thick, dark stream of red that stains the concrete below him.

Lionel is standing above, still raring to go and held back by Rafaela, who looks even tinier than usual. But she doesn't look scared. I'd be horrified if Emil had just been in a fight, but the look on her face is...not enchantment, but something close to it.

No one is helping the guy on the ground. I don't know what the story is, but I need to find out why Lionel is covered in this guy's blood. It's on his collar, his arm...his fist.

I want to ask him but as I step forward he glances at me, and the look in his eyes is wild. Not really seeing me. Not really in this moment except for his body.

I've seen that look before. It was the other time I saw him clenching a bloody fist.

Lionel once told me he didn't know why doctors bothered with explaining the difference in the types of mania since it all meant people with bipolar were crazy and, eventually, would end up depressed.

When I look at my brother, I see that he's sick. I see that he needs his meds to properly function.

I see that I have fucked up big-time and I have to fix it.

eighteen.

Emil drives Lionel and me home in Lion's car, not without protests from my brother.

He insists that he's fine, that he can get us home himself
after God knows how many drinks, that we should totally
fucking ignore that he's moving around like a can of com-
pressed air on the verge of bursting. He's mad that we left
Rafaela at Alicia's house and mad that we let that guy on the
garage floor get away from him.

"What was your problem with that guy?" I ask. He's in
the backseat, and I can't look at him. It's my fault that he's
like this right now and yet it's his fault, too, for involving me.
I'm mad at both of us, at what we've gotten ourselves into.

"He wouldn't leave my girlfriend alone," Lionel responds in a steely voice.

"He goes to school with Rafaela?"

"He's from the fucking Palisades."

Oh my God. *That* was the guy from the Palisades? How does he always know where Rafaela is? They don't have any friends in common.

Emil looks over at me, sensing that I know exactly who Lionel is talking about, but I shake my head and mouth *Later*. I don't want to get into the details now, not with Lion so amped up.

"We should stop at the Brite Spot, Suzette," Lion says as we drive past, the white sign with the huge orange dot looming behind the diner. "I could really go for some pancakes. And then we could go out again. It's still early—"

"It's time to go home, Lionel," I say in a voice that sounds like I'm his mother. I hate it, but it momentarily shuts him up. And I don't want to hear him talk right now because he called me by my name instead of Little. Yet another sign that says he's not okay.

As soon as we pull into the driveway, Lionel jumps out of the car and runs up to the front porch and for a moment, even though I know it would only make tonight even worse, I wish Mom and Saul were still up. Because then, after tonight, all of this would be over. But every floor of the house is dark, save for the lamp they've left on for us in the front room.

Emil watches me. "Do you want me to go in with you?"

I start to say no, that I can handle this myself. But I don't want to handle this by myself anymore. And Emil already knows everything. Justin pulls up to the curb then; he dims his lights but leaves the car idling. He sobered up pretty quickly once the fight started and promised he was okay to drive.

"Can you stay?" I ask, turning to Emil. "Tell your parents you're spending the night at Justin's?"

He looks up toward the turret and even though I'm filled with anxiety, I feel my body go warm as I think about him in my bedroom. "I want to, but...it's kinda hard to sneak out of a room like that."

Shit. He's right. There's only one way down that doesn't involve acrobatics and an extreme lack of good judgment. I think about the tree house, but I feel strange inviting him into my space with Lionel again, especially tonight. And I'd rather be close to Lion; the tree house is too far.

"We'll set an alarm," I say. "You're used to getting up early. You could even run home."

"Okay." He looks at me and shakes his head, smiling. "This is probably a really bad decision, but okay."

"This whole night has been a bad decision. Why stop

now?" I smile back at him before I get out of the car and wait for him to talk to Justin.

The house is quiet, and I click off the lamp as soon as we're inside. Emil takes off his shoes out of habit while I lock the door behind him. He holds the shoes in one hand and I take the other as I lead us up the first staircase, walking on the very tips of my toes. I pause in the hallway between Lionel's and our parents' room, but the strip of space under their door is dark and I don't hear voices on the other side. Lionel is still up, though, bumping around in his room.

I grab the tissue box from my nightstand and leave Emil alone, sitting barefoot on my bed. Then I march back down the stairs and knock as softly as possible on my brother's door while also trying to signal that I mean business. He pulls the door open immediately and walks over to his desk, as if he was already midtransit.

"What's up?" he says as soon as I close the door. "Change your mind about Brite Spot? I know you think I'm too fucked up to drive, but I can get us there. It's just up the street. Or we could walk! It's not too far. Not too late."

"Lion, this isn't okay. What happened tonight..." I swallow and set the tissue box on top of his bureau, dig out the pill bottles, and line them up next to each other. "You need to go back on these. I can't hide them for you anymore."

I expect him to be combative. I don't expect him to look

at the bottles and then me with a derisive smirk that makes me feel stupid for being here. For saying something. For caring.

"You were the one who offered to hide them," he says, his back to me as he plops down in front of his computer. "You can leave them here, but I'll get rid of them before I take them."

"Lionel, you got into a *fight*. You punched a guy so hard his nose might be broken."

"So? He should have left Rafaela alone."

I notice, as he types, that he hasn't bothered to clean off his knuckles. They're crusted with blood, the skin broken open in some places, but he's just clacking away on his keyboard as if this is all commonplace.

"Lion, this isn't *you*." I walk over to stand beside him, but still he doesn't look at me. "You don't drink like that. You don't get in fights. This is the bipolar."

"You think I don't know what I'm dealing with? It's *my* brain, Suzette." He pauses with his fingers above the keys. "Lots of people ride out their hypomania and they're fine. It's, like, increased energy. Nothing to worry about."

"It's not just increased energy!" I have to actively work to keep my voice down. "Not with you. You get irritable and angry and..." I stop myself from saying it scares me. "Lion." I take a deep breath even though I'm still looking at the back of his head and it's always easier to say something to someone when you don't have to make eye contact. "If you don't start taking your pills, I'm going to tell Mom and Saul."

His fingers start clicking over the keyboard again, as if I haven't spoken at all. Then: "You don't want to do that."

"No, I *don't* want to do it, but you're not giving me a choice!" I realize I'm breathing heavy, talking too loudly, and take a moment to calm down.

He whips around then, his eyes narrowed to slits. But still I can see the pure fury that lies behind them, and I can't believe that for the first time in his life, it's directed at me. "You think I don't know you told them last summer? All that stuff I said to you . . . You went right to them the next day."

I knew he knew about it, but I thought the fact that he didn't bring it up meant he was grateful, on some level, for my intervening. "I didn't tell them exactly what you said. I—"

"It was enough to make them decide I had bipolar! And then everything was worse than when they thought I just had fucking ADHD."

"The *doctors* decided that. What was I supposed to do? Pretend like what you said didn't scare the shit out of me? You were talking about *dying*."

"And I told you I didn't want to, but you still went right to the parents. I'm so fucking sick of this," he says, shaking his head. "Sick of everyone butting into my life, thinking they know what's best for me."

"But you're not getting better . . . you're getting worse."

"First of all, you don't get to fucking tell *me* how I'm doing. And second, do you really want to talk to them about me again? When you have some secrets of your own that they might want to know about?"

"Fine." I throw my hands in the air. "That would be really, really shitty of you, but fine. Out me to our parents if it makes you feel better, but—"

"No, what would make me feel better is if they knew how shady you're being with my girlfriend."

My skin turns cold. I want to hurt the person in front of me, the hard expression contrasting against lively freckles and bright, bright hair. But this isn't Lionel.

"I'm not doing anything with your girlfriend." My voice is shaking.

"You would if there was no way I'd find out." His voice is pure ice. And he doesn't give me a chance to protest. "I can't stop you from telling them," he says, his eyes boring into me. "But aren't they gonna wonder why it took you so long? And if you tell them . . . we're done."

"We're not *done*." The tears come fast and they're rolling over my cheeks, dripping down my chin and into the crease of my neck. "We can't be done. We're *family*."

"Yeah, well, family doesn't tell on each other. They keep secrets. They protect each other." He shrugs then, and that smirk pops back up, more mocking than before. "So go ahead and tell if you want, but we're done if you do. It's not like we're blood, anyway."

My knees buckle instantly; I barely catch the wall for support in time. I have nothing to say after that, but it doesn't matter because he doesn't look back again. I'm invisible to him. The sister he could disown in five seconds flat.

I stumble out to the hall, pause when I'm just a few feet from Mom and Saul's room. I could go in there now and tell them everything and hope that one day he'd be able to forgive me.

But I'm so weak, so tired, so hurt that I can't pile one more problem onto this day. Maybe when I wake up every-thing will be different. Lionel will be receptive to his meds and he will apologize and everything will be good between us again. And if he's not, then I have to think seriously about what my life would be like without him when boarding school isn't the reason keeping us apart.

I trudge up the stairs to my room. Emil has turned on the twinkle lights so everything is cast in a soft glow. He's sitting on my bed, on top of the covers, flipping through a book of poetry by Gwendolyn Brooks. His shoes are next to the bed.

"How'd it go?" he asks, lowering the book.

I undress immediately, dropping my clothes to the floor piece by piece until I'm standing in nothing but my underwear.

He looks at me—at my eyes, not my body. "Suzette?"

I start to answer him but my face crumples.

"It's okay." He comes to me, wraps his arms around my naked shoulders, and walks me toward the bed. "It's going to be okay."

"It's not, though," I say in a voice thick with tears. "He won't take his meds. He hates me, Emil."

"He doesn't hate you."

"He does."

"Come on," he says as I lie down. He pulls the covers over me gently, first the top sheet and then the duvet. "Appa always says everything will look better in the morning and . . . not to sound too much like my dad, but maybe that's true, okay? It's been a long night."

Emil turns off the lights and crawls in next to me. He seems hesitant to touch me when I move closer to him, and when I kiss him, he doesn't kiss me back. He pulls away and looks at me.

"What's wrong?" I ask.

"It feels like I'm taking advantage of you, when you're upset like this." His voice is quiet.

"You're not. I want this. I want you."

He slides his thumbs across my cheeks, brushing the tears away as he cups my face with his strong hands. He kisses me first this time and makes up for the kiss he didn't return. His lips are warm and understanding as they meet mine, as if he knows how much I need to be needed tonight.

I take my time removing his clothes, stopping to touch the parts of his body I haven't seen before. He sucks in a breath and releases it unevenly as my fingers glide across his skin. I've never seen a boy completely naked; even when we were up in the tree house that night, Emil never took off his boxers. Now he strokes the dimples at the small of my back as I look at him a little too long.

I ask if he has a condom and he nods, grabs one from his jeans on the floor. But he stops and asks if I'm sure before he puts it on. I'm no surer of what I'm doing than when I was with Iris, but like when I was with her, this feels right.

We go slow, and still sometimes it is so uncomfortable I have to bite my lip to keep from whimpering. I don't want him to think he's hurting me because he's so gentle the whole time, as if my body is sculpted of glass. He kisses and kisses me, and each time our lips meet, I think the strangest thing about being so close to Emil is that it's not strange at all.

And I don't think about Iris. Not until we're done and he is wrapped around me like a spoon, his arms holding me tight like she used to, like he'll never let me go.

nineteen.

I'm so sorry" are the first words out of Rafaela's mouth when she sees me.

I'm not working today, two days after the party, but when she asked me to meet her at the coffee shop next to Castillo Flowers, I obliged. I didn't have anything better to do than try not to drown in my worry, so it was good to hop on my butter-yellow beach cruiser and ride over here with the wind whipping through my dreads, the sun warming my skin as I cycled up Sunset. But now that I'm here, I wish I weren't. I know it's not Rafaela's fault that Lionel lost control, but I can't help feeling resentful.

Or that she's bad for him.

She slides into the seat across from me at the wrought-iron

table crammed into the small outdoor space and takes off her sunglasses. "I had no idea that guy was going to show up. I told you he'd texted me earlier and then he was just, like, *there* and..."

"But what *happened*?" I wrap my hands around my iced latte. "Something had to have set Lion off. I mean, he doesn't just go around punching people like that. And he won't tell me anything."

For the first time since I've met her, Rafaela blushes. It's subtle, but her skin pinkens and she stares down at her empty hands. "He's trying to protect me. That guy is bad news."

"Obviously," I say, and it's not lost on me how unkind my voice is. But I'm tired of secrets.

She purses her lips and stands. "I need coffee."

I'm slurping the last of mine through a straw when she returns, ignoring the annoyed glances of the dad type sitting to my left.

Rafaela sits down with a hot coffee, takes a sip, and looks at me. "The last time I saw that guy, he said he was going to 'fuck the gay' out of me."

The dad type huffs, not even trying to hide the fact that he's listening in.

"What?" I say, admittedly as shocked as he is.

"He knew about Grace, and he was always really weird when other girls were around. I told you how he'd get all possessive, and that was whether or not I even thought they were cute. Like, we could've been walking by a woman wearing mom jeans and driving a minivan, and he'd make sure I wasn't checking her out." She shudders. "It was really creepy, so I started ignoring him."

"And he couldn't handle it."

I remember Iris telling me something similar, about how the boys who'd flirted and tried to get her attention at her old school were angry when she rebuffed them, but especially so when they realized she wasn't into guys at all. Like it was a direct threat to their masculinity, and they were embarrassed that they'd wasted time on someone who didn't reciprocate their attraction. I feel lucky that Emil handled my confession so well, but I know I won't always be so fortunate.

"No, and seeing me with another guy was apparently the last straw." She sighs and looks at her coffee. "The night of your welcome-back party...when he showed up at DeeDee's...I may have told him I was going to be there."

"What?" I lean forward and lower my voice.

"I was bored," she says. "And drunk. And I knew he'd make a fool of himself in front of everyone. He did, but—"

"That only made it worse."

She nods. "And this last time...I don't know. I guess I wanted to see what he'd act like if he saw me with another guy. But he was drunker than I've ever seen him, at Alicia's. Calling me all sorts of names. Lionel defended me, of course, and then the next thing I know he's just whaling on him."

I could tell her, right now, how Lionel hasn't been taking his meds and how I think their relationship isn't good for him. But it's not my place to say something. If Lion was mad at the idea that I'd tell our parents, I can't imagine he'd be okay with me telling his new girlfriend. Just as with my parents, not telling her feels like watching a bomb slowly tick down to its explosion, but setting it off early seems just as, if not more, dangerous.

"Do you think it's because of his bipolar?" When I look up, she's leaning forward, eyes more golden than green and a little scared. "I didn't want to say anything, but I know mood swings are part of it. And he was fine that whole night and then he was so angry out of nowhere....Is that normal for him?"

But he wasn't fine. She doesn't know him well enough to read his moods, the slightest change in his behavior.

I touch my nose ring, tap it three times before I respond. "I don't know if I should get into that. Lion is kind of touchy about it. You should probably talk to him yourself."

She shakes her head. "I'm asking because I want to hear what *you* think, Suzette. Is this something I should be worried about? I really, really like him. A lot. But that scared me. And I feel shitty being scared. Lionel isn't a *scary* person. But he didn't seem like himself."

I shake the ice around in my cup as I weigh the good of telling Rafaela Lion's secret against the bad of facing him after he finds out. My lips choose for me.

"He's *not* himself. He's off his meds." I close my eyes for a second to regroup, because I felt dizzy, just saying those words. Telling Emil was different. Our families are close and they've always known our secrets. And Emil isn't dating my brother.

As I sit here, waiting for her response, I wonder how much longer they'll be together after this. I remember what DeeDee said, that Rafaela has a reputation for dating shitty guys, and my stomach hurts as I think about her putting Lionel into that category.

And when she still doesn't speak, I blurt, "You can't say anything to him, Rafaela. I'm not telling you this because of what you said the other night... in the bathroom. I don't want you to hate him. I want..."

I don't know what I want. I've mentally replayed that moment in the bathroom almost as often as my night with Emil. No one has ever implied that they wanted me when I couldn't have them. Are we just supposed to go on pretending that we're not attracted to each other now that she's put it out in the open?

"I know." Rafaela watches me over the lid of her coffee as she takes a long drink. "And I don't hate him. I...I feel relieved, actually."

"What?"

"Well, it would be pretty frightening if he was acting that way on medication."

"That still doesn't make it okay. Aren't you worried about him? Do you know what can happen if he doesn't get back on track?" I feel like my mother, like I'm lecturing someone younger than me on something she should already know.

"Suzette, lots of people don't take their meds and they're fine. It doesn't always have to end in some tragic story. Some of the best artists in history had mood disorders." She sighs. "You can't make someone do something they don't want to. If he doesn't want to take his meds…"

She trails off as if that's the end of it.

"You can if they might hurt themselves without it."

Rafaela frowns. "Has he ever been hospitalized?"

"No. But you haven't seen him depressed. You haven't heard him talking when it's really bad."

"Is he seeing a therapist?"

I nod.

"Well, then he can't be so bad, right? His shrink would let your parents know if something seemed off?"

I shrug. Maybe she's right. I'm the only one freaking out about him, but he's around other people every day. Mom and Saul know what to look out for, same as Dr. T. Maybe I'm overreacting. Maybe this is why Mom sent me away last year.

We sit in silence for a while. The man next to us leaves, but not before glancing over with an expression that rests somewhere between reproachful and curious. I glare at him until he walks away.

"Look, I have four tickets for the cemetery movie this weekend," Rafaela finally says. "*Dazed and Confused*. I bought them at the beginning of the summer, figuring I'd go with Grace and the girls. But I'd rather take Lionel and you. And you can bring your dude. Is that weird?"

I shake my head. Maybe it would have been, ten minutes ago. But her response to Lionel's secret isn't what I expected, and she lied to me soon after we met, about the guy from the Palisades. Something has changed, even if I can't just turn off my physical attraction to her. And the truth is that Lionel won't want to hang out with me if she's not around. I'm back to giving him a wide berth and he's back to letting me.

"So you'll go?"

"Sure," I say. "I'll ask Emil."

I should feel better, having told someone else the truth about my brother. Maybe the most important person to him right now, even if I don't want to admit it. But she doesn't agree with me or my parents or anyone else who really knows Lionel, so my effort seems futile.

I need to tell someone who will do something. As much as I hate to admit it to myself, I have to find a way to tell Saul.

twenty.

We can go anywhere on our adventures, as Saul calls the afternoons we spend together. We like to explore the city, all the corners of Los Angeles that people have forgotten or don't know about or have deemed too far to drive to. I feel most comfortable when we're at the museum, and this time he says we'll be uninterrupted and free to spend the day as we please.

"See? I even turned off my phone." He holds up the blank screen for proof.

"I'm holding you to that," I say, raising an eyebrow.

I'm trying to be normal with him, but there's nothing normal about how I feel. My stomach has been churning all day from nerves as I go over and over in my head how to tell him about Lionel. It would have been easier to tell my mother, but Saul deserves to hear it from me. I don't want to ruin our day, so I decide to wait until we've walked around awhile.

There's a Matisse exhibit I've wanted to check out, but we stop at the Tar Pits first, heading down the sidewalk along Wilshire. We cross the grassy entrance and find an empty bench in front of the models of the prehistoric animals.

"How's the flower shop?" Saul asks as we sit.

"Fine." I ignore how Rafaela's face flashes through my mind. I wish I'd never agreed to our double date this weekend. Maybe there won't even be a date, after Saul finds out about Lionel. "Good. Ora said my last arrangement was 'full of passion,' whatever that means."

Saul raises an eyebrow. "Could it be we have a budding florist in our midst?"

"Um, no." I make a face. "I mean, it's not a bad job, but I still don't know much about flowers. And it's not like they really mean anything. People get them to say they're sorry. Then they die."

"Come on, kiddo, you're too young to be so jaded," he says, sounding truly disappointed. "There used to be a whole language of flowers, in Victorian times."

"I know. Floriography." Ora has a couple of old books that her mother owned. She keeps them in the back room, on a shelf above the counter where we prepare the bouquets. I've paged through one of them when I was bored and I guess

I understand it—telling stories and expressing emotions through flowers. It's not so different from art, except paintings and sculptures and photography live on. Flowers dry out and the petals shrivel up and people throw them away when the water starts to smell.

"Well, you might miss the shop a little when you go back to Massachusetts, right? *If* you go back?"

"Oh," I say. "Yeah."

I haven't labored much over whether or not to return to Dinsmore since Mom mentioned the choice is mine. Not directly, anyway. But lately it seems like I can't do anything without being reminded of Iris; she's wrapped up in the safety of Emil and my attraction to Rafaela and my complicated feelings of betraying Lionel. Everything goes back to her and I know, for sure, that it's because I never apologized. I should have told those girls on our floor to go to hell. I should have been proud of what I had with Iris instead of trying to take the easy way out.

"Have you decided yet?" he asks after a pause. "We don't mean to push you, but there's always a lot of paperwork and phone calls involved with schools, and the summer is just about half over..."

"I don't know," I say. "I haven't...I can't decide."

"How about you let us know by next week?" Saul says easily. He believes Lionel is fine, that his health is stable, so he must think my decision is based on trivial factors, like missing the food and sunshine of L.A. and the comfort of my bedroom tower.

"Okay," I agree. In a week, maybe the choice will be made for me; maybe Lionel won't even want to look at me after his secret is out in the open.

A couple of guys saunter by with skateboards under their arms, nudging each other as they look through the bars of the fence at the woolly mammoth.

"You know we miss you when you're gone. So much, kiddo," Saul says, rubbing a hand over his face. Stubble is cropping up on his jawline, a darker red than the hair on his head. "But you shouldn't stay here for us, if you want to go back. We'll all be fine...Lionel included."

But he won't, not the way he is now. And not if he goes off his meds again when I'm gone.

I look down at a stray leaf skittering by my feet. "I know, I just...It's hard to know what to do sometimes."

Saul's arm goes around me. "I wish I could say that part of life gets easier."

I lean my head against his shoulder and close my eyes and we stay like that for a while. When I open my eyes, I notice a couple of women giving us strange looks. I stare back until they look away. Sometimes I feel as if I should wear a sign that says HE'S MY STEPDAD!!!! to combat the baffled looks we get when we're together. It's fucking gross.

I tell Saul I want to go see the big boulder at the edge of

the museum grounds, so we make our way over, stopping a few feet from the group of older people already congregated underneath. They walk through the tunnel super slowly, gazing up at the enormous rock suspended above. We stand back and wait, giving them space.

"Saul?"

"Suzette?" he says with a grin, imitating my serious tone.

I lick my lips and press them together before I ask him, "When Lion's older, what if… what if he decides to go off medication?"

Even that question sends terror zipping through me, but I hope he reads between the lines, because I don't know if I'm strong enough to blurt out what I want to tell him.

Saul turns to face me, his lips parted. "Well, I'm not sure there's anything we could do about that when he's an adult. Unless he was hurting himself, and then we could have him hospitalized, but that's not a long-term solution. And if he's still planning to go away for college, that's not something we could actively control once he's gone."

I nod.

Saul looks at me a long moment, as if he's trying to decide whether I'm mature enough to handle what he wants to say. I've noticed more looks like that from him and Mom in the last year or so, as if a line runs down the middle of my face, separating me into child on one side and adult on the opposite.

"You know, when Daphne and I split up, we had a lot of talks about our custody agreement. We both decided Lionel living with me would be the best thing for him at the time, and then he got along so well with you and Nadine that we decided he'd stay here permanently."

"But why did you decide it was best for him?"

He puts his hands in his pockets and blinks down at the ground. "Daph was going through some issues of her own. Not as intense as what Lionel has, but similar. Cyclothymia, another mood disorder. Some people call it a cousin of bi-polar. A mild form. There's no approved medication spe-cifically for cyclothymia, and Daphne didn't want to take a chance on the ones typically prescribed. She didn't want to go to therapy, either, and . . . I didn't feel like that was the best option with your brother around, so he came with me."

I twist my fingers around the hem of my black tank. "But she seems like she does okay."

He looks at me. "Daphne is a competent, amazing woman, just like Lionel is going to be a competent, amazing man. But I personally don't see the value in refusing treat-ment that could help someone live a more stable life."

I had no idea about Lionel's mother. He's never men-tioned it, and I wonder if they've ever spoken about the choice to not medicate, if she influenced his decision to stop or if the inclination runs in their blood, similar to their illnesses.

The people ahead of us eventually tire of the boulder's

wonder and head toward the museum, leaving us to take our turn. I feel unsteady on my feet as we walk, too much new information swimming through my mind.

"Stay right there," Saul says when I'm under the rock, and he jogs off a ways to take a picture of me with his phone's camera.

The installation is called *Levitated Mass*. I will look tiny beneath it. Extraordinarily small because of the massive stone balanced over my head, my features indistinguishable because of the distance between Saul and me. I curl into an even tighter version of myself. Holding on to one wall of the tunnel as if the boulder above will come crashing down when I let go.

I don't want to tell Saul yet. If Daphne can live and thrive without treatment, maybe Lionel can do the same. And maybe that means I need one more sign before I tell his secret and ruin everything between us. If he's able to manage on his own, like his mother, maybe I was never supposed to tell on him at all. Maybe we can keep this secret between us, just like the others we've kept, stored in the invisible vault that assembled itself when we became brother and sister.

Saul counts before he takes the photo.

I try to smile when he gets to *three*, but my lips won't turn up so I hide the bottom half of my face behind my shoulder a second before the shutter clicks.

twenty-one.

Cemetery movies are a summertime tradition, and they're exactly what they sound like: People pay money to watch movies in a cemetery.

But it's a pretty cemetery in Hollywood, a lot filled with gorgeous mausoleums and crypts belonging to old-time movie stars and important people of Los Angeles. The movie is set up away from the gravestones, which eliminates the creep factor. And I always think there's something peaceful about walking through the manicured grounds.

Lionel insists on driving to pick up Rafaela, but Emil wants to drive, too, so we take two cars. I have to wonder how much of Lionel's insistence is because he doesn't want to be trapped in a car with me. His energy level seems steady, like it hasn't increased since the evening of the fight. It hasn't gone down, either, but I'm waiting for that crash. Dreading its nearly inevitable arrival, no matter how unpredictable its timing.

He and Rafaela arrive first and we squeeze into the line ahead of them, ignoring the frowns of the people behind us. The gates don't open for a couple more hours, but everyone lines up early to get the best spot on the grass.

"We brought snacks." I hold up the paper bag in my hand.

"And we brought blankets and booze." Rafaela points to the canvas backpack on her shoulders. "Oh, and I got a joint from Alicia."

Lionel is in a good mood; I can see the energy behind his eyes, but he seems relatively calm. Sometimes I think about what he said to me that night, that we're not really family, and I wonder if it actually happened. I'd think I'd completely imagined it, but every time he and I make eye contact there's a hardness behind his gaze, and I know it was real. I suppose he realizes it was enough to get me to keep my mouth shut, because he doesn't seem at all concerned that I'll go to Mom and Saul. And I don't feel comforted by the fact that my brother knows me so well.

As soon as we get through the gates he grabs Rafaela's arm and they start running toward the viewing area. They push past people who were in line ahead of us, the blankets

Lionel was in charge of tucked under his arm like a football. Rafaela screams as they sprint away, wild and giddy, like she's tearing through the air on a roller coaster.

"Damn. Lionel might've missed his calling with track," Emil says, watching them go.

I take a deep breath and tell myself that's not the sign. Not yet.

By the time we find them, Lionel and Rafaela have already claimed a patch of grass big enough for the four of us to spread out. They're carefully smoothing out the wrinkles in the blankets when we arrive and Lionel looks up with a proud grin. "A pretty perfect spot, right?"

Rafaela doesn't wait for us to respond before she confirms this with a kiss. "The best, babe."

Babe? Wow. My eyebrows go up involuntarily and I feel Emil's hand slip into my free one. I glance at him, wondering why he chose that moment to take my hand. He only smiles.

The time before the movie is prime for people-watching, when the DJ is spinning and people are popping open bottles of wine and setting up full-fledged picnics. I'm always fascinated by the groups of people who sit together, how sometimes they all seem to look and dress alike, and then others appear to be a bunch of people who were randomly selected to be friends. I wonder what people think when they look at the four of us together.

Emil and I raided the shit out of our respective

refrigerators, so we have paper-thin slices of prosciutto, six different kinds of cheese, fancy crackers, and fig jam. There are red and green grapes and hard-boiled eggs and pickles and an entire loaf of French bread, along with some leftover challah I managed to save from last night's Shabbat dinner. Rafaela and Lionel produce small plastic cups and two bottles of red wine that look expensive; I don't ask how they got them.

"I've never seen *Dazed and Confused*," Emil says almost sheepishly as the film is about to begin.

"Me either," I admit.

"It's a classic," Rafaela declares. "Makes me wish I grew up in the seventies."

"I'm not laid-back enough for the seventies," Emil muses, moving a plate of cheese to the side.

"No free love for you?" she teases.

My eyes slide toward her. When she makes eye contact I know we're both thinking of that night in the bathroom, of how things would be different between us if we all believed in free love.

"Nah. I'm more of a one-woman kind of guy." Emil puts his arm around me and my face turns hot, as if he could read our thoughts. Rafaela smiles over at us and snuggles into Lionel, her palm grazing the freckles on his arm.

The audience is vocal, saying the lines with the characters or shouting them out before they've been recited. Rafaela pulls out the joint and sparks it up about a third of the way into the movie, but the smell of weed already permeates the air around us. She takes a long drag and passes it to me. I consider it for a moment, then take a small hit; it's been a while since I've smoked pot. And it's strong, but the small bit of smoke I inhale is smooth going down my throat. I hold out the joint to Emil, who shakes his head.

Lionel looks at me expectantly, but I hesitate before I hand it to him. I have no idea if he's ever smoked before. What if he has a bad reaction?

Then he snatches the joint out of my hand without a word, reminding me that he doesn't care what I think is best for him. I watch as he inspects it, puts it in his mouth, and sucks in. He repeats this two more times, and I think he'd have gone for a fourth hit if Rafaela hadn't said, "Yo, save some for the rest of us."

But I'm done. I can already feel it hitting me. Just strong enough to loosen my limbs and cloud my head with a delicious haziness, but not so much that I'm unaware of what's going on around me.

"Feeling good?" Emil whispers by my ear.

I nod and relax against him.

Halfway through the movie, I sit up to grab my bottle of water. My throat is parched. I can't find it next to me, and when I start searching the blanket, I look up and find Rafaela and Lionel making out. Not short, sweet kisses like before, but full-on lips melded together, his hands tangled in her hair with hers draped lazily around his waist. They're practically lying back on the blanket and it all makes my stomach turn, but I can't stop watching, either.

"Hey," Emil says, and when I don't reply, he lightly rubs my arm. "Hey, let's go for a walk."

I start to protest, point out that the movie is still playing, but both of us know I'm not even pretending to watch. So when he stands and holds out his hand, I take it and follow him off to the edge of the viewing area. We pass the portable toilets and stop next to the fat base of a date palm tree.

"What's going on?" Emil's voice is calm, but his face is unsmiling.

"What do you mean?" For some reason, I don't want to make this easy for him.

"I've been watching you watch them all night."

"I'm sorry if I'm worried about my brother, but—"

He shakes his head. "No, you were watching her."

I don't look at him as I speak. "I'm not checking out every girl just because I'm bi."

Everything freezes, just for a moment; this is the first time I've said it so definitively, without questioning what I am. Emil doesn't seem to notice or care.

"Come on, Suzette. Give me more credit than that." He shoves his hands into the pockets of his hoodie. "I've seen you around other girls. It's not the same."

284

"I don't know what you want me to say."

He exhales. "Do you like her?"

"No." Then, a second later: "I don't know."

"So, I guess that's a yes." He pauses. "That night at the party...did something happen with you and her? When you went upstairs?"

"Emil, no. Nothing has happened with Rafaela. Ever."

"But you've wanted it to." Not a question.

I look up at him, at his face twisted into an expression I hope to never see again, full of anger and hurt. And I'm the one causing him to look that way. "I like you. I'm here with *you*."

"I kind of feel like you're here for everyone *but* me."

"What?"

"Like you're keeping tabs on Rafaela because you like her. And listen...I get that you're close to your brother and you want to be there for him, but it's like you feel responsible for everything he does. He doesn't need to be looked after by his little sister. He needs real help, Suzette."

"He's still going to his therapist," I mumble to the tree. But I'm not even sure if that's true anymore.

"Seriously? Because as worried as you seem...wouldn't his therapist know something is wrong, too?"

"I don't *know*, Emil. He barely talks to me anymore." Maybe he's successfully managed to skip appointments or convinced Dr. T and my parents that he's ready to cut back on them, or perhaps he's simply so good at hiding his symptoms when he needs to that no one suspects anything is out of the ordinary. "I feel like shit."

"That's exactly my point. You don't deserve to feel that way."

"He's my brother!" I cry out so loudly that a man walking by jumps a little. "What am I supposed to do? Let him go through this alone? I was gone for the entire school year—the least I can do is be here for him now."

"You didn't abandon him, Suzette. He had your parents and doctors and...it's not like they couldn't get by without you here."

"Oh, so now it doesn't matter whether I'm around or not? Thanks, Emil." I start to stalk off, but he touches my elbow, gently pulls me back to him.

"You know I didn't mean it like that. You're..." He swallows hard. "You're one of the best people I know. I hate seeing you caught up in this shit. And I hate that I care so much."

"Well, I hate being caught up in it." I swallow before what I say next. And I say it softly. "Why *do* you care so much?"

"You mean why have I always liked you?" He laughs a little, but I know he doesn't think anything about this conversation is funny. "I would've turned it off a long time ago if I could have. I never thought you'd like me back and now... God, I sound like such an asshole."

I don't say anything in response and after a few seconds, he goes on.

"You know how our moms studied abroad in France their senior year?"

I nod. "Paris."

"They loved it so much they promised to give their first kids French names."

"What?" I take a step back.

"Emil and Suzette." He exhales, and now he's talking to the tree, too. "I've always thought it meant something, like we're cosmically linked. Our moms are best friends. They had us the same year and ended up living a couple of miles away from each other. Our names...I thought we were soul mates."

I blink, focused on his shoulder. "My mom never told me that."

He looks at me now. "You know, I always felt weird growing up, having a French first name and a Korean last name and dark skin. People don't know what to do with all that. But knowing you made me feel a little more normal. Like at least we shared two of those things."

"Emil..."

"I don't want to be with you if you're into someone else, Suzette. I'm not saying you have to choose, but I can't keep hanging out with you and her...not with the way you look at her. I like you too much to be okay with that."

His voice chokes at the end and he walks away then and he doesn't stop when I call his name.

I trail him back to the blanket, staying a few feet behind. I don't know what to say after that. I don't know how to feel about what he said. I've never seen Emil so upset, and I never thought I'd be the one to make him feel that way.

Lionel is gone when I get back to the blanket and I stop myself from asking where he is. Rafaela and Emil are sitting as far apart as possible, not talking.

She looks up when I sit down between them, her eyes asking me what's going on, but I give an almost imperceptible head shake and turn back toward the screen. The kids in the movie are all at some big party in a huge field not unlike the one we're currently gathered in, minus the gravestones and plus something called a moon tower. They're having a lot more fun than any of us on this blanket.

Rafaela starts to look around after a while. I'm now nervous about any interactions with her around Emil, but I'm almost relieved when she leans in to whisper because I'm so aware of how quiet he is on the other side of me. He hasn't looked my way once since I sat back down.

But then she says: "Lionel's been gone for kind of a long time."

"Where did he go?"

"To the bathroom, but that wasn't long after you guys left."

I frown. "I didn't see him."

Which doesn't mean anything. There are tons of people here, and the area by the toilets can get crowded. But I'm usually so good at spotting Lionel in a crowd.

"I've texted him a couple of times and he's not responding," she says, her own eyebrows scrunched together.

I pull out my phone and call him, but of course he doesn't pick up. If he's not responding to Rafaela, he's definitely not going to answer for me. Still, I leave a quick message telling him to call me. I keep my phone out.

"Maybe he went for a walk and lost track of time." She chews on her thumbnail.

"Maybe," I say, but it's obvious neither of us believes that. Emil finally glances over, but he remains silent.

By the time the credits begin to roll and people are packing up their things, I'm worried. Rafaela and I haven't stopped staring at our phones. Emil reluctantly asks what's going on without quite looking at either of us.

"Lionel's gone," she says.

"Well, he drove," Emil replies, "so as long as his car is still here, we know he hasn't gotten too far."

The three of us begin haphazardly shoving the remains of our feast back into the bags. Rafaela barely shakes out the blankets before sloppily throwing them over her arm.

"It's going to be okay," I say, though I'm not sure if it's more for my benefit or hers. "We'll find him."

"Yeah," she says as we march along through the departing crowd. "He's almost eighteen, not a little kid."

But of course what none of us says out loud is that he's off his meds, which changes everything.

We cross Santa Monica Boulevard, walking as fast as we can without running and stepping on the heels of people ahead of us. Emil still says nothing, but I see the concern on his face when I look at him.

"Shit." Rafaela stops when we get halfway down the street she says they parked on. "We were right there, under that tree."

There's an empty spot where she points, the pavement and curb illuminated by the streetlamp above.

"Are you sure it was this street?" Emil says.

"I'm positive. We were on Tamarind, because then we started talking about tamarind trees and how most people don't even know any other trees but, like, the really obvious ones.... *Shit*," she says again, closing her eyes for a moment.

"Let's take a look around, just to make sure he didn't move the car," Emil says, already walking.

"He wouldn't *move* the car," I say. "This is Hollywood. If you find a spot, you keep it."

"Suzette, I'm trying to be practical." He turns to look at me. "We need to go through this step by step because if we don't find him here, we have to tell your parents. And I think you know how well that's going to go over."

We look for Lionel on every side street around the cemetery, but he and his sedan are nowhere to be found. We loop back to the cemetery grounds to take one last look, but the security guards are kicking everyone out and say we can wait by the entrance for stragglers. We stand around for another twenty minutes, but no Lionel.

Emil looks at me. "What do you want to do?"

Rafaela is looking at me, too. I hate this. I shouldn't be the one in charge. Lionel is the older one. He should be looking out for me.

But he's sick, and that illness is currently untreated and I knew that. So this is partly, if not mostly, my fault. I pull out my phone and try him again; it goes straight to voice mail this time.

"Go home and tell my parents he's missing."

twenty-two.

Emil stops at every place I suggest on the way home, just in case we happen to find Lionel at one of his old haunts.

None of the bookstores or libraries he'd visit are open, so that knocks out three-quarters of his life right there. We check the school grounds and the taco truck. Live music makes him anxious, so that rules out any of the shows tonight. We take a lap around the reservoir, the same at the lake. Rafaela wants us to check the area around Castillo Flowers, just in case, and she calls Ora to see if he's at her house. The last stop before home is the Brite Spot. I'm hoping he'll be sitting in a huge booth by himself, surrounded by platters of pancakes and bacon and sausage and eggs. He's not there.

Emil shuts off the Jeep and jumps out when he pulls up to my house.

"You don't have to walk me up," I say. "I mean, that's nice, but—"

"I'm going in with you." He slams the Jeep's door.

I stare at him. He was so upset that he barely spoke for over an hour, but he's willing to take the fall with me?

He shrugs like it's no big deal. "You shouldn't have to do this by yourself." He looks at Rafaela in the backseat. "You coming?"

She gazes up at the house with wonder as we walk to the porch. "Holy shit. This is your home? You guys never said you live in a fucking fairy-tale house."

Emil shoots her a look, like maybe this isn't the time, and she keeps her mouth closed for the rest of our walk to the door.

Mom and Saul are sitting in the living room, curled up together on the couch. They're watching something on TV, a fast-moving scene that sends white light flashing across their faces.

"How was the movie?" Mom asks, wiggling her toes. She's relaxed into Saul, her knees tucked in so she's almost curled in a ball.

I don't say anything. I'm standing in front of Emil and Rafaela, but my mouth won't open. I look at Emil, who frowns a little but says, "Pretty good. Lot of people..."

"And who's with you?" Saul asks, trying to see behind me.

"Remember me? I'm Rafaela." She steps forward. "I met you at my aunt's flower shop."

"Of course," says Saul, and his face is so warm it makes me look away. I have a feeling I won't be seeing that grin much longer.

"We've heard so much about you, Rafaela," Mom says, smiling. "It's really nice to meet you."

"Did you ditch my son?" Saul glances toward the windows that overlook the front yard.

Emil nudges me into speaking.

"We, um...we sort of lost him at the movie," I finally say, my voice creaky.

Saul gives me a funny look. "You lost him?"

"He went to the bathroom and never came back," Rafaela says, and I want to squeeze her in gratitude for helping me out. "He drove the two of us, and when we went to look for the car after the movie, it was gone."

"He's not answering his phone," I say when Saul immediately pulls his out. "And we stopped by a few of the places we thought he might be, but..."

Saul is calling, and it must go straight to voice mail for him, too, because he hangs up without saying anything. Mom is sitting up now, checking her phone on the coffee table.

"Maybe he went for a drive. It's just barely past curfew,

so he'll probably turn up soon." But her voice doesn't sound as confident as her words. "You kids are welcome to wait here until he does."

"Is anyone hungry? I can make us some sandwiches," Saul says, getting up from the couch.

There's another silence, and now is the moment I should say something, but I've forgotten how to open my mouth.

Emil clears his throat just as Saul is almost out of the room. "You guys need to know something."

I know he will say it if I don't, and I think that's the moment I truly understand how difficult it is to stop caring for someone. My conversation with Emil was so painful, but here he is standing by me, willing to do the one thing I've been avoiding all summer, one of the hardest things I've ever had to tell my parents. But I can't let him, as much as I'd like to. I've been so busy trying not to betray Lion that I didn't realize I'm exactly the one who has to do it.

"Lionel is off his meds."

It is the longest sentence in the world and my voice shakes the whole way through, but I get it out.

Saul whips around so quickly it scares me. But not as much as the look on his face. "What did you say?"

I breathe out through my nose. "He's off his meds. He has been for a while."

Mom is standing now, too. My underarms are drenched

in sweat. I've never wanted to avoid my mother's gaze more than at this moment.

"He told me he was going to stop taking them, and he tried to get rid of them, but I convinced him to give me the bottles." My voice is raspy, as if my throat is resisting the words. "I thought he would realize he was better off with them and he'd want to take them again. I thought…"

It doesn't matter what I thought. I fucked up.

"How long has he been off them?" Mom's voice is so sharp that I flinch.

"I don't know. It's hard to keep track of days during the summer…" I think back to our walk on the trail. "He told me a couple of days after Saul and I went to Ora's shop. But he'd already stopped taking them before then. I don't know how long…"

"He has it written down," Rafaela says, and her voice sounds too loud. Like she's standing too close to me, even though none of us has moved since I told them.

We all stare at her until she goes on, but I'm staring because I wasn't aware he'd told her about the meds.

"He's been journaling…about being off the meds and how it makes him feel. He called it a mood journal. So that might be in there, exactly when he stopped."

"I'll go look in his room," I say at the same time Mom grabs her phone and says she's going to call Dr. Tarrasch.

Saul starts dialing the police.

Emil and Rafaela thunder up the stairs after me. I throw open Lionel's bedroom door, hoping, like I did at the Brite Spot, that the last place we look will be where he's been hiding the whole time. That there's some way he could have slipped past Mom and Saul without them knowing. But his room is empty. It smells mostly of books and a little like unwashed sheets. His computer hums on the desk and I look at the spot where I was standing when we had our last fight.

I feel guilty going through Lionel's things but we tear the room apart, leave nothing untouched. The mood journal never turns up—it's not in his nightstand or tucked under his mattress or squeezed between the spines in his bookshelves.

"Did you find it?" Mom asks as soon as she hears us coming down the stairs.

"He must have taken it with him," I reply, shaking my head.

"Dr. Tarrasch wants us to call her as soon as we hear something," she says.

"The police said there's not much we can do, but they've filed a report," Saul offers and then pauses. "He's still considered a child."

"Is there anything we can do?" Rafaela looks back and forth between my parents.

"Just keep our phones charged and on," Mom says. "And we need to make a list of his friends and start calling them."

"We *are* his friends," I say softly.

"I'll call Justin and Catie," Emil says.

I call DeeDee and Tommy, and Rafaela gets on the phone with Alicia and then Grace, trying to cover all our bases.

Eventually, we've gone through everyone he could possibly be with, even people he hasn't spoken to in years. Nobody has seen Lionel.

For a while, no one stops moving. Lists and calls are being made, and Mom jots down a time next to each person we call. Saul puts on a pot of coffee and makes sandwiches that nobody eats.

We take turns charging our phones, and everyone jumps when someone so much as receives a text, but it's a false alarm every time. And every time, my heart sinks further as I realize how very badly this could go.

"You kids should go home and get some rest," Mom says around two a.m., looking over at Emil and Rafaela.

She's been quiet for some time now. Same as Saul. I haven't said anything to either of them unless they speak first. And I don't want Emil and Rafaela to leave because I don't want to hear what my parents will have to say when we're alone.

"I don't need to go home," Emil says, scratching his arm.

Rafaela nods blearily. "Me either. I want to stay here until we find out something."

"Well, you should try to get some rest here, then," Mom

says. "Call home to let them know you're staying here. Emil, the couch pulls out, and Rafaela, you can take the guest room...."

I go to the linen closet upstairs without being asked and stuff my arms with a pile of sheets, blankets, and pillows. We didn't shut Lionel's door after we searched his room. I pull it closed and pass Saul on my way down, but he retreats to his and Mom's bedroom across the hall without another word. I can't tell how angry he is with me, but I know he'll have plenty of time to think about it. He won't be sleeping tonight.

Emil and Rafaela have pulled out the sofa bed and we all go to work, putting the sheets on the mattress and slipping the pillows into fresh cases. We don't talk but I'm sure they feel the same way, like it's good to have something to do, even for a couple of minutes.

When we're done I shift my weight, trying to figure out what to say before I leave the room. Apologizing for what I've put Emil through tonight doesn't seem like enough, and thanking Rafaela for sticking around seems like too much. I decide brevity is best and simply say good night.

Mom is in the kitchen, refilling her mug of coffee before she goes up to join Saul. She doesn't smile or frown. She just looks at me.

"I'm sorry." I look right at her as I say it, as much as I don't want to. "I know it's not enough, but I am."

She takes a sip of coffee, gives a brief nod. "I know."

"Should I go talk to Saul?"

"I think you should try to get some rest. He's not going to be up for talking much right now."

I remember the way he silently passed me on the stairs.

"Come here." She sets her mug on the counter next to the sandwiches nobody ate.

I walk across the room until I'm standing in front of her. Up close I see all the emotions her eyes convey, none of which I like: sadness, irritation, and a little bit of fear.

"I'm very unhappy with you for not telling us about Lionel," she says evenly. "It was beyond irresponsible and foolish. You know better than to keep something like that from us. Your brother's mental health is nothing to play around with, and I thought you understood that."

I feel tears rising up, but I know I don't deserve sympathy or even the release that comes with those tears, so I hold them in. Blink and blink and blink so they won't come.

"But you are not responsible for your brother, and we never expected you to be. This isn't your fault." She takes my cold hands in her warm ones and holds them. "I love you, okay? No matter what happens, I love you, Suz."

I'm lying in bed, not sleeping, when the door to my room opens.

I look at the clock. Four a.m.

The house is too still for this to be good news, but I'm hopeful. And if it's not good news, then I at least hope it's Emil, coming up to say that he doesn't hate me.

"You live in an actual princess tower," Rafaela stage-whispers once she's reached the top of the stairs.

I sit up. "It seemed a lot cooler when I was younger."

"It is still *plenty* cool." All I can see is the outline of her tiny figure and her curls. "The houses where I grew up look nothing like this, trust me."

She moves to the empty side of the bed, kicks off her shoes, and gets in under the covers without asking. A week ago, my heart would've been racing from her being so close to me, lying in bed with me like Iris and I did. But it's not the same as Iris and me. What Emil and I have—had?—is closer to what I had with Iris. When I think about being with Rafaela, I've never thought of anything deeper than how we would connect physically. I need more than that, I think— someone I can trust.

She shivers and moves closer. "I'm freezing."

I lie down again because it *is* cold, too cold to not have the blankets wrapped around me. But I look at her and say, "You should probably go back downstairs."

I can't see her face but I can feel her smiling when she says, "Would your parents freak out if they walked in right now?"

I'm not thinking about my parents, though. I'm thinking about Lionel's accusation, that I'd be with Rafaela if I could get away with it. I'm thinking about Emil, and what he would think if he saw us in my bed.

"I just really don't need anything else to go wrong right now, okay?"

"I don't like being in the guest room alone. It's too quiet. And I'm scared." She pauses. "What if we don't find him?"

"Don't say that."

"He didn't seem sick to me. If he had…"

"That's the thing. By the time we notice, he's usually already in the middle of an episode."

"He told me himself about the meds.…He told me everything, the day after you did. I didn't say I already knew. And he said he doesn't become totally manic."

"But it's still hypomania, and with him…he can get overly angry about things. And sometimes that's followed by really bad depression. We don't really know his patterns because he started taking meds as soon as he was diagnosed."

She sighs. "I hated being told what to do with my body and I thought it was the same with him and his meds. Like he should have the choice, you know? But I guess it's not the same."

"No, it's not. Not really."

"I'm sorry," she says. "If I made things worse for him."

"Lionel was going to do what he wanted no matter who was around." I don't say that maybe we wouldn't be lying here worrying about him if she'd used her powers for good and convinced him to get back on track with his treatment. Because that's not something she would have had to think about at all if I'd gone to Mom and Saul from the start. "He doesn't let himself get close to a lot of people. There was a girl before you—"

"Grayson?"

"Yeah," I say, surprised that they've talked about her. "And he liked her a lot... but not as much as you."

"Really?" Even through the exhaustion and concern, happiness comes through in her voice.

"Really."

"Emil is one of the good ones, too," she says after a pause.

"The best," I say without having to think about it.

She reaches out to touch me, but I lean away from her until she gets the hint and slowly slides her hand back to her side of the bed. I don't know what she was going to do—touch my hair, touch me, try to kiss me. I don't know if it was an innocent gesture or if she was testing my loyalty to Emil.

I don't want to know.

She gets up and smooths the covers back over that side of the bed and pads down the stairs to the guest room without another word.

I don't sleep. I just lie there, waiting for the sun to come up.

Waiting for my brother.

twenty-three.

I must have dozed off for a bit because the next thing I know, my room is bathed in sunlight.

I rub my eyes and look at my phone, charging on the nightstand next to me. Ringer turned all the way up. Nothing from Lionel, but there are a couple of texts from our friends, saying they'll let me know if they hear anything. It's eight o'clock; he's been missing for almost twelve hours now.

I don't have the energy to shower, but I change my clothes and brush my teeth before I go downstairs. The kitchen is a disaster, but there's fresh coffee and food everywhere. Most of it looks like it's hardly been touched. I have no appetite, so I pour a cup of coffee and head into the living room.

Mom, Saul, Emil, and Rafaela are all there, joined by

Emil's parents. Catherine immediately folds me into a hug, murmuring comfort in my ear. Emil's dad passes us on the way to get more coffee and squeezes my arm, giving me a kind smile.

"No news?" I say to the room, even though it's a stupid thing to say because I would know if there were news.

"None," Saul responds. He doesn't look in my direction, but at least he's still talking to me. Kind of.

"We're going to organize a search party for the afternoon," Mom says. "Emil told us you went to some of his favorite places, but it won't hurt to check again. And we should definitely look at as many parks and hiking trails as we can during the day—it'd be easy enough to hide out there at night."

A search party. For my brother. This isn't the first time I've wished I could turn back time and have a do-over, but it is the one I've most earnestly hoped for. My brother being gone is the biggest problem I've never been able to fix.

"Wait a minute." Emil's back goes straight, and I notice he's wearing different clothes. His parents must have brought them over, or maybe he went home and came back. Either way, I'm glad he's still here. "Has anyone checked the tree house?"

No one says anything—we just all get up and start running, a flurry of hope headed toward the backyard. Emil reaches the tree first and climbs up in record time. The rest of us wait below, breathless, but it's only a couple of seconds before he pops back out, shaking his head. "Empty."

He doesn't come down right away, and everyone goes back to the house, shoulders slumping. Hope gone.

I stay. And when Emil still doesn't come down, I go up.

He's sitting on the futon, his elbows on his knees, head resting in his hands. "I thought he could be up here, you know? That kind of shit that happens in the movies. People are always in the most obvious place you don't think to look."

"It was smart," I say. "We have to try to think of everywhere. No one else thought of it, not even me."

He doesn't respond.

"And it could be worse. You could be me. I really fucked up." The most obvious statement of the year, if not my lifetime.

I guess he's back to ignoring me. And I deserve the silent treatment, for a number of reasons. But I'm so relieved when I hear his voice. "We're sixteen. People expect us to fuck up."

I sit down next to him, tentatively. "They don't expect us to put someone's life in danger."

"You did what you thought was right. And yeah, it was fucked up, but I get it."

I look at him. "You do?"

He sighs and meets my gaze. "I'm sorry I said all those things to you. That wasn't cool. Especially..."

"You didn't know what was going to happen, Emil."

"It still wasn't cool."

"I didn't know all that stuff you said...about the French names."

"Mine isn't spelled the French way, but...yeah. Our moms made a pact." He licks his lips. "I guess I didn't realize the Rafaela shit was bugging me until last night, and then I just let everything out at once."

"There's nothing between me and Rafaela," I say quickly, and Emil looks as if he doesn't believe me. "It's not like what I have with you. And I don't know what that is, but...I care about you, Emil."

"You don't have to say that to make me feel better."

"I'm not. But that girl I told you about—my old roommate—I cared about her, too. And I feel like I need to figure things out with her before I start anything new."

"You still like her?"

"I don't know." And I don't. I don't even know if Iris will ever talk to me again, but I have to try to make things right with her, somehow. "But I like you. And I like being with you. And I don't know what I would've done without you this summer."

He looks at me warily. "Yeah?"

I'm out of words. I put my hands on either side of his face, lean in, and kiss him softly. He's still for a moment and I freeze, wondering if he's going to refuse me completely. But then his hands find the small of my back, grazing over my dimples of Venus.

Emil kisses me back and I know he believes me.

When we walk into the house, the mood is more somber than before. Mom is halfheartedly taking notes to organize the search party with Catherine by her side. Saul is zoned out on his phone, tapping endlessly at the screen. Kevin, Emil's dad, is staring at his hands, as if the solution to this predicament rests in his palms. Rafaela is pacing the room; I'd never take her for a pacer, but she's burning a path back and forth across the hardwood floor.

If we were in an actual fairy-tale house, like she said, there would be a fat, dark storm cloud hovering over our roof instead of sunbeams that won't quit slipping their way into every room of the house. Everyone loves L.A. for the warmth and sun, but sometimes I'd give anything for a proper dark, rainy day that matched my mood.

Emil and I sit next to each other. Not touching, but I'm glad he's next to me.

Saul's phone rings, scaring the shit out of him even though he was holding it in front of his face. He frantically pushes the talk button. "Hello? Hello?"

Everyone sits up. Rafaela stops pacing. I can't remember the last time I was in a room so silent.

"Yes, this is he. Yes...yes. No, I did not. Okay." Saul frowns. "Listen, I really don't have time for this.... Yes, I care about the security of my card, but you declined the transaction. Which is good, because I'm not in San Luis Obispo, I'm sitting in my home waiting for my son to—"

We all sit forward as he stops talking and then, when he starts again, as the tone of his voice noticeably changes, as light comes into his eyes for the first time since last night. He stands up and starts walking around aimlessly, and Mom somehow knows that translates into him needing a pen and shoves one at him, along with a piece of scrap paper. Saul scribbles something quickly and barely says good-bye before he hangs up.

"What happened?" Mom asked.

"Was that about Lionel?" I chime in from the couch.

Saul doesn't answer us, just begins frantically dialing a number. He's babbling, not completing a sentence before he gets to the next one. I manage to make out his name and something about the credit card company before he stops talking and starts nodding. Then smiling. Mom is next to him, frozen in place just like everyone in the room.

"He's there, with you?" Saul finally says. His voice rises with each word and the room is so quiet I'm sure all seven of us are collectively holding our breath. "You're sure it's him?" He pauses, then, "Yes, he does have some of the prettiest red hair we've ever seen. That's our boy."

Mom and Rafaela immediately begin crying tears of relief, but I can't move. My brother is alive, and it sounds like he's safe, too. Emil slips his fingers between mine and squeezes.

Saul finally hangs up and his eyes are wet, too. "That was a bookstore, up in SLO. They specialize in rare books and said Lionel came in this morning. He tried to purchase a book for twenty thousand dollars."

He's laughing, and I've never been so happy to hear it.

Luck was on our side. Lionel is safe. Even without his meds, he led us straight to him.

twenty-four.

The drive to San Luis Obispo is just over three hours, and we don't even run into bad traffic.

We take the 101 North all the way. I gaze out at the crystal-blue water of the Pacific as we drive along the coast for a stretch. I'm glad to have the sun on my face now. Lionel is safe.

The bookstore is a family-owned business. The woman who owns it said most of the people who try to use stolen cards get out as fast as they can after they're found out, but Lionel just stood there and started crying. Sobbing. She said she had a feeling someone might be looking for him, and her husband got him something to eat while she was trying to find Saul's number. Saul called while she was still looking.

I haven't said a word the whole trip, and Mom and Saul don't say much, either. We just want to get there, and somehow, not talking makes the drive seem faster. The bookstore people said they would take good care of Lionel, but three hours is a long time. Long enough to worry that they won't keep their promise.

Lionel picked one of the best places to get lost. San Luis Obispo is on the Central Coast, with a downtown area full of restaurants and boutiques and bars and shops. It has one of those old-time drive-in theaters, and DeeDee and her dad once stayed here at a famous hotel where all the rooms have different themes, with big stone walls like caves and shag carpet and brightly patterned wallpaper.

Mom and Saul don't let me go in with them when we get to the bookstore. I know it's because they don't want Lionel to get overwhelmed, but I'm antsy the entire time they're gone. I briefly consider trailing them in, hiding in a corner until they're ready to go. But they'd kill me. Mom looked back in at me before they left and said, "Don't go *anywhere.*"

And when they come back, it's not *they* at all. Just Mom. "Come sit next to me," she says once she's in the driver's seat. "Saul is taking Lionel back in his car."

"Oh." I want to see him, but by the shaken expression on Mom's face, maybe it's best that I don't. I slide into the passenger seat next to her. "How is he?"

"He's sick, sweet pea." She places her hands on the

steering wheel, even though the station wagon is still turned off. "But he's safe. Saul is driving him straight to the hospital when they get back, and Dr. Tarrasch will meet him there. Lionel talked to her on the phone for a few minutes. She doesn't believe he went into full-on mania, but we want to get him checked out. They're going to do some tests and get his meds adjusted, so he might be in the hospital for a day or so. Just as a precaution."

"I'm really, really sorry, Mom," I whisper.

"I know, baby." She turns to me and nods. "I know."

Saul comes home late from the hospital, so late that Mom is in bed already.

It's one in the morning, but I can't sleep. The house feels too quiet with everyone gone now. I'm sitting in the living room, by myself, because part of me is hoping that the doctors will say Lionel wasn't as sick as they thought, that he just had a bad lapse in judgment and he'll be fine without too many adjustments. But the other part knows how foolish that is. He drove to San Luis Obispo on a whim on a Saturday night when he was on a date. No matter how much I wanted to believe he could handle his illness on his own, I know it's not true.

I hear the engine of Lionel's car as it pulls up and Saul parks at the curb. His footsteps sound tired as they trudge up the steps and across the front porch. He struggles with the key for a few seconds before realizing the door is unlocked. He's not expecting to see me when he comes in; he's too tired to hide his expression, the one that says he's really not in the mood for me now.

He nods, but that's it. Drops his wallet and keys on the table by the door and walks straight back to the kitchen. I follow him.

Emil's family cleaned the kitchen while we were gone, and it was sparkling when Mom and I got home. We didn't have the energy to cook, so we ordered in Thai food that we picked over until she went to bed.

Saul takes down a pan from the rack hanging above the island. "Egg in a hole?" he asks without looking at me.

"Yes, please." Suddenly I'm famished.

He makes them wordlessly and they are perfect. The bread a buttery, golden brown on both sides, but still soft enough on the inside to soak up the runny egg in the middle. He gives me the first one and I wolf down half of it before he's started eating his.

I set down my fork when he stands across the island from me with his plate, taking his first bite. "I'm sorry, Saul. I... I should have said something, and I'm sorry."

"Have I ever made you feel like you can't talk to me, kiddo?" When I look at him, his eyes are almost overwhelmed by the bags under them, but they're also red-rimmed.

"That day at the museum, you could've told me. Any day, anytime... I've tried to make it clear how much you can trust me."

I've always known that. Practically from the minute I met him, which is what makes this all so much worse. But what Lionel said—just thinking about it makes tears well up. What if he still hates me? What if things are never the same between us?

"Lionel said he was done with me if I told you," I say, the tears bursting forth as soon as I speak. "He said we wouldn't be family anymore. I didn't want that to happen."

Saul pushes his plate away. "He didn't mean that. He was unmedicated and—he didn't mean it, Suzette. Lionel and I will always be your family."

"I trust you." I rub at my eyes but only succeed in smearing tears across my skin, making my face more of a wet mess. "I do. I won't do anything like that again. I promise."

He nods. "That's a promise I need you to keep."

"You're not mad at me?"

"A little bit, yes." He blinks. "And we're going to have some serious talks about this very soon. But I don't blame you for this. And I love you."

"I love you, too, Saul," I say as he wraps me in one of his hugs.

twenty-five.

Mom and Saul think it's best that I wait to see Lionel until he comes home in a few days, so I try to keep myself busy.

I go into the flower shop for my regular hours the day after we get him from San Luis Obispo. Things are different with Rafaela. She treats me the same and we have the same easy rapport, but she doesn't flirt with me and I don't really miss it. I wait for the usual flutter to arrive when I see her—it never does.

We mostly talk about my brother's health. She knows that my parents are wary of him dating anyone for a good long while, but she says she wants to be there for him. As his friend, if they can't be more.

That night, DeeDee comes over and we order a pizza, which we eat up in my room before we try to choose a movie.

"What's Alicia up to?" I ask, scrolling through our options on my laptop. We're sitting next to each other, one half of my computer balanced on each of our thighs as we lounge against my headboard.

"Hating me, probably." She sighs and presses Pause. "We broke up. For real, this time."

I stare at her. "For good?"

"I guess. She broke up with me."

"What'd you do?"

Dee rolls her eyes. "She said she could sense that I was bored. *Restless.* Said I should go sow my wild oats, like I'm some dude who can't keep his dick in his pants."

"Well." I give her a look.

"Shut up. There's a difference between being in an open relationship and cheating, you know."

"But Alicia doesn't think so?"

"She gets the difference." DeeDee shrugs. "She just doesn't want any part of it."

"Sorry," I say, lightly bumping her shoulder with mine. "Maybe she'll change her mind."

"Or maybe we weren't meant to be. Summer isn't a good time to be tied down, anyway."

"Said like a dude who can't keep his dick in his pants."

I grin and duck as she swats at me with a pillow.

Emil's parents treat us to dinner the next night. Steaks in Beverly Hills.

"We should be treating you," Mom says as we pore over the dessert menu. "You were so good to us when Lionel was missing."

"We didn't do anything you wouldn't have done for us." Catherine takes a long drink from her wineglass. "The most important thing is that he's back and he's getting better."

"How was he today?" I ask Saul, who spent a couple of hours with him this afternoon.

"Good. So good, in fact, that he's coming home tomorrow."

"Really?" I'm still worried he'll be mad at me, but I want to see him. It's only been three days since he disappeared, but it seems like I haven't seen him in months.

Saul says yes, that he'll be home by lunchtime. He looks as happy as I feel.

Later, while we're waiting in line with our parents to give the valet our tickets, I tap Emil on the arm. When he looks at me, I start walking and motion for him to follow. We go down the sidewalk a bit, stopping once we're around the side of the building.

We've texted a few times since Lionel was found, but we haven't seen each other since then. I've missed him. And though we don't have a lot of time before they pull the cars around, I'm happy to be alone with him, even for a few minutes.

"I have to tell you something but I wanted to do it in person. Not over text or the phone or whatever," I say, and I wipe my palms on my flowered skirt.

He looks at me, wary and expectant at once.

"I'm going back to Dinsmore. To Massachusetts."

He exhales, nods. "For her?"

"Yes and no. I need closure. Not just with her, but... I wasn't honest about who I was when I was there." I finger the Magen David hanging from the silver chain around my neck. "I need to try to make things good with her... Iris... And I need to go back and see what it's like living there when I'm not hiding who I am."

Emil nods again. "When do you leave?"

"Not for a while. I have a few weeks here..." I take a breath. "What you said to me, back at the cemetery movie— I think you're one of the best people I know, too. I don't want to leave you hanging and I don't want you to feel like you have to wait for me. I just..."

"You've gotta figure shit out. I get it." He looks down at his shoes before his gaze finds its way back to me. "Do you have to figure it out before you go?"

I stare at him, not sure what he's saying.

"I mean, can we hang out until you leave? It doesn't have

to be... It can be whatever you want. I just don't want to stop talking to you."

"I don't want to stop talking to you, either. Or seeing you."

We move toward each other. We kiss. I'm worried it's going to feel like a good-bye, like a farewell to everything we built this summer. But it's sweet. Hopeful. And I feel certain that it won't be our last.

twenty-six.

Mom and I make lunch while Saul goes to pick up Lionel from the hospital.

We'll grill the shrimp when they're back, when it's almost time to eat, but we start making the salad while we wait. Mom puts me in charge of the avocados.

"Did you get a chance to talk to Iris about rooming together?" she asks, rinsing a colander full of radishes. "The school emailed me. They said they need your roommate request as soon as possible."

Mom and Saul seemed genuinely sad when I told them I've decided to return to Dinsmore. They asked if I was sure, and told me that whatever challenges we had to get through with Lionel, they knew we could do it together. I'll be sad to leave them again, too, and Lionel, of course, but it feels like the right decision—going because I want to.

"I haven't talked to her." I slide a knife carefully along the edge of the bumpy avocado skin, trying to keep the blade moving in a straight line.

Mom frowns. "I know you just decided for sure that you're going back, but honey, you're going to end up living with someone you don't know if you don't tell them something soon."

"I…" I swallow hard. There's never going to be a good time to do this, and if I do it now, that's one less thing to worry about for the rest of the summer. So I start talking. "Iris wasn't just my roommate. She was sort of my girlfriend. Second semester."

If my mother is surprised by the news, it doesn't show on her face. She turns off the water. Her voice is soft as she says, "And you two broke up?"

"Yes, but…there's more to it. We were kind of shamed into breaking up, right before school ended. Someone caught us together, and the girls in our dorm…Well, if the school brochure had a section highlighting the bigots, they'd be front and center."

"Oh, sweet pea." Mom walks over so we're standing next to each other. "I'm sorry. Do you want to talk about it?"

"Not really," I say.

"You know, now I'm not sure I want you going back there

if it was so bad. Maybe I should have a talk with the administration about those girls."

"No, Mom. I want to go back. . . . I can handle it myself."

"You're sure?"

"Yes, but... only if you and Saul promise not to shut me out about Lionel." I'm nervous to say it, but it's something I've worried about ever since I made my decision. It would be easy for them to say things will be different and then not follow through once I'm three thousand miles away. "I know I messed up, but... I want to feel like I'm still a part of this family, even if I'm not here."

She nods. "Of course. You'll always be part of this family, sweet pea."

"I don't know if Iris wants to see me again. I wasn't brave enough to stand up for us."

She smooths her hand across my forehead. "Bravery doesn't always look like you think it will. And it's never too late to stand up for the right thing. You're a good girl, Suz. Something tells me she's going to forgive you. And if it takes her some time, I'm sure you'll understand."

I nod, realizing I have no idea how Iris will react to me. All I can do is hope for the best.

Mom looks at me very seriously. "I know we've said this before, but I am okay with whatever sexuality you identify with. So is Saul."

"I think I'm bi," I say. "I like Emil. I've…had crushes on other girls."

"Well, I've never understood the whole issue some parents have with their kids not being straight." She hugs me and then pulls away to look at me again. "It shouldn't be the default, baby. I want you to be you, whoever that is."

My throat goes dry when I hear Saul's car pull into the driveway.

Mom and I wait for them in the living room and when Lion walks in, I feel overwhelmed. From pangs of missing him and relief that he's here in the flesh and the anxiety that he'll be angry with me. Mom hugs him and then takes Saul by the elbow and says, "We'll finish making lunch. It'll be ready in about ten minutes."

Lionel looks at me and I stand in place, looking back. He smiles and I take a tentative step forward.

"Hey, Little," he says with the ease of his old self.

My whole body relaxes. "You look good."

He nods. "I'm all right. I mean, not all the time. I'm still adjusting."

"That's normal, though, right?"

He smiles again. "Yeah. I guess it is."

I feel weird standing here in the living room with him. Too

formal. As if he's reading my mind, he opens the front door and we walk outside, sit on the front steps of our fairy-tale house.

"They said you're going back to boarding school." I can't read his tone. It's factual more than anything.

"Yeah. I think it's what I need to do."

"I hope it's not because of me. I promise—" He stops, like he needs to catch his breath. "I promise not to put you through this again."

"No. No...Lion. This is about Iris and making things right. With her and with myself." I nudge him in the side. "You can't scare me off that easily."

He gives me a grudging smile that turns into a grimace. "I'm sorry, Little. Really fucking sorry. It was shitty of me to ask you to keep that secret."

I shake my head. "You don't have to say that."

"No, it wasn't fair. And God, I feel like the biggest asshole for what I said...when you came in my room." He closes his eyes for a couple of seconds and when he opens them and looks at me, their color is somehow bright and soft at the same time. "That was the worst thing I could have said to you, and I knew it. I would never be done with you. Ever."

"Same here," I say, releasing a breath. Then: "I'm never keeping a secret like that again. If anything ever happened to you..."

For the first time in a long time, the air is peaceful

between Lionel and me. Maybe neither of us has much else to say, but it feels good to sit here like this, with nothing bad or secret or unspoken between us.

"Did the parents tell you about my Central Coast road trip?" he asks.

"Kind of, but they didn't say much. What happened?"

"It's all kind of hazy, but I don't even know how I ended up in San Luis Obispo. I think Rafaela and I were talking about it and I thought how cool it would be to go on a trip there, and then I just sort of took off." He shakes his head like it was years ago instead of a few days. "Guess I took a detour and camped out on Pismo Beach overnight. That's where I lost my phone."

"You spent the night at the beach?"

He shrugs. "That's what I told the guy at the bookstore. I was waiting on the doorstep when they opened. Got caught trying to buy a book with Dad's credit card."

"A twenty-thousand-dollar book."

"Not just any book. A 1969 copy of *Alice's Adventures in Wonderland* with illustrations by Salvador Dalí," he says, still awestruck. "He signed it, too. Dalí! It was amazing."

"It was twenty thousand dollars," I say in disbelief.

"Well, the hypomania thought I should have it."

"At least your hypomania has good taste." I shoot him a wry smile.

We're quiet again, until Mom sticks her head out the

front door and says lunch is ready. The smell of spicy grilled shrimp wafts out the door and lingers on the porch, reminding me of the tacos we ate when I arrived from Massachusetts at the start of the summer. That feels like a lifetime ago.

"I'm glad you're back," I say to Lionel as we stand.

"Yeah...me too."

He gestures for me to walk in ahead of him. I think about how easily we could have lost him, both physically and mentally. But then I stop myself.

Right now, I just want to look at my brother, be at peace with the fact that he's going to get better. We didn't lose him.

He's still my brother.

He's still here.

Acknowledgments

Thank you to my brilliant editor, Alvina Ling, for loving this story from the start and helping me shape it into the book I always wanted it to be. Many thanks also to Kheryn Callender for your sharp eye, fresh perspective, and overall enthusiasm.

And thank you to the entire team at Little, Brown Books for Young Readers for all your hard work and dedication to this book.

Thank you to Corey Haydu for understanding me and supporting me and listening to me beyond reason. And for being my Life Twin. I am so grateful to know you.

Thank you to my dear friend Kristen Kittscher for your steadfast friendship, constant encouragement, and eternal kindness.

For friendship and first reads, thank you to Courtney Summers, Stephanie Kuehn, Sarah McCarry, Maurene Goo, Kirsten Hubbard, Elissa Sussman, and Justina Ireland.

Thank you to my parents for being my biggest fans.

And all the gratitude in the world to Tina Wexler for always believing in me and pushing me to do my best work. I am so honored to call you my literary agent and friend.

Turn the page for a sneak preview of

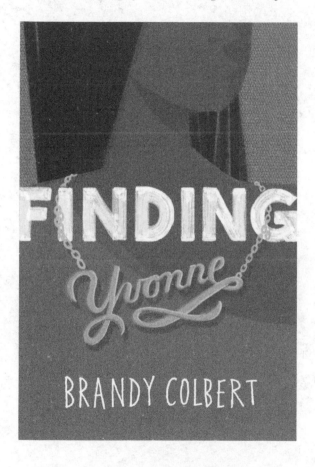

Available August 2018

1.

There are three things I know about my father: He smokes pot daily, he doesn't like to speak unless he really has something to say, and he is one of the most respected chefs in Los Angeles.

I also know that the best time to see him is at Sunday breakfast. We aren't around each other much; Dad gets home from work so late during the week that he's rarely up in time to make a proper breakfast. He usually grabs something light when he gets up, around noon, and then eats family meal with the staff before the restaurant opens for dinner. But Sundays are special. He reserves Sunday mornings for an actual meal that he plans in advance, and there's always plenty to eat.

Sometimes I want to skip it on principle alone. I shouldn't have to set aside one day a week to see my own dad for more than a few minutes. But I love Sunday breakfast, and he's usually in a good mood because he gets the day to himself, so I find myself at the table every week.

He's standing at the counter when I stumble into the kitchen this morning, coating pieces of chicken in a mixture of flour and seasonings.

"Morning," he says over his shoulder. "Coffee's on."

"Thanks." I pour a mug and stand next to the fridge, watching him. "Is Warren coming over?"

"Should be here any minute."

Which means I'll need to down this cup of coffee if I want to brush my teeth again before he gets here. I slurp steadily at the mug, but the doorbell rings before I can finish. Well, it's not like anything is going to happen with my father here.

Warren Engel is standing on the porch in jeans and a plaid button-down with the sleeves rolled up. He smiles and wordlessly reaches for my hands. I pull him inside and we stand looking at each other for a moment, his big tea-colored eyes roaming softly over me before we hug.

"Missed you last night," he says in a low voice, though Dad couldn't hear us over all the banging around he's doing in the kitchen anyway.

"Sorry I didn't make it over. The party went late, and then I just wanted to sleep in my own bed."

"It's cool. I was at the restaurant until late." Warren was promoted to sous chef at my father's restaurant a couple of months ago, a big honor in itself but especially since he's just barely twenty-one. "What's Sinclair making today?"

"Come see for yourself," I say, leading him back through the hallway. His hands trail lightly over my hips as we walk, sending warm shivers up the small of my back, but it ends as quickly as it started. We break apart when we're standing in the same room as my father.

We're not official, Warren and I. We probably would be if he weren't so paranoid about our age difference. We're only three years apart, and I don't think my father would care. He basically thinks Warren can do no wrong.

Dad is carefully placing chicken legs and thighs into a skillet of hot oil as we walk in.

"Chicken and waffles?" Warren says, grinning like the day just turned into Christmas. My father has a lot of fans, known and unknown, but I think Warren might still be his biggest.

"You know it." My father moves the skillet to a cool burner. "Want to get the waffles going? Iron's already hot, and the batter's in the fridge."

I reach into the refrigerator to hand Warren the pitcher of

batter, then grab the jug of orange juice, too. "Isn't he off the clock?"

"Happy to let you take over if you're so concerned about Warren," Dad says, smirking as he heads over to the sunroom.

Not two minutes later, the skunky scent of marijuana wafts through the air above us. Neither Warren nor I bat an eye. My father's frequent pot-smoking isn't exactly public knowledge, but it's certainly no secret around here. He says it's mostly to combat the stress that comes with owning a successful restaurant, but he also swears that he's created some of his most iconic dishes while stoned. He probably knows that I've smoked, but we don't talk about it and we've certainly never done so together.

Dad is what I call a professional stoner. He's been smoking for so long that it's hard to tell when he's high. The whites of his eyes turn just slightly pink, and sometimes he takes a little longer between thoughts, but other than that he's completely functional. Almost disturbingly so. I've seen him carry on extremely involved conversations when I know he's blazed up pretty recently.

I down a glass of orange juice while Warren tends to the waffles, creating a generous stack on a plate next to the chicken. Dad comes back in just as they're ready, and we all help transport everything to the table. I carry plates and silverware and quickly set the table as they place the food.

Eating with my father and Warren isn't like sharing a meal with anyone else I've ever known. Usually people taste a few bites of their food, declare how good it is or what it's lacking, then move on to more stimulating conversation. Warren and my dad analyze each bite, discussing which spices were or were not used and what they've changed since the last time they made the meal. Sometimes Dad gives him tips on his method, but I realized how much he respects Warren when he started asking for his opinion.

I grew up in the restaurant industry, but I don't understand food the way they do. Except for sweets. Baking makes sense to me, maybe because there's science behind it. There's so much trial and error with cooking. I get frustrated when a recipe doesn't turn out right the first time, even when I follow it to the letter.

"I was thinking about going to check out that new spot in Venice," Dad says to Warren. "The one Courtney Winters just opened up."

"Oh, that place is supposed to be the real deal." Warren wipes his mouth and takes a long drink of water. "You're going today?"

"She has a Sunday supper. What do you think?"

"Yeah, sure." Warren pauses and looks at my dad first, then me. "You want to come?"

I pour more syrup over my waffle and take a bite. Even I

can't help but stop and think how perfectly light and fluffy it is as I chew. "I don't know," I say, looking at my father. "Am I invited?"

"Of course you are, Yvonne. I thought you'd be practicing," Dad says with a shrug.

I do usually practice my violin on Sunday. It feels like a good end to the weekend. A structured start to the week. But I need a break from the routine sometimes. And now that I'm no longer taking private lessons, I can make my own practice schedule.

"Can we stop at the boardwalk?"

"Yeah, sure." Dad waves one hand in the air as he drags a forkful of chicken and waffles through a pool of syrup with the other. He's already done with this conversation, ready to get back to food talk.

The meal with them tonight will be almost exactly like the scene at this kitchen table, only they'll sample an unreasonable amount of food, and my father will go back to the kitchen to talk to the chef, and I'll have to hear everything from why he thinks the dining-room sconces are incompatible with the space to him breaking down the components of a sauce.

It's exhausting, but I know the meal will be good. My father won't try just anyone's food. And I'll get to spend time with Warren, which always makes me happy. He works such long hours that we don't get to see each other as often as I'd like.

Besides, I don't have anything else to do today. My Sundays used to be filled with violin practice, but with Denis no longer around to crack the whip, I don't see much of a point.

It's hard not to give up on yourself when the person who's supposed to believe in you the most already has.

Jessie Weinberg

Brandy Colbert

is the author of *Pointe, Little & Lion,* and *Finding Yvonne.*
Born and raised in Springfield, Missouri, she has worked as
an editor for several national magazines, and now lives and
writes in Los Angeles.